BEYOND EVERLASTING

By
Lara Nance

Dear Simon,
Matt and I thoroughly
injoyed our tour with you.
It's something I will always
remember.
Here's the book I promised,
and hope you enjoy the tale.
Best!
Lara

Beyond Everlasting
By Lara Nance

PRINT:
13 – ISBN - 978-1492137054
10 – ISBN - 1492137057

Dedication:

To Jason Atkins who believed in dreams and in me.
To Karen who loved this story as much as I did.

4

Chapter 1

"*Merde!*" Etienne stared at a dress design from his new collection. "What am I doing? If I present this I'll be a laughing stock in the fashion world." He tossed the illustration onto his drawing table and stared into the distance. *My show is going to be a total disaster. That's it, I'm finished.*

After a second, he grabbed his jacket and ran down the spiral stairs of his atelier and to the street to hail a taxi. *I have to get out of here. I'm going crazy.*

"To The Louvre." A rush of adrenaline electrified him for the first time in months. He didn't even know why he mentioned the museum. But it sounded right. At least it was an escape from thinking about his doomed spring show.

Once he arrived, he paced back and forth as he waited in queue to enter the famous museum. What was he thinking? Could he really find inspiration here? He repeatedly glanced at his watch as the line snaked forward. So much work to do, and here he wasted time on a whim. Coward. Just go back and face the fact his career as a designer was over. He exhaled, desperation overcoming reason, and became resigned to the winding line's slow pace as it approached the great glass pyramid.

Finally, he entered and strode across the shiny floor of Hall Napoleon beneath the pyramid. Pausing, he turned in a circle, considering escalators leading to three wings. After a slight hesitation, he headed to the right into the Denon Wing. He'd visited the museum many times in his youth, and one of his favorite sites was still the impressive staircase rising to a glorious winged statue of the Victory of Samothrace.

A slight surge of latent warrior passion from the past stirred him where he gazed up the stairs at that famous symbol of victory. But it didn't offer the type of inspiration he needed. Something else pulled at his memory. He ran fingers through his already tousled hair. His eyes burned from months of staring at his tired unimaginative designs.

After a second of consideration, he remained on the ground floor and headed into the Sully Wing. He hurried through arched hallways with walls of red/gray marble and geometrically patterned black and white marble floors. He scanned Roman reproductions of Greek statues in the Melpomene Gallery with cursory glances, but no muse reached out from these ancient images.

This is nuts. What am I going to find here? He turned in a circle then went left and passed under an arched passageway to enter the Venus D'Milo Gallery. A calming sense of peace enveloped him facing one of his favorite pieces of art. He let out a deep breath and stood against a window away from the crowd. Even as a child, he'd admired the slope of her shoulders, the long line of her classic Greek nose, and the graceful bend of her neck.

He closed his eyes seeking influence and inspiration. If she were clothed, what would she wear? The cloth that draped her hips where it had fallen; was it a robe or just necessary covering improvised by the artist to conceal her most private parts? What had she worn to social gatherings, to the forum or to seduce her lover?

He opened his eyes, still caught in the intimacy of the imaginary scene. As his vision refocused, it fell on a striking woman dressed in white who stared at him, her pink lips slightly parted. Her light brown hair, piled in curls atop her head, framed a pale face with enormous blue-green eyes and full, heart-shaped lips. Tendrils of hair escaped a red ribbon running through her curls and tickled her cheeks and neck. His throat constricted.

Now here was inspiration. She was the most beautiful woman he'd ever seen, but with an aura that was ethereal, otherworldly. Her eyes widened in surprise, and then she blinked, confusion shading her expression. Thick brown lashes lowered to cover her eyes as she quickly averted her gaze.

Etienne moved toward her and admired her slender neck, so much like the famous statue. Her dress appeared made of a thin linen or organza trimmed in gold ribbon. It floated about her like a cloud. A golden ribbon cinched the material under her breasts, and the gown fell in layers to her ankles from there. Her feet peeped from the hem, elegantly displayed in white satin slippers with kitten heels and diamond buckles on the toes. He moved closer. It was crazy, but he half expected her to run or fade away. When he reached a hand in entreaty, she swayed backward.

"Hello. I'm Etienne. I'm sorry. I didn't mean to stare at you. Are you enjoying the museum?"

Slowly she smiled, a glowing brightness that lit her eyes. Her gaze darted to different areas and then shyly lowered, hidden by the curtain of her lashes.

"I...I like the statue." The words floated, soft, haltingly, as if she tested each word for its correctness. "It is beautiful," came out stronger.

Etienne inhaled a deep breath. Relief flooded him. She'd made no move to leave. He took another step closer, mesmerized by the alabaster gleam of her skin. Her eyes changed from blue to green depending on the reflection of light. *My God, Venus D'Milo is nothing compared to this woman.*

"Are you from Paris?"

Although she spoke perfect French, her accent sounded strange, formal.

"Yes, oh, I am not sure, but I think so. I ... I cannot remember." She shook her head. "And you?"

"Parisian to the core," he said, charmed at her pretty confusion. How could she not know from where she came? He had to know more.

She laughed with him, but then put a hand to her mouth as if surprised by her response. Her green eyes sparkled like emeralds.

"Would you join me for a cup of coffee or tea?" Beyond fascinated, he needed to continue this encounter. Her presence energized him as nothing had in years. He was a broken down, empty hull of machinery lacking power, and she was a glowing source of fuel that could ignite his inner workings.

Her smile faded and confusion clouded her expression.

"Please, I'd like to talk with you." He took another step forward, but she retreated.

"I ... I am not sure." She gazed into his eyes and blinked several times, like a deer facing a headlight. "It is merely that ... I need to go now. I am sorry, I cannot stay."

"Can we meet?" He held out a hand, desperate not to lose her. If she left, the light would go with her.

"Oh, I do not think that would be a good idea." She took another step of retreat.

"What could it hurt to have a cup of tea together?" He tried his most charming smile. "I really would like to see you again. How about tomorrow?"

"Tomorrow?" She chewed a fingernail, but a flicker of interest flared in her eyes. It gave him hope.

"Yes. Wherever you'd like."

She paused, biting her bottom lip. People milled about the Venus, oblivious to the interaction between them. Focus in that gallery centered on the famous statue. Slowly, a smile spread over her lips and she raised her chin. "Very well. We shall meet tomorrow, here at this place, at the same time."

Etienne let out a deep breath. She hadn't refused. At one point, he'd thought she might leave and he'd never see her again. He nodded. "Yes, I'll be here. I promise." He glanced at his watch, marking the time.

"Until then, Etienne." She turned in a sweep of white filmy fabric.

"Wait." He stretched out both hands as she moved away. "What's your name?"

The lady in white paused and tilted her head to one side. She wistfully gazed at him, and then waved a hand before disappearing into the crowded halls of the Louvre. Her dress swayed with her movement in an alluring way that captivated the creative element of Etienne's imagination.

He remained rooted to the spot as his brain whirled with the appearance of this mysterious lady, so odd but intriguing. She was out of place here, with her elegant gown and coiffure. A character from another era. She belonged in a ballroom, surrounded by candlelight and elegant dancers. Was she a hallucination? He knew he was near mad with worry over his upcoming disaster of a show. He shook his head, but her image remained in front of his eyes, unforgettable.

An idea flickered. Vintage dresses in a modern setting, the flavor of history reflected in clothing. He retraced his steps to the entrance, oblivious to his surroundings. Dresses and flowing fabrics shaded his vision. He stopped when he reached the Hall Napoleon, trying to reorient. People pushed past, and he became aware of their laughter, conversations, footsteps on the marble floor. What should he do? He placed his hand over his forehead, feeling feverish.

A woman entering the museum gave him a brief glance on her way toward the information desk. He lowered his hand and stared after her. Another vision? She had straight brown hair pulled into a ponytail and wore jeans and a white shirt covered with a navy blazer. A camera with a long lens on a strap hung over one shoulder, and she carried a soft briefcase in one hand. He shook his head, perplexed. She looked exactly like the woman he'd seen at the Venus.

She turned, studying a map the receptionist had given her. No, he couldn't mistake it. She held an uncanny physical resemblance to the woman in white. After a quick glance over her shoulder, she took the elevator to the Denon Wing. Curious, he almost followed her for another look, but the designs forming in his mind urged him to take action before they fled.

He headed outside and emerged, blinking, into the bright sunshine. A surge of enthusiasm propelled him forward as swirling designs began to take definite shape. The image of her figure remained before him, elegant and alluring, a timeless beauty. Inspiration flooded him as he reached the sidewalk and waved energetically for a taxi to take him to his office.

***

The woman in white bothered no one as she hurried from the Sully Wing to the Denon Wing of the museum. When she wanted, she could travel in the walking movement of the living. As time passed, she tended to float or glide as she moved from one spot to the next. Still, she always tried to avoid gliding through the living so as not to disturb them with the intense cold of contact with the dead. Now, she flew along the hallways. Her feet never touched the floor, one hand over her mouth, the other clutching her chest. Her filmy dress flowed behind her.

The man had seen her. He lived and he had seen her. More startling than that, he had talked to her. The encounter left her with pleasurable sensations long forgotten –giddiness and anticipation. He was so handsome with his dark hair and classic features, surely the sign of a gentleman. His jacket couldn't hide evidence of broad shoulders, and strong muscular thighs moved beneath the fabric of his black trousers. Did he remind her of someone? A rush of familiarity compelled her to remember, but her memory remained hazy.

She slowed as she entered the Michelangelo Gallery, searching until she found the blonde-haired woman sitting against the corner wall. She sank beside her, sending frantic thoughts out. Blonde Hair preferred to speak through their minds as she focused on fading. She insisted it helped distance her from the world of the living.

What is my name? What is my name? I cannot remember it. She leaned toward the other woman and waved a hand in front of her remote gaze.

Your name? Blonde Hair's faraway stare sharpened into focus and she pressed her hands to her cheeks.

I cannot remember my name, she said again.

The blonde woman gave a faint smile, but her eyes remained sad. *Of course, dear, our memories fade: pains, hurts as well as the good times. After a while even our names are gone. Then you fade away to Everlasting.*

Her hands flew to her face as a chill of fear and despair gripped her. That's what had been happening to her. She was forgetting. She could no longer remember how long ago she'd died, how it happened, or who she left behind, if anyone. She'd become content to float around the museum looking at beautiful objects over and over because it soothed her. And now she'd forgotten her name. Jane, Jean, Jan, something like that.

Do you remember your *name*? She turned to Blonde Hair. If only the other woman had some advice that would help her with this dilemma.

Her friend narrowed her eyes in concentration and then smiled. *No, I cannot remember it at all. What does it matter? I think of you as Green Eyes and that is all I know of a name.* She floated to a standing position and moved to glide away. Her pale blue gown reached the floor and flowed behind her in sinuous waves. A lacy white shawl draped her arms and bunched where she held it close to her chest. Her eyes began to lose their focus.

I think of you as Blonde Hair, she admitted then followed

her friend as they floated along the corridor. Then she remembered why she'd sought the other soul. *Blonde Hair, I met a man today.*

Oh? The other soul paused.

Yes, he asked me my name, but I could not remember so I ran away.

He must be new, but no need to run away, my dear. Just tell him how it is with us. He will appreciate a guiding hand. It is always hard for newcomers. Her friend smiled and moved ahead.

She floated in front of Blonde Hair to halt her progress. *You do not understand. He is living.*

And he saw you? The other woman's blue eyes grew wide and penetrating.

Just imagine, to converse with a real person after all this time. It made me feel so wonderful. I must try to talk to him again. She closed her eyes and put both hands to her throat as she remembered words slipping through when she'd spoken to him in a louder voice than the one she used for other souls. Etienne, that's what he said his name was. Etienne. Etienne. What a beautiful name.

No, no, no! her friend admonished. *You must not. You cannot get involved with the living. It can only cause problems.*

Surely it cannot hurt to talk.

No, Green Eyes, that is not our purpose. We are here to forget, and when we finally forget everything, we fade away. She shook her head vehemently, and her blond curls flipped about. Fear flickered in her eyes.

"Forget him, Green Eyes. I mean it. Now leave me alone," Blonde Hair yelled aloud before she retreated in a huff. She actually took four steps before slipping into a glide.

Two living women nearby visibly startled and looked about in confusion.

Stunned, she froze as Blonde Hair floated away. Sadness descended over her like a dark, heavy curtain separating her from the possibility of happiness. She'd never seen the other soul so upset. What could it harm to talk with Etienne? Was her friend right? If the dead were meant to speak to those still alive, she supposed it would be normal to chat back and forth, which it wasn't. Could meddling in the affairs of the living invoke some malevolence? She shivered at the thought.

She'd been peaceful before she met Etienne, sad for some reason, but peaceful. Maybe that was best. And yet, she experienced such a thrill of pleasure and excitement as she conversed with the man, as though warm blood flowed through her veins again and passion existed in her soul. It was impossible to deny she greatly anticipated their meeting tomorrow. She needed to explore the stimulating sensation of familiarity again. The lure enticed her too much to ignore.

Ah…..Ja, Je, Jen, yes! That was it. Jeanne! That was her name. She'd remembered after all. She hid her smile behind one hand as Blonde Hair floated along the hall into the next room. She couldn't wait to tell Etienne.

**

Margot pushed through the door of her townhouse and tossed her camera case and purse on the sofa. She shrugged out of her jacket and rubbed her aching shoulders with both hands. It had been a long day at the museum but she knew her pictures would turn out well.

Her cell rang and she dug it out of her purse. "Hello?"

"How was your day?" Her mother's cheery voice made her smile.

"It was good. I only have a couple more days of work to finish the assignment."

"I'm glad. I'm hoping this job will lead to more steady work. I'm so glad your father ran into Professor Galen."

A twinge of irritation made her let out a huff. "Mom, my work is going well anyway. Weddings are a great source of business. I have two next week."

Her mother sighed. "I suppose. It just seems that working for the university would be more...I don't know...respectable."

Margot flopped on the couch, sick of having this same conversation over and over. When would her mother let it go? "I want to work in fashion, and I meet interesting people at weddings that have connections. Trust me, no one at the university will be an entrance to the world of *haute couture*."

"Fashion seems too frivolous. I should think you'd want to do something more artistic. You're a very talented photographer."

"So you think me taking pictures of great art from the past is artistic? She snorted. "They can only pose one way, Mom. Let's not get into this again, okay? I'll help out Professor Galen as a favor to Dad but I'm not looking for more work helping academics produce research papers."

"Maybe you could write a magazine article and use your pictures."

"Let me worry about my career. Please?" She ran the back of her hand over her forehead.

"What are you saying? I've never been one to butt in on my children's lives."

"Right. Good-bye, Mom."

She leaned her head back on the sofa. Making photos at weddings was lucrative and despite her mother's worries, it produced a dependable living for her. But her dream was to work in fashion. She'd love to hook up with one of the famous designers and become their house photographer. The one opportunity she'd had to work with one of her friends at a fashion shoot had been the most exciting job she'd ever had. Unfortunately, breaking into that business as an unknown wedding photographer was nearly impossible.

No matter how impossible, she wasn't going to give up on her dream.

Chapter 2

Etienne's staff called greetings when he arrived at his atelier, but he hurried through the first floor workroom without answering. The trip to the museum left him jittery with the need to put some of his ideas on paper before they disappeared. He climbed the spiral staircase to the loft where he worked, taking two steps at a time. After threading his way through bolts of fabric, stacks of his drawings, and dress mannequins, he sat on a stool behind his drafting table. A glance at his shaking hands made him tuck them under the table.

"Hey, boss, do you need anything?" His long-time assistant, Chloe, followed him upstairs.

He waved a hand of dismissal at her and she retreated, frowning. He sat for several minutes with his head in his hands, elbows propped on the drawing board. Slowly, the swirling images formed into concrete ideas. He pulled a clean sheet of paper onto the board and grabbed a pencil. His hand moved rapidly with a sureness he'd not experienced in years. He grinned. This is how it had been in the beginning, before his first show, before he became jaded and empty.

By seven o'clock, everyone left. In their favor, they made numerous attempts to offer assistance and sustenance, but he waved them each away, desperate not to lose his visions - his mystery lady in a variety of different outfits.

He drew with a sureness long dormant as images flowed from his imagination onto the paper before him. It was Great Gatsby meets Erte'. Art deco swirling with prim linens and cottons contrasted with velvet and satin. It was Regency period, but with headbands, feathers, swinging beads, all accented by luminous, soulful eyes full of mystery and passion. Not just fashion, but art.

The best work of his life.

As the reddened tint of morning sunlight gleamed in his windows, he glanced at the brightness, disoriented. The night passed so quickly he hadn't noticed. He lowered his pencil and stared at the drawings on the table. Twenty-two designs of perfection. The pinnacle of his creativity, and *she* stared at him from every one. He sat back and admired the work. Ball gowns to city dresses, slacks, hats and coats. It was all there. A complete collection.

Unfortunately, in four weeks he would present his spring line at Fashion Week. His House had entered the final stage of preparations with a collection he'd worked on for six agonizing months, none of it worth a tenth of what he'd designed in this one night.

He rubbed his eyes and pushed his fingers through his hair. Did hope exist that he could put this new collection together in time? Maybe, just maybe, with a miracle or two. But he required one element to assure his success. Her. She was the soul of every single design.

"Etienne?" Chloe tentatively poked her head up the spiral stairs. "It's seven o'clock in the morning. Have you been here all night?"

"Come up." He gestured her toward him and stood from the table. "Come look at this." Eagerness like electric shocks ran through him. He needed someone to verify the quality of the work. No one knew the scope of his talent better than her.

She came forward, speculation in her eyes. Her bobbed, dark hair flipped as she glanced around the room. When she reached his side, her gaze followed his pointed finger to the scattered pages on the drawing board. With eyes growing wider, she sifted through the pages faster and faster until her mouth fell open.

"What, what have you done, Etienne? What have you done?" She tore her eyes from the images to stare at him in wonder. "It's a miracle! Fabulous. What happened?"

He grinned bigger at each of her utterances. He knew it. It was good. No, it was great.

"Chloe, listen to me." He pulled her by the arm to tear her away from the designs. He took her to the desk he used for his business matters and sat, pulling a notepad to him. "We have to scrap the collection we're working on. We have to use these new designs. Do you hear?"

She nodded as if in a trance, eyes still wide. He knew it constituted madness, but his old designs were crap. With this new work, House Etienne would return to its former glory. He detected the spark of passion in her eyes, something he hadn't seen since they'd offered their first collection to the fashion world years ago. Sleepless nights. Days without eating. It was suicide, but what they lived for -to present a vision the world would not soon forget. — To create a spectacle of great fashion.

He smiled and nodded, knowing exactly what she experienced. The rush of anticipation swelled in him as well. If they could pull it off, this show would rock Paris, rock the world. The scent of success filled him with strength and power, like he could accomplish anything.

"There are twenty-two drawings. Have Sean and Lola start the patterns at once. I made notes on fabrics beside each design. Have fabric samples here this afternoon and we'll choose what to use. We'll leave the accessories to last. If there are any gaps, we'll pull the best pieces from the old collection, but I don't think we'll have to."

Chloe nodded eagerly. "What models do you want? The ones we booked for the old collection are all wrong for this. We need timeless looks. Jane Austin, not *Blade Runner*."

"Yes, excellent. You have the right idea. Call Alan at the agency. Do whatever you have to. I want the best. We'll need hair extensions. Sophia is unsurpassed in that area. I'll need vintage jewelry. Make a note, and get Claudette for the fittings. She can keep her mouth shut."

"Venue? Do we have time to change?" She bit the end of her pen.

"Damn!" Etienne pounded the desk with his fist. "The warehouse is completely wrong. Damn." He stood and paced, one hand to his head. His previous collection had a modernistic tone, with metal, skintight leathers and primary colors. He'd rented a large manufacturing warehouse to show the collection, using machines and clutter as a backdrop for the futuristic designs he'd produced. Now, he needed a showplace to reflect the timeless, genteel sophistication of his new collection.

"Chloe, don't worry about that yet. I'll think of something. Get going. We have an impossible task ahead of us. If we pull it off, it'll be worth it."

"Don't worry, we'll do it," she promised.

She would work her fingers to nubs now that she had something to be proud of. He smiled. She turned to hurry downstairs.

"Chloe, one more thing. Keep this a secret. Not a word outside the House. Let the vulture media and the other houses think we'll still have the other collection. I want to shock everyone." He gave her a conspiratorial wink.

She grinned in agreement and rushed away to start the madness.

***

Jeanne needed to find Francois. He might help her make sense of this dilemma of interacting with the living. He'd died a long time ago, longer than most here, but he still knew his name. Stories spread that he talked to the living and traveled outside the museum. She'd never met him, but rumors circulated among the dead as they did among those alive.

She moved to an alcove and paused, away from the crush of people circulating to and fro. The movement of the masses stimulated confusion, and she needed quiet to contemplate. Why had she wanted to forget the past so badly? She remembered sadness, but not the reason for it. She had loved art in her former life. That much she remembered. When she died, she'd focused on the art to such an extent the details of her living existence faded quickly. She now realized that had been a subtle but purposeful move on her part. There was something horrible she didn't want to remember.

"Green Eyes?"

One of her acquaintances hailed her. "Brown Boy", the soul of a young man with brown hair and eyes, in a brown suit and bowler hat. Jeanne smiled and waved to him.

He floated to her alcove and gave her a questioning look. "You seem different."

"Oh?" She put her hands to her cheeks. "How is that?"

"I am not sure." He scanned her face. "Maybe you do not appear as sad as usual."

"Do I always look sad?"

"Well, yes, actually. Now that I think of it. I always

thought of you as having a sad face." He cocked his head to once side, considering her. He laughed. "Now you're happy, as if expecting a present."

She laughed with him. He'd described her mood exactly. Without knowing why, she'd always been gloomy. However, Etienne filled her with an eager anticipation full of delightful stimulation.

"I have a secret," she said, leaning close.

"A secret? I love secrets. Tell me what it is."

"Hmm, I am not sure I should." She backed away and crossed her arms. "You may not approve. Blonde Hair didn't."

"Come on, Green Eyes. Please tell me."

"You must call me Jeanne. I have remembered my name and I want to use it. It is Jeanne," she proclaimed triumphantly.

"Jeanne? That's pretty. I like it. I wonder what my name is. I shall have to try to remember. If you can, maybe so will I." He seemed intrigued with this idea, momentarily diverted from her news. After a pause, he persisted. "Now what is the secret?"

"I was on the ground floor of Sully with the Venus statue, and I noticed a man. His face seemed familiar." She remembered straight black hair falling across his forehead, blue eyes, and chiseled features giving him the air of an aristocrat. But more importantly, she found his eyes alluring, drawing her into their depths. "I stared at him, and then I realized he could see me. He talked to me and said his name was Etienne. I have never had something like that happen before. Have you?"

Brown Boy rubbed his chin. "I find that very interesting. I have never experienced such a thing, but the living are so fascinating. I wish I could talk to one of them."

"I am going to meet him. He wants to see me again." Jeanne tingled in pleasurable anticipation.

"Well, how about that. I'm impressed."

"Some souls here think it is a bad idea." She paused and looked around. "When I told Blonde Hair, she became angry. She feels it will cause problems. What could possibly concern her so much?"

Brown Boy shook his head. "There are vague warnings and stories carried among the dead. I have always listened to the warnings because I want to fade as soon as possible to be with my

love again." He paused and shot her a speculative look.
"Nevertheless, I cannot help but be intrigued by this incident. I do
not know how anything bad could happen. Perhaps Blonde Hair is
frightened about stories of ghosts and possessions she heard while
in the living world."

Jeanne considered this. It was possible, but her worry
didn't ease. "I want to talk to Francois. Maybe he will know more
about this." She glanced sideways at him. "What do you think?"

His eyes brightened. "It is a good idea. I have to admit, I
have wanted to meet him, but the warnings kept me away." His
eyes narrowed, but after a second his face relaxed. "I would go
with you if you do not mind. Do you know where we can find
him?"

A tingle of pleasure made her shiver. She'd hoped he
would accompany her. Francois might have the answers she
needed, but she was a little frightened as well, especially after
Blonde Hair's warnings. She smiled and nodded. "I have a good
idea where he is. I will find you tomorrow after I meet with
Etienne, and we will seek Francois."

Chapter 3

Etienne's eyes burned from no sleep, but adrenaline kept him energized. He visited his friend Gaston to discuss the bizarre encounter at The Louvre. No one could understand the need for inspiration better than his old friend.

He climbed the stairs to Gaston's third floor garret studio and paused as shouts filtered down.

"You listen to me, you big.....oaf. No one needs to be up at three a.m. playing opera on the stereo. Are you crazy?" an angry female shouted.

"I couldn't sleep," Gaston responded in a loud but placating tone.

"If you can't sleep, read a book, drink warm milk, take a walk. But don't make noise. I just moved in yesterday and already I don't like you."

"Opera is the only thing that works," Gaston insisted.

"Then buy some headphones, and if you don't have money, trade one of these awful paintings for a pair."

Etienne reached the garret door. Inside, a tall, shapely woman with short spiked red hair confronted his friend. Gaston was a big man, but he shrank before her like a child whose hand had been caught in the cookie jar. In his typical paint splattered jeans and old T-shirt, he stood with a paintbrush in one hand and the other stretched in entreaty.

"Are they really...awful?" Gaston asked when she paused for breath. He glanced around at numerous fake Monets, Rembrandts and Reubens propped against the walls.

She bit her bottom lip, studying him. "Just keep it quiet from eleven p.m. to seven a.m. I don't think that's too much to ask. Don't make me come up here again." She turned in a huff and pushed past Etienne with a glare as she headed for the stairs.

"Hey, old friend. What have you done?" Etienne watched her exit, chuckling. "She was really, um, pissed off."

"She's magnificent." Gaston stared after her.

"I believe you've met your match." He laughed at Gaston's

cowed expression.

"Have you ever seen such a woman?" His friend sank into a chair beside a small table at the window, eyes unfocused after the encounter. "A glorious goddess with flaming hair."

"And temper to match. I assume she's your new downstairs neighbor?"

"Apparently so," Gaston replied. "I really didn't know anyone had moved in. I swear."

"Liar." He chuckled. "You've never cared what your neighbors thought, or anyone else for that matter."

His friend gave a rumble of low laughter. It started as a chuckle and grew to a hearty guffaw that made his belly shake. Etienne joined in. It seemed like years since they'd laughed so hard like this, slapping their knees and tears rolling down their cheeks. Finally the joviality dissipated and left them gasping for breath and wiping their eyes. A cathartic experience.

"My God, that felt good," Gaston said, brushing at his eyes. "All the weight on me lifted for a second. I miss that feeling of lightness—having no cares. Why can't I feel like that all the time?"

Etienne took a deep breath and slapped his friend on the back. "Like old times at art school," he agreed, wiping a last tear. "When we had dreams and thought they might come true."

"I wonder if she likes poetry," Gaston pursed his lips and crossed his arms over his chest.

"You really must ask her, my friend."

"So what are you doing here? I thought you were knee-deep in your spring collection." Gaston rose and placed a new canvas on his easel. "Did you bring any wine?"

"I have some exciting news I've been dying to tell you. Yesterday, I went to The Louvre."

"The Louvre? What for?" His friend raised a brow.

"I went crazy in search of inspiration, anything to bring back the spark of creativity I lost. I can't seem to find it in the present, so I thought maybe I should look in the past. Where is there more past in one place than The Louvre?"

"Hmm." Gaston shrugged. "Very true."

"Anyway, I wandered around for a while, and then I found myself at the Venus d' Milo. I noticed a gorgeous woman there. She was incredible. A knockout. I can't describe the feeling I had when I saw her. It was like when I was young, driving fast with the top down and my favorite rock song playing full blast. Pure adrenaline. I had to meet her. When I approached to talk, she acted shy."

"So, what happened?"

"We talked, that's all. Then last night, I went to my office and designed the best collection of my life."

His friend's expression remained blank. "You talked? That's it?"

"You're missing the point. I have my spark back. I have my inspiration."

"But what about the girl?"

"I'm seeing her again today."

"You're going to see her and then...?"

"Yes. What are you trying to say?"

Gaston sat and poured them red wine. He gestured for Etienne to sit in the other chair.

"Here." The big man pushed one of the glasses across the table. "So, you meet a gloriously beautiful woman, and all you talk about is your collection. Don't you see a problem with this?"

"What's wrong? I didn't talk about my collection to her. We barely spoke." He shook his head and ran fingers through his hair. Describing that moment of basking in her beauty seemed beyond him right now. The overwhelming glow of attraction and salvation had changed his life.

"Did you kiss her? Caress her arm? Whisper in her ear?" his friend asked.

"Ahh, so that's what you're getting at. Look, we talked for maybe five minutes at most. You don't get it. She made such an impact in that short time I was able to create an entire collection around her. It's good, Gaston. It's really good. She saved me."

"Hmm." His friend's eyes narrowed. "Is she an angel?"

"I'll try to explain in terms you can understand. It would be like you meeting someone at the market and coming home to paint the greatest masterpiece of your life after years of painting these reproductions." He waved an arm around the room. "She's a muse. The inspiration I needed. Don't you see?"

Gaston took a deep breath then nodded. "I think I understand. It's a spiritual thing."

He put his head in his hands in exasperation.

"It's okay. Really. I know you have trouble attracting women. You don't have my charm." Gaston patted his arm.

"Okay, forget it." He looked at his watch. "I have to go, anyway. I'm going to meet her again at The Louvre." He stood and moved to the door.

"Good luck, then, old friend. You should think about somewhere more romantic for your next date though," Gaston called after him as he hurried down the stairs.

He literally ran into the red-haired woman carrying a box in the front door as he rushed out.

"I'm sorry. I didn't see you," he said. "Here, let me hold the door for you."

She scowled at first, but then nodded as she passed inside.

"I'm Etienne, a friend of Gaston's. We weren't properly introduced before." He followed her to a first floor apartment and opened that door for her as well.

"Thank you. I'm Vivienne. You didn't exactly see me at my best up there. I'm not trying to be rude, but your friend woke me in the middle of the night. I had an important interview today." She put down the box and offered a hand.

He smiled and warmly shook it. "Oh, I think you were *very* good up there, just what Gaston needs. Don't give him any slack and he'll be eating out of your hand in no time."

Vivienne's façade of reserve melted and she laughed. "I'm not sure that's what I'm after, but if it will make him behave, I'll take your advice. What's up with the paintings? All those reproductions. I didn't mean to offend him, but what's he doing?" She wrinkled her nose.

"He makes a lot of money painting them while he's waiting for inspiration. He's really a good guy. You should go later and have a glass of wine with him. I think he'll behave from now on."

She gave him the once over, but said, "If you say so, I'll do that. I don't want to have bad relations with my neighbors."

"Good. Sorry, I have to leave. I'm sure I'll see you again. Very pleased to meet you, Vivienne." He smiled and waved as he headed for the front door to look for his taxi. He had to meet his mystery lady.

24

***

Jeanne strolled around the Venus statue, counting her circles. She'd reached two thousand and forty-nine when Etienne appeared. He hastened and appeared anxious, glancing about the room. That thrilled her. He searched in every direction, brow furrowed. She went around the statue and his gaze found her.

His face lit up and he came toward her smiling. *"Mademoiselle.* I'm so happy to see you again."

"Jeanne," she said, a flutter of happiness at saying her name made her grin.

"Pardon me?"

"My name. It is Jeanne," she replied, proudly.

"Ah. So, Jeanne is it? Very pretty." Etienne glanced around and fidgeted with the lapel of his jacket. He started to speak then looked down.

"I am happy to see you again, Etienne," she said, amused at his nervousness.

"Thanks. I'm glad you decided to meet me." He took a deep breath. "Would you like to join me for a cup of tea? There's a café at the entrance." He pointed behind him.

She paused only a second before nodding. She couldn't drink tea but she could watch him.

They moved among the crowd to the café, and Etienne found a table for them then purchased two cups of tea. The deep aroma of fresh brewed espresso wafted around them along with a touch of cinnamon.

Jeanne swiveled her head, flooded with interest. She didn't frequent this part of the museum. It was fascinating to watch the living here, so busy and interactive. Until yesterday, her life had been absorbed in works of art, and she usually ignored people except to avoid moving through them. This was very different. Exhilarating.

She studied Etienne as he took the seat opposite her. Handsome chiseled features were accented by his nearly black hair. Once again a wave of familiarity, even intimacy, washed over her. She almost felt the heat of his arms imagining them wrapped around her. She closed her eyes, savoring this encounter. Happiness. The way he gazed at her filled her with a joy she couldn't remember from her past. Surely this wasn't a bad thing.

"You look very beautiful today," he said, rubbing his fingers over his cup.

"And you look very handsome." An insistent tug of memory continued. It had to be that she had seen him or known him in the past, but how could that be possible?

"I have to tell you, you made such an impression on me yesterday. It was amazing. Tell me about yourself." He took a drink of tea.

"Oh, no. You must tell me your story first," she countered. It flustered her to be asked to reveal a past she didn't remember.

"Very well, if you insist. I'm determined to please you." He told of his passion to be a fashion designer, how he'd made an impact on the fashion world with his first collection and then the subsequent failures over the last few years.

"Fashion, that is so exciting. You must be very talented. I would love to see some of your work," Jeanne said, leaning toward him over the table. "I am very interested in art. I used to paint—" She sat back in her chair, stunned. She hadn't remembered that information until now. She used to paint. Yes, that's right. She'd painted landscapes in oil paint. This new memory told her she'd enjoyed it, although she believed she hadn't been very good.

"You painted?" he asked.

"Yes, yes I did. Landscapes."

"Why did you stop?"

Why did she stop? Was it because she'd died, or was there another reason? A faint memory struggled to the surface, a vision of someone who'd insisted on her ending her attempt at painting. But why? The full memory lay hidden.

"I am not sure why," she responded. "I still love art. That has not changed. Will you allow me to see some of your designs?"

His hands shook as he pulled papers from his coat pocket. He gazed at them, then hesitantly unfolded the sheets and smoothed the creases. Finally, he slid them across the table to her. She could feel his gaze as she studied the drawings and his notes of fabrics along the edges.

The first, an evening gown of white chiffon reminded her of her own dress, only this design draped from one shoulder and sparkled with golden glints that scattered sparsely at the waist to a denser patter at the hem. She gasped in delight.

"Oh my." She motioned for him to reveal the next picture.

He slid that sheet away and their gazes met briefly before she lowered hers to the design. This one was a short cocktail dress of black taffeta mixed with white satin and lace inserts. Amazed at the geometric effect, she shook her head, speechless.

When he removed the last sheet, she continued to stare at the table. Such beautiful ideas. He'd skillfully combined art and comfort in each design. Women would love them. She raised her gaze to his. "They are genius, Etienne. Truly genius. You have combined so many elegant nuances. I am very impressed."

He nodded eagerly. "I'm so glad you like them."

"You tell me you have not been successful lately, but these designs are wonderful. Surely this will be a triumph," she said.

"I'm pinning all my hopes on them, actually. Otherwise it'll be the end of my career."

"But the sketches." She paused and glanced at the figure on the last drawing. "There is one part of them I find confusing."

"Yes? What is that?"

"The face. Each figure has the same face and it is mine."

He opened his mouth, but no sound emerged.

"Etienne?"

A play of confusion, guilt, and elation crossed his features. "Yes? I'm sorry. I'm having trouble finding the words to relay the significance of meeting you yesterday."

"Just tell me."

He looked away for a moment, and after a deep breath, said, "I told you about my current design slump. I'd already designed a spring collection for this year and am only four weeks away from presenting it. When I saw you yesterday, everything I'd been searching for came into focus. Jeanne, you are the inspiration for this collection. Not just the collection, but, well, I know this will sound crazy, but you also helped me believe in myself again. I thought I no longer had the ability to innovate, to truly create. I cannot thank you enough for that gift."

His earnest declaration filled her with glowing elation. An unexpected urge to weep followed the initial rush of pleasure thinking she'd instigated his redemption. As an artist, she understood the need to celebrate one's unique abilities and the impact of creations on others.

"I feel honored and inadequate for this praise." She shook her head and pressed her hands to her cheeks.

He leaned forward, his eyes sharp and intent. "No, Jeanne. You're way more than adequate. In fact, I want you to be the focus of the collection. You should be the face of House Etienne."

She raised her head and blinked rapidly. "What do you mean?"

"I mean that without you, there is no collection. I want you to be the heart. — Your face on billboards, in ads for Vogue and W, on the red carpet at the showing of the collection. Without you, each creation is incomplete. I need you." He reached across the table, but she pulled away.

She stared at him, speechless, startled. His interest had been about how she could help him profit from this new collection? Had she imagined the romantic connection between them? The attraction? Confusion stripped her of her fantasy and left her vulnerable. Maybe Blonde Hair was right about the dangers of getting involved with the living. He'd been so earnest; she hadn't anticipated this revelation.

"I ... I don't know what to say. This is unexpected." She stood and glanced around.

He stood, rubbed his chin and placed his hands on his hips.

"I need to go now," she whispered. A crushing sense of disappointment overwhelmed her.

"No, please," he entreated. "Have I offended you? I'm sorry. Please, don't leave."

People at adjacent tables glanced at him, brows raised.

"I have to go now." She headed to the café exit. As a soul, she moved faster than he could follow. When she passed under the pyramid, she flitted left into the Richelieu wing. He called after her, but she had to get away and sort through her emotions. The happiness and fulfillment she'd sought had evaporated in minutes. She needed to find Brown Boy. Maybe he could help her make sense of Etienne's actions.

Chapter 4

Jeanne glided aimlessly along the Richelieu wing, floating through people instead of moving around them as she would normally. She barely noticed that the living shivered and glanced around as she passed. Etienne's comments and her disappointment kept her preoccupied.

As she neared the end of the wing, her surroundings returned to focus. She backed against a wall and studied the throngs of people. Perhaps she'd been too abrupt in her judgment of him. Had she let Blonde Hair's warning instill an excess of caution?

There was no disguising the earnest appeal in Etienne's eyes. Surely she'd not been so mistaken in his character. A connection existed between them, she was sure of it, and it wasn't only for his commercial needs. What should she do?

She needed to find Brown Boy. After floating to Sully, she located him near where they'd met yesterday.

"I am glad to see you," he exclaimed.

"Brown Boy, I need to talk with you," she said urgently.

"It is George," he announced.

"George? What do you mean? Who is he?"

"My name. I remembered it. After talking to you yesterday, I decided I needed to try and remember more of my history if I am to discover why I am not able to fade. I focused on what memories I still had, and then more emerged. Of course I remember my fiancé. That was easy. Then I remembered my name is George Spillwell. I am from London, England. I was visiting Paris when a carriage accident happened. I was killed in front of the Louvre. That is all I know so far, but I am going to keep at it until I can discover my fade-block."

"Fade-block?" Jeanne drew a blank.

"That is what I call it. Each person who cannot fade must have a fade-block. A specific reason or purpose they must understand and resolve before they are able to pass to Everlasting."

"Ahh," Jeanne said, dazed by this rush of information.

"So, what about you? Did you meet Etienne?"

She twisted her hands together. "Oh, George, I have been foolish, I am afraid." She explained what had occurred in the café and how she'd run away. "I was hurt thinking he only wanted me to be a figure for the benefit of his collection. I so hoped he liked me. I need to be liked. Of course, I kept thinking about what Blonde Hair had said, too. Now I may never see him again. What shall I do?"

George stroked his chin, considering this dilemma with appropriate seriousness. "Now, the way I see it, this situation may be what you need to break your fade-block."

"How can that make a difference?" she asked.

"Helping Etienne. Maybe you have a purpose to aid him. He says he is on the brink of disaster. Your assistance would provide him a way to survive. From what you told me, he seems a good sort - someone who deserves to be helped. See what I mean? I cannot believe helping someone could lead to something horrible."

Her hope burned brighter. "If only that were possible. I should be pleased to help him."

"This is a good question to ask Francois when we see him, but why else would this interaction have happened?"

"True, this is an unusual occurrence. It is not every day a soul talks with a living person." She was finding more to commend this idea of George's. Why would she have met Etienne and have him be able to see her and talk to her if their interaction wasn't important? Even fated?

Her friend beamed. She put a hand on his arm, grateful for his interest in helping her. "I must make contact with him again. How will I find him?"

"He might return to the place you first met. It's the only connection between the two of you. You must go to the Venus."

"Yes, yes. That is what I must do. Thank you, George." She waved a hand in farewell and rushed to the scene of their first meeting.

***

Etienne stood in the middle of Hall Napoleon. He slowly

spun, searching for Jeanne. She'd disappeared. He slapped his hands to his thighs in frustration. Damn it. Why was he such a fool? He'd lost her.

He rubbed his burning eyelids. She'd gotten under his skin with her mystery. Today, she wore the same dress she'd worn yesterday. What reason could there be for that? He couldn't deny the connection between them. She'd captivated him like no other woman. When he considered the rich socialites and leggy models who'd thrown themselves at him over the years, he realized he'd had no trouble avoiding entanglement with any of them. Jeanne was different. Every time he directed his thoughts elsewhere, her lovely face intruded. Her elegant movements, graceful as a dancer, fascinated him.

Across the hall stood the woman who looked like Jeanne but wore modern clothes. Startled, he froze. Perhaps the lack of sleep made him hallucinate. But no, there she was, carrying the camera in her hands and taking pictures of different aspects of the entrance area. Then she headed into the Denon Wing, quickly gone from his sight. He couldn't believe it. Who was she and why did she look so much like Jeanne? A pounding throb began behind his eyes. He had to get out of there.

He left the museum, frustrated and confused, gravitating to Gaston's place in a daze. Self-directed anger burned at the disaster he'd made of the meeting with Jeanne. Had he lost her forever?

Gaston wasn't in his garret, so he knocked on the door of his friend's second floor apartment. Voices and laughter emerged from behind the door.

"Etienne," Gaston bellowed after opening the door. "Come in, come in, my friend."

Vivienne had taken his advice to give Gaston another chance. They shared an artistically arranged bread and cheese tray while drinking red wine. She lounged on the sofa and gave Etienne a conspiratorial wink.

"This is Vivienne." His friend gestured to his guest. "I didn't have a chance to introduce you when you were here earlier." Then he pulled him into a bear hug. "And this is my best friend in the world, Etienne."

His eyes bulged at the strength of the embrace. Clearly this was not their first bottle of wine. Drinking made Gaston either

sentimental or suicidal. He was grateful he wouldn't have to deal
with a tearful friend today.

"It's a pleasure to meet you." She handed him a glass of the
wine.

"Thanks. Glad you two are having a better visit than the
last time I was here." He broke from Gaston's hold and settled in a
chair beside the sofa.

"Have some of this wonderful cheese." His friend gestured
to the tray. "Vivienne brought it. She's a chef. Isn't that great?"

"Really? Where are you working?" He took a piece of
cheese from the tray and savored the rich nutty taste.

"Nowhere yet. I'm looking." She grinned. "I just graduated
from the Cordon Bleu. It's hard to find a job when you haven't
worked as a chef yet. All they want to offer new graduates is *sous*
chef."

"Isn't that how it works, though? You work as a *sous* chef
for a while to gain experience in the real world, and then get your
own place?" He reached for more cheese and a piece of bread,
realizing he hadn't eaten much today. His stomach rumbled in
gratitude.

She shrugged. "I suppose that is the path for most, but I've
been cooking a long time. I had a small café in Provence before I
came to school. I want to be a chef and create, not just chop
vegetables. I want to have a five-star restaurant right here in Paris."

He and Gaston shared a glance. Another person seeking
fame for their art. She fit right in.

They were interrupted by a knock on the door, and his
friend got up to see who it was.

"Thanks for the tip about your friend," she whispered.
"He's funny. I like him as long as he doesn't wake me up again."

"I'm glad. If you continue to feed him, your sleep will be
sacred, I promise."

She put a hand over her mouth, stifling a laugh.

Gaston pulled open a crate that had been delivered. He
stripped away packing and revealed a small painting about a foot
square in an elaborately carved vintage frame. "Ah, you beauty."
He held the picture at arm's length and stared at it, then bestowed a
kiss inches from its surface. "Mmmwhaa."

"Another piece for your mystery collection?" Etienne went

to inspect the new painting.

"Yes, and I have a place already reserved for it." Gaston crossed to the wall behind an easy chair and placed the small painting in an open space between two similar paintings.

"It's nice," Vivienne commented, cocking her head to one side in consideration. "I was worried about your judgment when I saw those reproductions upstairs. This choice redeems you. Is it the same artist as these others?" She gestured to the various small-framed pictures that hung around Gaston's apartment. "I don't recognize the artist. Are they famous?"

"Only to Gaston." Etienne laughed.

"Come on, they're great. Admit it," his friend protested.

"Yes, they're very well done, but you don't know who painted them. I don't understand your fascination, that's all. With your connections, you could've made some good investments over the years with well-known artists. These will never be worth anything."

"I don't care. I like them. The mystery of the painter is part of the allure. Finding them is one of the few pleasures left in my life. Don't deprive me of that," Gaston grumbled.

"Well, I like them, too," she declared, earning a grateful smile from their host. "But how do you know they're from the same person?"

"First of all, I know the style of this artist so well I could identify them anywhere. But, they do have a clue." He motioned for her to come closer to the new painting. "There in the left-hand corner is a small "V." Do you see it?" He pointed to the area.

"Ah, yes, there it is. It's very small, and faint, almost as if the artist wanted it unnoticed. Why would that be?"

His friend shrugged. "Who knows? It's part of the mystery, which appeals to me. One day I'll uncover the secret. I'm determined."

"But I see what you mean. Up-close the brush work is exquisite," she said with her nose inches from the canvas.

The big man nodded approval.

She hesitated, then turned from her perusal. "I'd better get back to unpacking. I'll leave you two alone for now."

Gaston began to protest, but she remained firm. After telling them to finish off the cheese and bread, she departed.

"She's really something," Gaston declared after the door closed.

"You're clearly smitten."

"What's wrong with that? You have your mystery Louvre lady, why can't I have a female diversion?"

"I don't have the mystery lady anymore, I'm afraid. Her name is Jeanne, by the way," he said. The hurt look in her eyes haunted him.

"I told you it wasn't a good idea to have a date at the Louvre. You need a nice restaurant, candlelight, flowers ..."

"Oh, stop it," Etienne exclaimed in exasperation. "It had nothing to do with that. Everything was going well until I stuck my foot in my mouth."

"You do that a lot, my friend. What did you do this time?"

"I showed her copies of the sketches I did last night. I was trying to relay how important she was to me and it came out as if I was only there to ask for her to help in promoting the collection. I said it all wrong." He dropped his head into his hands and mumbled, "I think I love her."

"What did you say?" Gaston demanded.

"I said, I think I love her," he shouted. "Haven't you ever heard of love at first sight?"

The big man blinked in surprise and said solemnly, "I never thought I would hear those words cross your lips." His friend grabbed him in another bear hug, pounding his back until he nearly choked. "Congratulations, my friend. I'm very happy for you."

"St-st-stop!" He finally got out and pushed the big man away.

"What? I can't be happy my best friend has finally found love? This is Paris, the city of love. We celebrate love here." He began to hum a popular love song, waving his hands in time to the tune.

"If you will please brew a pot of coffee and drink some, I will tell you why we cannot celebrate." Etienne coughed, struggling to get his breath back.

"All right, all right. If that's what you want. Come sit at the bar and tell me your tragic story while I put on the coffee." Gaston went into the kitchen.

He followed and took a seat on a stool.

"As I was saying, we were having a great conversation until I screwed up what I was trying to tell her. I guess it offended her and she ran away."

"She ran away? That's too bad." He clicked his tongue.

"Yes," he said, miserable.

"Women. They love to run away."

"They do?"

"Yes, yes. They're passionate about it."

"But why? I don't understand."

"Because they want you to chase them, you idiot. Don't you know anything about women?"

"Chase them? That doesn't make any sense."

"Yes, for them it means commitment or something." His friend gestured with the coffee pot. "You know, like when knights would kill dragons for princesses. It's like that."

"So chasing after them is like slaying a dragon," Etienne stated uncertainly. "Some form of gallantry."

"Ex-actly. Now you're getting it."

"I'm not sure ..."

"Well, I'm sure. You need to take my advice for once. Go after her and everything will be fine."

"That's the problem," Etienne said. "I don't know how to find her. I don't even know her last name."

His friend's brow in concentration. Then a broad smile broke across his face. "So, you don't know how to find her and she doesn't know how to find you, right?" He swayed on his feet and reached for the counter to steady himself.

"Right."

"Wrong." Gaston continued to grin. "The only place in common is where you first met."

"Venus di' Milo," Etienne said after a few seconds.

"Venus di' Milo." Gaston nodded.

He bolted from his stool and headed for the door.

"Wait. What about the coffee?" his friend called.

"It was for you, buddy. Thanks," he yelled from the hall.

He had to find Jeanne.

Chapter 5

Jeanne returned to circling the statue to pass time. With each step, she pondered everything Etienne had said during their brief *tête-à-tête*. She was now committed to help him, but she faced a large impediment. He was the only one who could see her. She would be forced to tell him the truth—that she was a ghost. That would be difficult. He said he wanted her as the face of House Etienne, but she had no way to accomplish this. Hopefully, moral support and creative inspiration would be gift enough for him to succeed.

At her four hundred, twenty-fifth circle, he rushed through the room entrance headed for the statue. An internal glow suffused her soul as it did whenever she saw him. She smiled and went to meet him. Their eyes locked at once, and she could see in his that she had done right in giving him another chance. Nobody could fake such relief. His face radiated sheer joy.

"Jeanne," he said when she neared. "I'm so sorry. Everything I was trying to tell you came out wrong. I want to be with you. That's what's important."

She stopped a few steps away. "It is my fault, Etienne. I should not have run away. I should have let you finish. I do want to help you, if you still need me."

He closed his eyes. "There will be no living with Gaston after he was right about this." His laughter resonated with relief.

She laughed with him, filled with happiness again. Now she had the difficult task of enlightening him about her afterlife existence. She couldn't predict how he would react to this news, but she had to disclose her true nature. It wasn't fair to lead him to believe she could accomplish something impossible. He might be the one to run away this time, and she was desperate not to lose him. She motioned him to follow her into the hall and gestured to a bench in an alcove where they could talk.

"Etienne, I have to tell you something important," she began.

"Oh, my God," he exclaimed, dismay darkening his eyes.

"What?" She jerked back in surprise.

"You're married, aren't you? That's what all the mystery is about."

"No, that is not it. I am not married. At least I do not think so." Her eyes widened and she bit a fingernail.

"What do you mean? You don't know if you're married or not? Why are you being so mysterious?"

"That is what I want to talk to you about. I have to explain." She knew he must be exasperated, but it made telling him the truth proved more difficult than she'd imagined. She wished she could touch him, take his hand, and reassure him of her regard for him.

"Please," he said, eyes pleading.

"Etienne, I am not like you." She paused. "I...well, I come from another time."

He shook his head.

"Oh, I am making a sad botch of this," she exclaimed. "Look, I will just say it. There is no way to make this less shocking. I am dead."

"Dead." He blinked several times, and his mouth opened and closed.

"Yes. I am what you call a ghost or a spirit."

"A ghost," he repeated.

"I died a long time ago, and I am caught here for some reason. I do not know why, but I really do want to help you. However, I cannot be the face of House Etienne, because, well, because no one can see me." She broke off and placed a hand over her mouth to stop her nervous babbling.

He started to laugh. "Okay. That's fair. I deserved it."

"What are you talking about?" She leaned back, surprised by his reaction.

"This is a prank. I get it. You wanted to have a joke on me for how I bungled our date this afternoon. That's really good. You had me going there for a minute. You should be an actress."

"Etienne, it is not a joke. I am serious." She stared at him until his chuckles faded away and his face went slack.

"What are you saying? You're dead and no one can see you? But that's not true. I can see you."

"I know. That is a mystery, but we have a connection, you

and I. We were meant to meet for some reason," she said, leaning forward.

"There are no such thing as ghosts," he said.

"Take my hand." She held out her right hand.

He glanced at her, hesitating.

"Take my hand," she repeated.

His fingers inched toward hers, and he when he tried to grasp her...nothing. He gasped.

She nodded.

He tried to touch her face and met air. He shivered. "It-it-it's true," he stammered. "But it's impossible. How is this happening? I can see you. You look as real as me, but you're not there." He reached for her shoulder and his hand passed through her body. He scooted, putting more bench between them.

"Yes, it is true. I am sorry to cause a complication when I truly mean to help."

Conflicting emotions warred in his expression: disbelief, fear, hurt.

"I just can't believe it." He stared at her, his eyes moving back and forth as he studied her face. "Why can't anyone else see you?"

"I do not know." She shrugged. "This situation never happened to me before, and it happens rarely to other ghosts."

"There are others?" He glanced around.

"Yes, but you cannot see them." She sighed. "Let me explain." It took a while, but she relayed the story of the souls and what happened after death, how they were supposed to fade, but some didn't.

"So, you haven't, what do you call it, *faded* yet?"

"No. I was beginning to forget, and then I met you. Now I feel I have some purpose to fulfill. Until yesterday, I didn't even remember my name. Memories are starting to return, but it is a slow process."

"You don't know who you are," he stated.

She shook her head. "No."

"That has to be distressing."

She nodded.

He rubbed his eyes. "This is a lot to comprehend."

"Etienne, are you all right?" She pressed a hand to her

chest, leaning forward.

"I don't know. I just don't know." He stood and gazed down at her. "I need to think about all this. I'm...I'm confused."

She reached for him then drew back, understanding. "Is there any way I can still help with your collection? I want you to succeed. I care for you."

He seemed not to hear her as he scanned the area. "Do you stay here all the time?"

"Yes. This is all I remember since my death."

He winced. He ran fingers through his hair, closed his eyes then suddenly opened them. "Jeanne, something strange happened twice while I was here in the museum. I saw a woman who looked almost exactly like you, but she wore jeans, modern clothes. Do you know who she is? Have you seen her?"

"A woman who resembles me?" She searched for such a memory. "No, I have no idea. Before yesterday, I was so focused on fading I really did not notice much until I saw you."

"This is all so bizarre. I can't help wondering if she's involved in this strangeness. Why would I see two women who look alike, and one is a ghost?"

"I must agree it is puzzling."

"Hey, I'm sorry. I need time to deal with this. Nothing is making sense. I'll come back tomorrow. Will you be here?"

"Come to the Venus. I shall be there. Will you be all right?"

"I guess. I have to think. I'll see you tomorrow." With a shaky smile that didn't reach his eyes, he headed toward the exit.

***

Once out on the street, Etienne signaled a taxi and gave the address of his shop. He'd arrive later than planned, but he needed to see what his staff had accomplished on the new collection. He had nothing else now. How could he have fallen in love with a ghost? Just as his life took on new meaning, a huge chunk of that meaning disintegrated. He shook his head. Somehow he must put this fantasy aside and focus on reality. It didn't help that he suffered from exhaustion, skewing his judgment and concentration.

The atelier swirled in a storm of activity. People ran, yelled and tossed papers, fabric and other objects back and forth. In the midst of the chaos, Chloe stood directing traffic, a tape measure around her neck, two pens stuck in her hair at odd angles, and a cell phone in one hand. A chuckle rose in his gut. She was truly in her element—a tiny Amazon of organization.

When her gaze met his, she smiled in relief and motioned him forward. The sketches he'd done last night were each posted on individual easels set in a semicircle. At the base of each easel sat bolts of fabric. Chloe motioned for an assistant to bring him a chair.

"I was afraid you weren't coming back," she whispered in his ear as he sat. "I was going to kill you."

"And miss all this madness? Never." He focused and pushed fatigue aside.

They spent the rest of the evening discussing what fabrics to use for each design. The paper patterns were finished. Tomorrow they would start preliminary cuttings, using muslin so they could make adjustments on the fitting models. The fabrics they chose tonight would then be cut from the final muslin patterns. They dispensed with steps that might have made the process smoother, but they had to save time. Chloe chose this less common route to the finished product. She would oversee every phase, so precision would not be lost in deleted steps. The finished clothes had to be perfect.

"So, we meet back here tomorrow," Chloe announced to the remaining workers. "Pattern cutting begins."

Cheers sounded from the group.

The applause made Etienne realize they were as excited about this new collection as Chloe and he. It shouldn't have surprised him. They took pride in House Etienne and wanted to be winners. Their enthusiasm reminded him their careers were as much on the line as his. If he went down, they did too. He needed this new perspective right now, and it spurred him onward. The disappointment over Jeanne weighed on him, but he had to succeed for his House, not just for his pride.

"What's wrong?" Chloe sat in a chair beside him, concern lighting her eyes. "Where have you been all day?"

He leaned back in his chair and stared at the ceiling then glanced at Chloe. "Do you believe in ghosts?"

"I don't know. Maybe. Why?" Her brown eyes slid away and then back.

"I just wondered if you had ever thought about it."

"Are you serious?" She searched his face.

He nodded, solemn.

"I've never seen one, if that's what you mean," she said. "But I have a friend whose aunt is a medium. She's told me a lot of things that can't be explained any other way. Her aunt has séances for people who want to contact dead relatives. You would be amazed at what has taken place during some of those." She tucked a short lock of brown hair behind one ear. "I guess it's possible for there to be ghosts. Who could really know unless you had seen one yourself?"

He started to tell her about Jeanne, but changed his mind and remained silent. It was a burden he couldn't share.

"So, why are you asking?" she prodded.

"I don't know, Chloe. Maybe I've gone crazy. I think I need to get some sleep." He stood and started for the door then glanced at her. "You did a great job today, by the way. I couldn't do this without you, you know."

She snorted. "Yeah, I know."

He gave a wave and headed out. All he wanted now was to have a glass of wine, collapse under the covers of his bed and try to make sense of everything that had happened today. How had he ended up in such a bizarre situation? In love with a ghost - his muse, a ghost - the hope of his collection, a ghost. Not to mention some living woman walking around in the Louvre who looked just like her. Maybe he would wake in the morning and learn this had been a bizarre dream.

Still, he couldn't regret the unique encounter. Jeanne had inspired his greatest work so far and pulled him from a deadly slump. Ghost or not, they shared some connection. She even offered to help him despite how he'd initially presented his proposal. Maybe she was right about a reason for their encounter. Meeting her had already produced results which were tremendously beneficial for him and his career. If only the world could see her as he did, her beauty, her essence of perfection. His arms ache to hold her. If only he could touch her, be with her ... ah, well. He could dream.

***

Margot hit SEND on her computer to transfer her photos of The Louvre to Professor Galen. She sighed. It had been interesting spending time in the famous museum again, but taking pictures of pictures wasn't very stimulating. Still, the money for the project would be good and she could afford the new lens for her camera she'd been lusting after.

She picked up her mail from the coffee table and sank to the couch beside it. Bills, bills and bills. Ah, and the new copy of Vogue. She tossed the other envelopes aside and settled back to immerse herself in the latest fashions. She didn't make enough money to own any of these glorious designs, but she certainly enjoyed looking at them.

Her doorbell rang. She rose and opened it to reveal her friend Lily, a petite blond with big blue eyes and tiny frame. She wore red leggings and a black silk tunic belted with a gold medallion chain.

"I've got tickets to see Maroon 5 tomorrow night. Want to come?" her friend gushed and hurried in. "I know you love them."

Her heart leapt. That was her favorite band. "Of course I want to go."

"Great. I have to take you away from your boring pastime listening to old jazz." Lily gave her a hug.

She laughed. "It's not boring. Those are classics. I like a broad range of music."

Her friend plopped herself on the sofa. "Yeah, modern jazz and classic jazz."

"That's an exaggeration. Want some wine?" She headed for the kitchen.

"Red," Lily called. "Got any exciting jobs coming up? I love being your assistant at weddings. I get to graze the buffets and the hot men."

Margot returned with two glasses of wine. "Two next week. I could use another pair of hands."

"Sure. I'm happy to help. It's fun." She took a glass and clinked it against hers. "Cheers."

"Cheers. Did you hear anything from your cousin?"

"Yes, sorry. He said they don't need any more photographers for the fashion shoot."

"Oh." Her heart sank. Another opportunity shot down.

"He said he'd keep you in mind for the future, though." Lily rested a hand on her arm. "I know how much you wanted to do it."

"It's okay." She shrugged, trying to produce a smile. Another hit to her dream.

Chapter 6

Jeanne set out to find George and discuss what had occurred. Elation invaded her like bubbles of light flooding her being. Etienne had not deserted her. George was right. Their meeting was no mistake. She surely had a purpose to fulfill. It was important for Etienne to succeed, and she was going to help him in any way she could. Now, she had no desire to fade. She wanted to stay in the present with Etienne.

She found George staring at the Mona Lisa, and called a greeting.

"I am glad you found me, Jeanne. I have been worried about you," he said, turning to meet her.

"I returned to the Venus as you suggested, George. You were right. Etienne came full of apologies."

"That is good," he exclaimed. "It is what you wanted, right?"

"Well, yes. I agree our meeting has a purpose, and I want to help him. The problem is he needs me as a model for his collection, and as you well know, no one can see me but him."

He pursed his lips, pressing a forefinger against them. "Hmm, I think now is the time to find Francois. Maybe he can help us with these questions."

"Yes," she agreed. "That is exactly what we need to do. Another soul told me he's in the Napoleon Salon today."

They floated up the stairs to the first floor where the decorative art collections were housed. Both the Grand Salon of Napoleon in Richelieu and the Salle Grog-Carven in Sully housed expansive collections of elaborate chairs and cabinetry. These collections also displayed priceless rugs, tapestries, chandeliers and mirrors. They were cordoned from the public, and the spirits could gather undisturbed. The souls arranged their bodies in positions of sitting or lounging on the historic furniture.

Francois had settled in the Napoleon Grande Salon re-creation. He stood beside the fireplace, one leg crossed in front of the other as he took a position leaning against its ornately carved frame. His dress dated from the period of the late eighteenth century: black pantaloons that came to his knees, white hose and brown buckled shoes with heels. His coat was an elaborate embroidered affair with large cuffs over a ruffled white shirt. A wig of white hair had a ponytail pulled back at the nape of his neck. A jewel-encrusted sword hung from a leather belt about his hips. He spoke softly, and the twenty or so souls gathered there leaned forward intently. To the living, their speech would sound like no more than the faintest whisper, a murmur not unexpected in a place of such history.

Jeanne and her friend sat on a rounded settee with silk ferns in its center. No one seemed to notice their arrival or either didn't care enough to miss anything uttered by Francois. Fascination with the man overcame her at once. His countenance exuded confidence and wisdom. No arrogance or condescension appeared in his manner. He spoke with genuine sincerity, and a light of compassion shone in his eyes. Blonde Hair insisted he lured new souls with grand tales and dangerous falsehoods that caused confusion and pain. She saw no evidence of malicious intent in his demeanor, at least so far.

"What if someone we left behind needs contact? What if they're suffering? If we communicate with them in some way to comfort them, is that so wrong?" A young woman wearing a bridal gown asked. Her face squeezed in an agonized countenance of unresolved pain.

Francois looked to see who had spoken. The young bride sat in a chair to his right, still clutching a bouquet of white roses in one hand as the other clasped her chest. He smiled gently, his expression of benevolent patience indicated he'd heard this same question many times over the past centuries.

"My dear," he said as he floated to her side. "Tell me the story of your death." He held out one hand and took her trembling fingers.

"I was only twenty years old." She smiled tremulously as she glanced at the others. "It was my dream wedding, held here in the courtyard of the Louvre. I was marrying my childhood boyfriend, with friends and family here to celebrate. I couldn't have been happier." She paused and looked down. "What a freak thing to happen, I had an aneurysm in my brain. I said 'I do' and I fell dead at his feet." She gazed at Francois whose eyes held empathy. "My new husband, the love of my life, fell across my lifeless body, sobbing. I couldn't stand to see him suffer like that. I want to tell him I'm okay, that he has to go on living and try to be happy. Is that so terrible?" The expression in her eyes pleaded.

"You have been to see him?" Francois asked gently, kneeling beside her.

She nodded, head hanging low. "Yes, many times."

"And what do you propose? Should you appear to him as an apparition and give him this message? You envisioned a note perhaps? How long has it been?" Francois questioned in his soft voice.

The bride looked up, her brow furrowed. "I'd never want to frighten him. Is that what would happen? He'd think I was just some, some, *ghost*?"

Jeanne stared, entranced. When she glanced at George beside her, his face held the same rapt expression as the others.

"It's been a year. I...I don't know what I should do. I just don't want him to suffer," the bride stammered.

"I think it is you who suffers now, my child. You are living the same memory over and over. You must understand the living can go on and have memories past the point of your death. After a year, your beloved is well along the path of healing. If you appear to him now, will it not make him suffer again as it did that fatal day?" Francois' hand tenderly moved over hers.

The bride raised her head, eyes brightened.

"You seek absolution for dying and causing pain to those you left behind. You must let go of this guilt. It was not by your desire that you died. You suffered from the death as well. Look how you have agonized over this," he exclaimed. "Poor child, you have suffered enough. The living will heal and go on, and so must you. Do you understand?"

She nodded. "Thank you. Thank you," she said fervently, grasping his hand. She smiled then and it seemed every soul present breathed a sigh of relief. She rose from her chair still smiling and strolled down the hall. As she retreated, her form became more transparent, and then disappeared completely. She had faded.

Jeanne moved to the edge of her seat. The bride passed in serenity. She was more convinced than ever that she had to talk to this man about her own lack of contentment, and the fear Blonde Hair had instilled in her.

Many other souls brought questions to him. She was impressed with how he individualized his response to each situation. In some cases, he urged contact. In others, he discouraged it. He was very intuitive about the living and clearly maintained a passion to help distressed souls.

As the day progressed to evening, the number of souls present dwindled to four or five. Francois moved about the room answering questions, standing close to those with whom he spoke. He came at last to the rounded settee where she and George sat.

"Monsieur, and mademoiselle." Francois gave a half bow. "I have not seen you here before."

"No, we came today for the first time," George answered with a gesture to include her.

"My name is George and this is my friend, Jeanne. If I may be so bold, will you tell us of your own death?" he asked, eyes intent on the older soul.

Francois paused, appearing taken aback. He studied George then nodded.

"It has been many years since I have related the details of my living existence to anyone. Most souls who visit me have so many questions of their own that there is no time for my own sorrow." A shiver shook him, and he straightened his shoulders.

Francois sat in a chair close by and gazed into the distance for a space of time before facing her. When he scanned her face, a surprised flicker of recognition crossed his features.

"Monsieur, do you know me?" she asked eagerly. What if he knew her from the past? He could help her remember.

Francois' eyes widened, but he shook his head, closing his eyes. "No, my dear. It is merely that you look so much like my darling Gabrielle." A flash of pain crossed his face.

Jeanne leaned forward, troubled. "Monsieur, please, if we are causing you distress, do not concern yourself with this request."

He took a few seconds to school his features. Did he attempt to ease the reflection of his inner turmoil? What had he

47

suffered?

"Well, perhaps it could be beneficial to speak of my pain. I have spent so much time helping others, I have not dealt with my own difficulties for quite a long time. I will tell you my story if you wish. Perhaps it is time. My own death, or what led to it...that is quite a story." He crossed one leg over the other.

"I must start when I was alive for you to understand. Back then, this museum was used for many purposes. Sometimes it was a royal residence, part of it was a museum of collected royal art, and part of it was a hall of artists actively pursuing their craft. When Louis XIV moved the court to Versailles, everything deteriorated. Soon, Paris changed and the mood of the people darkened. It took years, but that was the beginning of unrest and dissatisfaction among our people for the nobility."

The four or five souls who had lingered in the Salle moved closer and settled on nearby chairs.

"I was a captain in the guard of Louis XVI, and I was in love with a beautiful woman who was a lady-in-waiting to Queen Marie Antoinette." He paused. "I don't have to tell you what a volatile period in our history that was, the time of the great Revolution.

"Ahh, my Gabrielle. She was misunderstood. She loved her queen so desperately." He seemed lost in thought for several moments until one of the souls moved across his field of vision and broke his trance.

"I believe my mother and I existed during that period. I am most interested in your story and those involved," Jeanne said.

"Forgive me. It has been many years since I have dredged these memories." He refocused and glanced at his audience. "Yes, I was in love with Gabrielle de Polignac. She was a favorite of the queen. They had a close relationship, like sisters. Marie settled Gabrielle's family's debts, and Gabrielle helped Marie through her many emotional battles with the king and her difficult births. She stood beside her in the end when the mob ousted the royal family.

"Gabrielle was married, yes, that is true. But her much older husband obsessed over his position at court and how to gain advancement. He did not spend time with her, and she was lonely and afraid during those turbulent times.

"As captain of the guard, I was frequently in charge of

escorting the queen and her entourage as they traveled away from the palace or to the Queen's private estate, La Petit Trianon. I could not help but notice the queen's beautiful companion. They were very alike. They could have been twin sisters. Always they were together, sharing their secrets, their hopes and fears.

"It was inevitable Gabrielle and I fell in love. I was strong and protective of her, as her husband should have been. Rumors of unrest began to reach the palace. She feared greatly for her mistress. Marie acted oblivious to the danger until it was too late to escape. Gabrielle pleaded with her to take some action and convince the king to placate the mobs, but Marie could not seem to comprehend the thought of a common rebellion and continued to spend her isolated happy existence at La Petite Trianon, surrounded by sycophants who told her only what she wanted to hear.

"All too soon, the mobs of commoners would not be denied. Louis, Marie and their children were imprisoned. Finally, the queen acknowledged the danger. She wanted to escape and go into exile with her children, but that was impossible. Gabrielle was distraught. She had escaped capture but continued to serve her queen. Disguised as a common servant, she attended Marie in prison. I was also free, but in hiding as a loyal supporter of the king. We found a way to see each other every week despite the danger. Gabrielle was heartbroken. Her queen and friend faced a death sentence."

"How horrible," Jeanne exclaimed. The story chilled her, spurred by the passion with which Francois recounted his tale.

"Yes," Francois said sadly. "We had little opportunity for love, but the few moments we spent together were like heaven to me. We tried to find time for each other, but she had a duty to help the queen. I was constantly on the move to avoid arrest. I was much hated by the citizen soldiers, I can tell you."

"I understand it was a horrible time," George said in a low voice.

"Indeed. Paris became a city of mass murders. The aristocracy, along with those accused of helping them, were beheaded daily. My loyalty to the king and my passion to protect Gabrielle and her mistress required I help men who formed a secret society to save innocent noble families from the embrace of

Madam Guillotine. The leader was an English nobleman who became my dear friend. We did what we could to help the innocent aristocrats escape to England, although for every one we helped, there were ten we could not.

"The king and queen were finally condemned to death. The king went first. Nine months later, they pronounced death for the queen. Gabrielle was grief stricken. Not only was she distraught to lose someone who had become a friend, she was a loyalist and could not accept that an anointed queen of France would perish on the guillotine. She decided to switch places with Marie, and died in her place so the queen could escape." He bowed his head.

Silence reigned for several minutes as Jeanne digested this unexpected revelation.

George exclaimed, "Marie Antoinette did not die?"

Jeanne glanced to George and back at Francois. The other souls shared confounded looks.

"Yes, that is the truth. No one knows, for at the time, only I recognized the woman who rode in the cart that day wearing the queen's clothes and wig as my brave Gabrielle, not Marie Antoinette."

Not one soul moved for many minutes as Francois stood and paced. This news astonished her. With such horrific memories behind him, no wonder he hadn't faded.

"No one knew?" George asked. "No one discovered they had traded places?"

He stopped pacing. "No, no one. Had I known beforehand, I would have tried to stop it. She did not tell me. She made the arrangements herself so no traitor could interfere. They switched clothes, and Marie left the jail at day's end with everyone thinking her the maid."

"How did you learn about this?" Jeanne asked.

"I recognized Gabrielle riding bravely in that cart, hands crossed over her white gown. Her posture was so well beloved by me. I knew every nuance of her movements as no one else did. She was not Marie, and I was too far away to stop her. Our group held no hope of saving the queen due to the security in the Place de la Revolution for the event, so I stood in the Hotel de Crillon watching out a window over the heads of hundreds of screaming Parisians in the square. I could do nothing. She sent me a letter through the underground, which I received the day after her death. It said simply, 'Forgive me, your beloved Gabrielle.'"

Jeanne sank against the backrest of the settee, and George shifted in his chair beside her. No one spoke for a long time. The throb of emotion hung heavy around them.

"I didn't tell anyone," Francois said. "To me, the secret was her legacy. I would not dishonor her sacrifice by letting anyone know the queen had lived. She gave a tremendous gift with her life and I could not, in all good conscience, take it away."

"What happened to the queen?" George asked. "Did she escape and live?"

"I do not know for certain." He shrugged. "I suppose she went to Switzerland and took on Gabrielle's identity. In truth, I did not care. After Gabrielle's death, I became devoted to saving the *aristos*, but without regard for my own safety. I was captured as I escorted a Comte's family out of Paris six months after my love's death. My friends wanted to rescue me, but I refused. I did not want anyone put in danger for me when I did not want to live anymore anyway."

"How... how did it ... happen?" Jeanne asked softly.

"Oh, death did not come for me then. Eventually, my friends prevailed and rescued me. I went to Austria and spent some years trying to raise an army of loyalists, but to no avail. I had no heart for living after Gabrielle's tragic end. Eventually, I died a meaningless death. I do not even remember the details of it. The events leading to death shaped my life and kept me in this place, I believe."

"Yet, you are still here," she said.

He nodded. "Yes, and I pray every day that I will be able to fade to Everlasting and be with my beloved."

"Why can you not fade? Your past memories were appalling, of course, but if ever one had reason not to linger, it is you," she said. "You must want to be with Gabrielle very much."

"True. I help others, but cannot help myself. I suppose there is a reason I do not understand, but I have yet to find it. I have found some purpose in assisting others as they struggle with the time between living and fading, but my own questions I cannot answer."

"You did not see Gabrielle ... after ... she did not linger?"

one of the other souls asked.

He shook his head. "No, her spirit did not linger. It seems she was at peace with her death and her decision. I am glad for her. I assume she went directly from the guillotine to Everlasting. I believe she had been tortured enough and was spared this uncertain interlude in which we find ourselves." He gestured around him.

"But enough about me. These are old stories I only tell those who ask. Did you have some need I might be able to address?" He gave an encouraging look to George and Jeanne.

"No," she said quickly. "No, we only wanted to hear your story, monsieur. Ours is of no consequence. We appreciate the gift of your history, but we do not want to take more of your time. Perhaps we shall attend your salon again."

Francois inclined his head and honored her with a bow. "Very well, mademoiselle. Your regard was very kind. Please visit me again. I am charmed by your presence, and your beauty is a comfort to me – so like my Gabrielle. If I can ever be of service, do not hesitate to ask."

Jeanne clutched a hand against her chest, emotion welling like a storm inside her. How could she share her inconsequential problems with one who had suffered such tragedy? Her issues seemed trivial compared to his past. She hurried away, her heart aching for this brave man and all he had endured. Would he ever find peace?

Chapter 7

George sent her a quizzical look, but he followed as she went along the hall away from the salon.

"Why did you not speak to him of your questions?" he asked when they passed out of range of Francois' hearing.

"I could not. After hearing of his misery, my own needs seem frivolous. I would have been embarrassed to speak of my situation," she answered.

George nodded. "I understand. I am stunned at what he revealed. He suffered so much and yet helps others. He is most admirable."

They continued along the hall from Richelieu to Sully. Her heart wrenched, disturbed and weighed down by Francois' dark story.

"Are you going to continue to meet Etienne?" her friend asked after a while.

She paused, staring into the distance. All she'd learned tonight insisted that one should take advantage of opportunities when they arose and not put them off. Disasters happened to destroy opportunities, and then it was too late. She faced her friend with calm resolution. "Oh, yes. If I learned anything from Francois' story, it is that we must not waste opportunities for happiness. You said I have been sad since being here, and you are right. I am ready to be happy. If it means I need to become involved with the living, then so be it. I cannot feel that it will lead to anything evil. In fact, this interaction may lead to the fulfillment I need to fade."

George put a hand on her arm. "Then Jeanne, I really think you should talk to Francois. Counseling souls is what he does. Let us go back and speak to him."

She paused, but since she really wanted Francois' advice, she had to admit George was right. "Fine. We will go back."

They found Francois alone, sitting in a chair as if waiting for them.

"*Monsieur*, forgive me. I really do have something I need

to ask you. I hope I am not imposing." Jeanne moved to a chair beside him, and George sat on the other side.

Francois watched her with a kind expression. "I had a feeling you might return. I could see turmoil in your eyes. Tell me your problem and I will see if I can help."

She heaved a sigh of relief, and began her experiences of meeting Etienne. She told him how she and George had discussed whether this was a way for her to find resolution and fade.

When she finished, she glanced to her friend for encouragement then turned to the older soul. "Francois, now that you are aware of my situation, does your experience lead you to believe Etienne's ability to see me is an indication I am meant to assist him in some way?"

He stroked his chin and glanced sideways at her. "I must say it has the touch of destiny. Interactions of this type are rare. I do believe this is a case where you should pursue the relationship. Where it may lead, I cannot predict, but I am convinced the outcome will be fortuitous."

George motioned her to continue, so she asked, "Is there any way my interacting with him could cause something bad to happen?"

"What do you mean?" Francois' brows went up.

She explained what Blonde Hair had said, and her fear that malevolence could come from the interaction.

He stood and paced, his eyes fixed on the floor. She twisted her hands together then ran her palms down the sides of her skirt.

He finally came and stood before her. "You should not feel any remorse for your actions. I have no reason to believe such interaction can lead to any aberration of the spirit world."

"But there are situations where an aberration can occur?" George quickly asked.

"Yes." Francois nodded. "There are instances where spirits act outside what nature intended and this can lead to, ah… let us just say it could lead to problems. I do not see how talking to this man could lead to that sort of encounter. What part do you foresee playing if you help him?"

"That is yet to be determined. He says I inspired him to create his new collection when he was about to suffer financial ruin, so I have helped in that respect."

54

"Spiritual inspiration," George proclaimed, giving her a wink.

She smiled. Her friend was always full of enthusiasm. She loved that about him.

"Also, more of my past memories have surfaced as a result of our discussion. I discovered a clue to why I am here in the Louvre. I was a painter in my living life," she reported. "It is important somehow. My history must be revealed. I need to know more."

"I think your intuition is valid. Something from an earlier time is keeping you here, and it appears Etienne is your path to discovery," Francois mused.

"Can you help by teaching her the techniques for remembering?" George asked.

Jeanne eagerly turned to Francois. "Would you be so kind?"

"Of course, my dear. It would be my pleasure. It may help to some degree, but I still suspect Etienne is the key," he said.

"There is one other small detail I should mention," she said nervously. "I knew that if I continued to interact with him, he had to know I am no longer among the living."

"And?" Francois stared intently at her.

"So, I told him the truth," she said.

No one spoke. The two men stared at her, eyes wide.

"What did he say?" George finally asked.

"He was extremely shocked, of course. At first he thought I played a joke. When he tried to touch me, he could not deny the truth. I think he took it well, considering." She spread her hands. "He went home to think and is supposed to meet me here tomorrow."

"That is most interesting," Francois said, tugging at his cravat. "Unprecedented, in fact. There is really no telling where this will lead. Be careful, Jeanne."

He gave her another bow. "You must keep me updated on your progress. I am most interested in this situation. Now, if George will excuse us, I will try to facilitate your memories. You have some work to do before your next meeting with Etienne."

George rose and said good-bye before floating away.

"Come with me, my dear." Francois gestured.

She followed him to a more secluded corner at the back of the Salle, an area bathed in deeper shadows.

He motioned her to a chair in front of his own. He directed her to close her eyes and try to clear her mind of all current thought.

"Now, focus only on memories that belong to the past. Keep going over and over them. I find when I do this, it puts me in touch with the past and pulls more memories to me. See if that happens for you. But you must tell me if anything occurs which alarms you."

She had only a few past memories. One was of a female voice saying her name. Then came a vision when she painted a picture of a flowery meadow. Next she remembered an angry male voice telling her if she continued to paint, he would leave her. She maintained a firm rotation of those three memories.

Her best memory was the female voice. It comforted her. She concentrated on that voice and saw a face: a woman who smiled and called, "Jeanne? Jeanne Juliette! Where are you?" That face resonated familiarity. Next, she sat before an easel, a brush in one hand. She felt warm sun, smelled the heady aroma of roses, and stood at the edge of a meadow. This memory suffused her with joy.

A new memory arose. A different woman than the first, richly dressed and beautiful. She spoke in a foreign language, English. Her face floated in a vague mist, not as familiar as the first woman. Jeanne was a small child. The woman hugged her tight to her chest and tears sparkled in her eyes. "Goodbye, my little darling. I may never see you again. I am so sorry! This is for your safety. Please forgive me. I must send you away."

Jeanne opened her eyes. How fascinating. She had to find out about these people and what had happened in her life. Her heart ached with the need to unfold the history of her earlier years.

"Did you have any success?" Francois inquired, leaning forward.

"Yes, thank you so much. Your technique works. I saw two women who were part of my life. I must discover who they were."

"Be patient." He held up a cautioning hand. "These memories come slowly, one leading to another. It may take some time."

She nodded, understanding. "I will. This is important, I feel it. I can't thank you enough."

"Then come to me tomorrow and let me know what happens when you meet Etienne. I must confess I have ulterior motives. I have no idea why I am still here myself. What we learn as souls should be shared so we can help each other."

"I will. I want to help you as you have helped me and countless others." She vowed, "I will find you tomorrow."

"Thank you." He smiled. "Until then, *cherie*."

"Wait," she called as he moved away. He paused and turned, eyebrows raised. "I have one other question. Is it possible for us to leave the museum? Is there a reason we stay in one place?"

"Yes, you may leave. You can go anywhere you desire. The reason souls stay in one place is for comfort, an environment that facilitates fading. Usually it is where death occurred or a place that held special meaning, but not always. As you know, with fading we soon forget an outside world exists. Does that answer your question?"

"I believe so. Thank you," she replied.

He nodded and floated away. She returned to her contemplation of the past. She had hours before Etienne returned, and she was eager to delve into more memories. A part of her feared seeking these memories, though. Because somewhere in her past was buried something so painful it resisted remembering.

Chapter 8

Etienne stretched, surprised he'd actually slept well. The dreams and reflections he'd dreaded were lulled by an excellent bottle of red wine. He was still no closer to resolving Jeanne's entrance into his life, but he was in a more positive frame of mind because of the new collection. For the first time in years, eagerness spurred him to dive into the creation of new designs.

Chloe had beaten him in and already worked to pin muslin to the paper patterns. She had a cell phone pressed to one ear as she carefully observed Sean and Lola cutting and marking the fabric.

"No, Alan," she said. "Five is not enough. We need at least ten models. Who can do a major show with five models? What? What?" Her voice rose. "Are you suggesting House Etienne needs fewer models than Chanel because our collection is not expected to do well? Is that what you're saying?"

He froze. Redness inched up Chloe's neck. It seemed the fashion world had already written off House Etienne as a failure before seeing his collection this year. His heart skipped a beat, and his own face heated in anger.

"Very well," Chloe's tone changed from red hot to ice cold. "If that's how you feel, then we'll find another agency for our models. But I can tell you, Alan, House Etienne will not forget this insult." She punched the END button and crossed her arms.

Sean and Lola stopped cutting and gazed at her. In fact, everyone ceased work as she ended the call. Without saying a word, she strode into her office and closed the door.

Etienne coughed. Everyone quickly returned to their appointed tasks, although many threw speculative glances at him as well as Chloe's closed door. He headed across the floor, stopping to observe several areas and chatting with workers before making his way to Chloe's office. His presence among them settled the charged atmosphere and soon a genial chatter overtook the silence.

He knocked and, at her low response to enter, opened the door.

She sat behind her desk, arms still crossed, her eyes lowered. "I'm so sorry, Etienne."

"For what?" he asked.

"I let my anger completely override my reason. I should've pleaded with Alan, anything to get the models we need. Now we have no models. I've failed you." She gulped on a sob. "And that's not all. He's not the only one to assume we're finished. Cherese, one of our seamstresses, turned in her notice today. I'm afraid we'll lose others before this is done. How can we make a new collection from the ground up in record time with less than a full staff?"

"Are you kidding?" He came around the desk and sat on the edge, facing her. "That prick Alan has really begun to think too much of himself. He should be begging us, not the other way around. I'm glad to be rid of him."

She stopped crying and stared at him.

"Look, all of this is my fault. If I had been able to maintain my momentum and design better collections the last few years, we wouldn't be in this situation. We both know that's about to change. We just have to find a way to present this collection the way it's meant to be seen. Then everything will be different."

"I know that, Etienne. I have faith, but there's so much to do. We need a new venue, we need models, and all the agency models have already been booked at this late date. We can't have second-rate models for this collection. It wouldn't be fair to the designs." She rubbed moisture from her eyes.

"Don't worry about anything but the clothes. I want that to be your focus. Your magic will bring them to life. Leave the venue and the models to me. I have an idea."

Her expression brightened, and she swiped a hand across her eyes.

"Tell everyone there will be a large bonus for those who help us complete the collection. That should stall any ideas about jumping ship," he added. "Now, get out there and make the magic happen."

Her face glowed, and she nodded eagerly. She stood and enveloped him in a hug. "Thank you, Etienne. I can't wait to rub Alan's face in the reviews after our show."

"Were you able to get Claudette as our fitting model?"

"Oh, yes. One bit of good news. Seems she was booked for Gaultier, but they had a huge fight two days ago and she walked out. She has a crush on you, you know. She was thrilled with the offer. No begging needed there." She chortled.

"Excellent. Have her here tomorrow. I want to start the fittings as soon as possible."

Chloe gave him an affirmative salute and then returned to the workroom.

He climbed the stairs to his office, irritation and panic warred in his stomach causing a surge of bile in his throat. What if he was wrong? Doubt crept in like an evil shadow raising goose bumps on his arms. He rushed to his drawing table and flipped through his sketches. He hadn't been wrong. A light coolness of relief washed away the heavy misgivings. They really were good. Now he had to use every speck of his ingenuity to bring these creations to the world as befitted their significance. He'd been successful in calming his assistant's panic, but he really didn't have an idea about venue or models.

Suddenly, Jeanne's face flashed before him. Could she be right, that their meeting had a purpose? She'd already inspired the collection. Maybe talking with her could help him solve his other myriad dilemmas. It was worth a try. Even spiritual advice was welcome at this point. Crazy as it seemed, he still felt the pull of attraction, despite the impossibility of a physical relationship. For whatever reason, being drawn to her seemed right. He took a deep breath and headed downstairs. He hoped Jeanne would be waiting when he returned to the Louvre. Already her absence made his heart ache.

Chapter 9

Jeanne hurried through halls of the Louvre to reach the Venus. She'd become engrossed in the process of exploring her memories and hoped she hadn't tarried too long. It would not do to miss Etienne. At the same time, excitement filled her at the progress she'd made in recovering pieces of her past. She sailed along above the floor bouncing every few feet in delight.

The woman whose voice she remembered calling her Jeanne Juliette with such warmth was surely her mother. Memories of her returned with more ease than others she tried to explore, such as the rich woman telling her good-bye. She remembered that her mother painted. She painted portraits, and a man who she thought was her father helped her sell her work. She had been a child then, and those memories were happy and full of love.

The rich woman who told her good-bye and spoke English was a vague memory, perhaps because she had been so young. But that memory was most bewildering. The woman was not her mother, she knew instinctively. She had been with this woman and then the woman sent her away and was no longer a part of her life. She had said it was for Jeanne's safety. What could that possibly mean? How had she been in danger as a baby?

She had also explored the memory of the angry male voice telling her not to paint. A dark face, indistinct, had arisen with memories of cold and snow. She remembered buildings against a backdrop of whiteness, with large onion shaped turrets in brilliant colors. That remembrance, above the others, resisted recovery. She was certain such memories led to the path of her sadness, and investigating that course would likely prove difficult and even painful.

Her most exciting memory was of a new man. His features were not developed yet, but she had visions of showing him her paintings and him praising her. He'd encouraged her to paint and express herself. She remembered dancing with him by candlelight at Versailles, and a tingle of pleasured warmth spread through her. Had they been in love? Who was he?

She had no glimmer of her death or the events surrounding it. Perhaps the most painful memories were buried the deepest. No matter, she would keep digging until she found the truth and knew the secret of those forgotten times. In the interim, she remained committed to helping Etienne, besides the fact that being with him made her feel alive and happy.

When she reached the Venus, he'd already arrived and paced the floor as his eyes searched the perimeter though a tangle of people. When he detected her presence, he smiled and waved. A surge of happiness warmed her at this sign of his acceptance. She weaved through the mass of tourists to his side.

"Oh, Etienne, I am so glad to see you. Are you well?"

"I'm happy to see you as well, Jeanne. I have a lot to tell you," he replied. His gaze scanned her features. "I've done a lot of thinking. It's been hard to get my head straight, I must admit. As fantastic as this is, I'm still glad you appeared to me. I only regret you won't be seen and appreciated by the world as the face of House Etienne. My collection could frame your beauty like the elegant setting of a magnificent jewel. I really want to tell you more about the collection."

"First, I want to ask you a favor," she said.

"Of course."

"I want to leave the Louvre for a while and go somewhere quiet where we can talk. You see, I am trying to recover my memories. I cannot explain the importance of this fully, because I am not certain of the reason myself. I can only say that whatever destiny brought you and me together is urging me to explore my past as well. You see, this museum is a haven for me, a place of safety. If I am in another environment, it might stimulate more memories."

"Why do you think your past has become important all of a sudden?" he asked.

"Partially because something from the past is keeping me from fading, and partially because I think the knowledge may help you. I am not sure." She frowned. "I have to keep exploring and let the memories lead where they may."

"Okay. My apartment is way across town. But my friend, Gaston, lives near here. He's usually painting in his garret studio, so we could go to his apartment. How does that sound?"

"All right, let us do that," she said. The thought of leaving the Louvre frightened her, but she felt safer going with someone who could guide her in this modern world.

They stood on the curb as he raised his arm and whistled for a taxi. She hadn't really known what to expect, but the hustle and noise of the outside world made her want to scurry to the security of the museum. With great effort, she remained calm as she took in this transformed city.

As she scanned the avenue, her gaze was drawn to a face far down the sidewalk. A gray haired woman stared intently at her, sending chills down her back. Tourists passed between them and the woman disappeared. The woman resembled the vision she'd had of her mother, only older. That could not be possible, could it? She shook her head. The likeness had to be a coincidence or the intrusion of her dreams.

"Come on," Etienne said. He pointed to a taxi and got into the back seat, motioning for her to join him.

She quickly forgot the strange encounter in the novelty of a moving vehicle.

The driver stared at him, and she put a finger to her lips to remind Etienne not to speak since the driver couldn't see her. Etienne gave him Gaston's address.

She pressed her face to the window as scenes of modern Paris flashed by. The world had changed so much since her time. It was as if they were flying, a bit frightening but exhilarating.

A ringing sounded, and he pulled a device from his jacket pocket and talked into it. After the taxi dropped them off, he explained about his phone. His assistant, Chloe, had called with questions about one of the designs. Jeanne shook her head in amazement.

When they reached Gaston's apartment, he wasn't upstairs painting as Etienne had anticipated. No sound came from the apartment either.

"He must have gone out." He listened from the hall. "It's okay. He never locks his door." Etienne opened it and led her in.

He stopped after crossing the threshold, and she paused by his side. Her gaze settled on small paintings covering his walls, and a glow of excitement lit in her chest.

"Hello, Etienne. I didn't know you were coming by today,"

a man said. He sat reading a newspaper and drinking hot tea in an easy chair across from the door.

"What are you doing here, Gaston?" Etienne demanded.

"What do you mean? This is my apartment," his friend exclaimed.

"I know, but you're always in the garret. Why aren't you painting?"

"Why are you asking me all these questions? I don't have to paint every minute of the day. I wanted to take a break and have some tea."

"Tea? Are you kidding me? Tea? You never drink tea."

"What's wrong with that? Vivienne gave it to me. It's a special blend."

"Ah ha. So that's it. Vivienne. I should've known." Etienne pointed a finger at him.

Gaston threw up a hand. "Look, if you wanted to have a tryst with your lady friend, all you had to do was call. I can be gone for an hour or two. Just don't barge in and make a scene because I'm drinking tea for a change. I happen to like it."

"What did you say?" Etienne froze.

Jeanne stared at the big man.

"I said, don't come barging in here—"

"No, not that part, the part about my lady friend," he said slowly.

"Well, you come in here with this beautiful woman, whom you don't even bother to introduce, by the way, and obviously you came for a—"

"You can see her?" Etienne's voice rose. He glanced at her.

She smiled and nodded. Her heart soared as she moved to circle the room, gazing at the paintings.

"Of course I can see her, you idiot. Have you lost your mind? Ahh, I know what it is. The stress of this new collection has finally sent you over the deep end. I told you about that pressure."

"No, no, you don't understand. I have to explain something to you. You see, this is Jeanne," Etienne said.

"Of course it is. No one else could fit the description you gave me. She's the knockout."

"But, you see, yesterday when I went to see her, I found out that she's..."

"Yes, yes, she's what? Can you please make some sense, Etienne," Gaston demanded throwing his newspaper on the floor.

"I'm trying to tell you, but you're not going to believe it." He shook his head.

"Oh, go ahead, tell me and then bring your beautiful lady to me so I can meet her properly."

"She's a ghost."

The big man stared at him.

Jeanne finally tore her gaze away from scrutiny of Gaston's collection.

"He can see you," Etienne told her.

"I heard," she said. She searched his friend's eyes for a secret to what he had done without knowing. How did he have these pictures?

"I thought you said it was rare for a living person to see a ghost," he commented.

"Yes, it is very rare," she replied, eerily calm now.

Etienne studied her, wrinkles between his brows. "Are you okay?"

"Yes, I am fine."

"You're not stunned that he can see you?"

"Not really, now that I am here."

"Why not? You felt that way when I saw you the first time."

"It is because your friend has a piece of my soul," she responded.

"A piece of your soul," he repeated, looking from Gaston to Jeanne.

"Yes, you see these paintings?" She gestured to the small exquisite landscapes Gaston collected. "They are all mine. I painted them."

Chapter 10

Jeanne walked the room, studying the paintings through the adoring eyes of an artist who'd loved her work. She couldn't believe they had survived all these years, but was thrilled they had. Someone had preserved them, a gift from the past, and now Gaston kept them safe.

It took Gaston's attempting to touch her to finally convince him she was indeed a ghost. She giggled as he passed a hand through her body and nearly fainted. They administered brandy for the shock, the tea clearly not sufficient for an event of this magnitude. The big man broke into a sweat, and Etienne fanned him with the abandoned newspaper.

Etienne patted him on the back, grinning. "Old buddy, take it easy or the shock and your unhealthy lifestyle, might combine to do you in. Have another drink."

She couldn't tell which surprise was greater: the realization she was really a ghost, or that she was the artist behind his beloved collection.

Gaston took a gulp of brandy, and his color slowly returned. He stared at her then at Etienne. "This is unbelievable," he said, and took another drink.

"I know how you feel," Etienne commiserated. "I had the same experience last night."

"So, er, uh, Jeanne, you say you painted these?" Gaston stammered.

She reluctantly left one of the beloved paintings. She had memories associated with each one and the emotions flooded her.

She had to block the deluge of images that pushed at her mind. The sheer magnitude overwhelmed her. She would have to find a way to filter the images slowly and deal with the memories. Right now she basked in elation over her reunion with them and recalled the pleasure in their creation.

"Yes, Gaston. They are indeed my paintings. I remember painting each one like it was yesterday."

"But they're old, hundreds of years old," he protested.

"Hundreds?" She fought tugs from all directions as memories continued to emerge.

"Yes, I've had them tested in my attempt to find the name of the artist. Given the age and the style of the paintings, the type of paint and even the original frames, I can assure you they were painted sometime between 1792 and 1820."

He had just provided vital information that could help determine her identity.

Etienne watched her closely.

"Have you remembered something?" he asked.

She shook her head. "These paintings hold memories, but only about the actual painting times, very distracting and disjointed. Gaston's information narrows the search for my identity. I cannot believe this is coincidence, my coming here, my meeting you, all of it. Some purpose must emerge eventually."

"It's like a puzzle coming together," Etienne mused. "Mind if I have some of that brandy, old friend?"

"Help yourself. You bought it." Gaston gestured to the bottle.

"I thought it looked familiar." He scrutinized the label. He poured a glass and sipped. "You know, we need to explore that period of time, who the painters were and that sort of thing. And we need to uncover your last name," he said to her. "Wait, Gaston, didn't you say that there is a "V" on each painting?" He came to his feet and moved to the nearest painting.

"Yes, every one of them. I've already tried to determine the last name. The only painter of talent with a "V" during that period was a woman named Vigee Le Brun. This is definitely not her work. Besides, the start of the time frame coincides with the beginning of the French revolution. With all the turmoil of that period, I'm not surprised some talented artists disappeared from history. Some of them probably had their heads chopped off, if you want to know the truth."

She rested her hand on her throat. Francois and his horrific story came to mind. She had no memory of the guillotine or the hungry mobs that had delighted in it. The name of the painter Gaston had mentioned, Vigee Le Brun, had a definite ring of familiarity, though.

"Gaston, what about this Vigee Le Brun? Tell me about her. What was her first name?" She went to the sofa and sat beside Etienne.

Gaston started to offer her brandy, then rolled his eyes and threw up a hand, muttering, "Ghosts."

"Yes, what do you know about her?" Etienne queried.

"Vigee Le Brun? Her name was Elizabeth Louise and she was extremely famous for her portraits," Gaston said.

"Really? Portraits? That is very interesting, because the woman who I believe was my mother painted portraits," she exclaimed, tingling with excitement. She also thought she remembered the person who might have been her father calling the woman Elizabeth.

"Yes, she painted Marie Antoinette and many other nobles in a variety of countries," Gaston continued.

Jeanne froze. Now Marie Antoinette's name emerged - another connection to Francois. Was this mere coincidence?

"She lived in this city until the mob stormed Versailles and forced the royal family to move to the Tuileries. Seeing the writing on the wall, she went to Italy and continued to paint. She did a lot of traveling throughout Europe, Russia ..."

"Russia," she exclaimed. "Oh, my."

"What?" Etienne asked.

"I have a memory of snow and cold and buildings with onion shaped roofs. That can only be Russia." She put hands to her cheeks. They seemed to be onto something with this Vigee Le Brun. "Did she ever return to Paris?"

"Yes, when the revolution ended, she returned," Gaston replied. "I don't know exactly when. I'd have to refresh my memory. I'm telling you, there is no way Vigee Le Brun painted those pictures."

"Yes, but did she have a daughter?" A thrill of anticipation ran through her at the possibility she'd discovered her mother.

"I don't know," Gaston replied stroking his chin. "If she did, she was never known as an artist, I can tell you that."

"Let me borrow your laptop," Etienne said.

He brought the computer in from his bedroom.

She stared warily at the object. "What is that?"

"Oh, sorry. I keep forgetting about your lack of technology.

This is a computer. I can't possibly explain how it works, but it's a way to connect to sources of information. We can Google Vigee Le Brun and see her biography," he replied as he began the search.

"Google?"

"It's a term we use to search for something. In this case, a person. And, here we go..." He scrolled through the page, scanning for any mention of a daughter. "Ah ha! It says here that she had a daughter in 1780!"

"What was her name? What was her name?" She rose from the couch and floated up and down, eager to hear.

"Her name was…," Etienne looked up at her. "Jeanne Julie Louise."

They went motionless. She moved first, returning to her seat beside Etienne, stunned. Her mouth opened and closed several times before she was able to speak.

"She really was my mother," she whispered. The dull emptiness inside her filled with calming certainty. If she could find the other pieces, she'd be complete.

Etienne nodded. "Here's her picture." He turned the screen so she could see the self-portrait of Vigee Le Brun that accompanied the biography.

She stared at the rendering of the woman she had seen in her memory who'd called her name. A tangle of emotions erupted in her breast - joy, excitement, longing. She'd suspected the woman was her mother. "I want to read this."

He showed her how to scroll with the curser. Gaston sat forward, eyes intent.

It took some time for her to complete the whole entry of the fascinating woman who'd endured in a world dominated by male artists. She had become famous and successful by the sheer strength of her talent and determination.

"There are a few pictures of other people she knew and painted," Jeanne said with excitement. "I cannot believe it! Look, this is a picture of Francois. And this woman named Gabrielle was his love. Oh, and there are several pictures of the queen. How wonderful." When she finished, she looked up at them. "Thank you, both of you, for helping find my mother," she stated with sincerity. "Do you think you can Google me also and find out about my life?"

"Of course," Etienne said. He took the laptop and began typing. He silently scanned the results. He clicked to read some of them, and then shook his head. "There's very little here other than name, dates of death and birth. No mention of fame as an artist or how you died. All of this was in the biography of your mother. It's interesting that you died before your mother, though."

"That writing said I married a man while we were in Russia, and my mother did not like it. Then it says we later joined her in Paris for a while, until my husband left and returned to Russia. That is an interesting detail." She wondered if her husband was the angry dark face or the other man who radiated kindness and love.

She had a lot to think about and explore now that she knew this much. Also, she still didn't know who the rich, foreign woman was she had been with as a baby. In any event, she was grateful for the progress made this morning.

"Etienne, we have spent all this time talking about my past. I really wanted to hear about the collection." She had guilt for becoming so consumed with her past, but what a tremendous discovery they had made today. "I am sorry, but this was unexpected. What has happened?"

He threw up his hands. "Ah, that disaster. Where do I begin?"

He relayed what had occurred that morning. How the Paris fashion world had given up on him-the details of the show that had not been completed, the crises of having no models, losing employees and having a completely inappropriate venue.

"I'm actually glad for the diversion you provided today. It took my mind off of my own problems." He rubbed his chin. "At this point, no one of any importance will attend my show. The press will probably send junior reporters, and the fashion magazines will send secretaries looking for free clothes. It's beyond a nightmare."

"That's very bad, my friend," Gaston said, pouring another glass of brandy. "What are you going to do?"

"I don't know. I can't think straight. If I didn't have Chloe, I would give up at this point. At least I know she will make the clothes come to life."

"Etienne, where were you going to have the show before

you had the new designs?" she asked.

"In a warehouse. The look was ultra-futuristic. It's all wrong for this collection. This collection is about the past. It's more genteel but with flair. The warehouse simply won't work."

"Hmm," she mused. Where would such creations be best presented?

"Even if I find an appropriate place, I can't be sure anyone will come who's of any consequence," he added.

"Maybe you should back out. Save your money and try again in the fall," Gaston suggested.

"No," he stated vehemently. "This collection's time is now. I'm determined it must be seen."

"Etienne," she broke in. "Is Versailles still a royal residence?"

"No, we have no king. It's more of a museum or showplace for the public to tour."

"Then that is the site for your show," she announced.

"What? It's not even in Paris. No one will come."

"It is not that far. You must make them want to come. That is the secret."

"How? No one will drive to Versailles to see a show everyone thinks is a failure. They'll think it's too much trouble. I'm sorry, but I know these people."

"But you have to admit it is the perfect place," Gaston interjected.

"Listen, Etienne, these designs are about the past. That is what you said, right?" Excitement bubbled inside her. More ideas popped into her head.

Etienne nodded.

"Then if the people will not come for the show, you will make them come for something entirely different, something no one else will think of." A rush of exhilaration surged through her.

"What would that be?"

"A ball," she exclaimed. "A period dress ball. The show will be first, followed by the ball. Anyone would love to attend a ball at Versailles, and it would be fun to attend a show in period dress, no? So they come to the ball, but they must see the show first. You will have the finest food and wine, you will have an orchestra for music, and it will be known ahead of time that famous people will be there."

"If it could happen like that, then sure, it's a hit. I can get an orchestra because no one books them for fashion week, but the good caterers are already booked, and famous people who would be willing to come will be hard to convince."

"Can you rent Versailles?" she asked.

"There are certain areas you can rent with enough money and the right connections, I think."

"And the orchestra you say is no problem. Then I will take care of the famous people. I have an idea of how to entice them to come. Now, that just leaves the caterer."

There was a knock at the door and Gaston called to enter.

A strange-looking red-haired woman walked in, a bright expression on her face. "Hello guys, what's up? My interview for chef at Café Mirabel was horrible. But I made a pot of delicious bouillabaisse and some sour dough bread. Want to join me for dinner?"

They simply stared at her. Jeanne slowly smiled. A miracle had occurred.

"What?" the redhead asked. "Why are you staring at me?"

Chapter 11

At first, Vivienne appeared skeptical about the offer of a job catering a masquerade ball for Etienne. She accused him of feeling sorry for her lack of employment and offering a charity job. It took a lot of convincing on his part to make her believe he really needed her. Once persuaded of his desperation, she enthusiastically joined in the planning. She never mentioned Jeanne, which told him she could not see her. Best leave that revelation to a later date.

He and Jeanne departed to return to The Louvre. She appeared edgy, and he needed to return to the atelier to monitor progress on the collection.

Chloe motioned to him when he arrived, and her lips trembled.

"What's wrong?" He closed the door of her office once inside.

"I spoke to my friend, Claudia, at Vogue today. They aren't sending anyone to our show." Her bottom eyelids were red and moisture pooled there, about to spill over. She blotted them with a squished tissue.

He blew out a deep breath. He'd been expecting something of this nature after learning of Alan's sentiments yesterday. Fashion was a small world, and news traveled fast. Soon, the press, celebrities, and everyone of importance, would count House Etienne out for the spring show. He had to act quickly to stem the tide.

"Chloe, don't worry. That's not going to happen. Listen to this idea." He described the plan to hold the show at Versailles and tie it to a period dress ball. He hinted at celebrity appearances but failed to mention names. Chloe's mood changed dramatically.

"That's fantastic, Etienne," she said enthusiastically. "I love it!"

"So you think it will work?"

"Absolutely. This idea will bring everyone to our show. It can't fail."

"Okay, I'm going to take care of the details. How are the

clothes coming?"

"Great! The muslin is cut. We've almost finished basting them together. You can begin fittings tomorrow morning."

"Excellent. Keep your focus on the clothes. I'll take care of the rest. How are the employees handling everything?"

"Your promise of a bonus helped settle doubts for now. There's been nothing but enthusiasm today."

"Good. Let's keep any doubts to ourselves."

She nodded. Keeping the staff centered and focused was vital to delivering the collection on time.

"All that's left is finding models. I wanted to run an idea by you. What would you think of using British models?"

"What? Why?" Chloe asked, crossing her arms over her chest.

"Well, first of all, we have to admit that the local models of any talent are already booked."

Chloe nodded miserably.

"Also, I think the look of the clothes may lend themselves to a British bearing. You said we needed Jane Austen, not *Blade Runner*, right?"

She grew thoughtful. "Okay, your idea has merit, and in all honesty, we're desperate. But surely even the good British models are already booked."

"I have a friend with an agency in London. It's new and small, but Paul has an eye for quality talent. I'll call him tomorrow and discuss our needs. They may not be the most experienced, but I can count on him to bring them up to speed. Now, the only item we need to settle is when to have the show. Given all the issues we face, timing is paramount. I can't decide if it would be better to have our show before all the others or at the end."

"I hate to lose even a week of preparation time, but I have to say it will be better to present the collection at the beginning of the week. This year we know everyone will be in town for the Chanel show on Monday. Everyone would arrive on Friday for interviews and parties. Saturday night is taken by the Paris Vogue party, but Sunday night has no event that would keep people from our show with the proper publicity," she replied. "Especially if a few key celebrities let it be known they'll attend."

He nodded. "I agree. It's settled. I'll try to book Versailles for Sunday night. Now, I want to see the muslin patterns."

He entered the feverish activity of the workroom and began his analysis of the embryos of his collection. Despite his assurances to Chloe, a cold hand of doubt clutched his gut. But the charm of Jeanne's appearance gave him hope.

***

After returning to the Louvre, Jeanne immediately headed for the areas where she was most likely to find George and Francois. Excitement continued to fizz about her with all that had happened last night in her memories, and today with the revealing of her mother's identity.

More than anything, she was elated to discover her paintings. It was like finding all her best friends in one room after a long absence. What a tremendous coincidence to have her interaction with Etienne lead to these revelations. Or was it destiny? She leaned toward the latter as it fell in with her idea of having a purpose to fulfill.

She passed a cross-hall and noticed Blonde Hair floating aimlessly along one corridor, eyes unfocused. She was so transparent it was possible to see objects through her body. Jeanne sighed. Blonde Hair was on the verge of fading. It was right for her. She was prepared and eager for the process.

She wondered if she would ever want to fade. At this point, she was too elated with her new recollections and the ability to talk to Etienne and Gaston. Every moment was precious and filled with adventure. She had not felt sad for days. Fading to Everlasting did not hold the allure it once had.

She took a second look down the hall after Blonde Hair, and startled at the sight of the older woman who resembled her mother. The woman had vaguely distinguishable features, but sparked of familiarity. She was some distance away, so Jeanne moved closer. Before she took more than a few steps, the figure scowled and disappeared.

The woman was a soul. Surely if she had been her mother, she would've approached. Why had she disappeared? She rubbed her arms against an unaccustomed chill.

She continued toward Richelieu to find her friends. Was

she mistaken? Perhaps the time she had spent recalling her memories had caused her to see features of her mother. Besides, unfaded souls couldn't disappear like that.

Consideration of the mystery faded at the appearance of a woman with a striking resemblance to her. The one Etienne had mentioned. The woman wrote in a notebook. Jeanne couldn't deny the resemblance in their facial features, but the woman's hair was darker and straighter than hers.

Curious, she followed the woman from room to room. Her look-alike paused now and then to sit on a bench and write. Jeanne studied her from all angles. Who could she be? She moved closer until she could have touched her. A strange urge to walk through the women urged her a step forward until she caught herself. What was she doing? She raised a fluttering hand to her heart and retreated until she pressed against a wall. She'd never felt such a compulsion before. How bizarre.

After wandering through a few more rooms, the woman left the museum. Jeanne stared after her, experiencing a sense of loss. What did this mean? Now both she and Etienne had both seen her. Everything seemed connected somehow. More and more, recent events interrelated. She could make no sense of it at this point, so she went to find her friends.

George and Francois sat in the Napoleon suite. Two other souls lingered as well, listening intently to their conversation.

"But when do you know if it is right to have contact with the living?" George asked.

"It depends on each individual story. In some cases, there is truly a reason for the interaction. In others, the soul needs to acknowledge contact can be harmful for both parties and prolong the fading process," Francois answered.

"What if you do not know why you have not faded?" Her friend tugged on his earlobe.

Something in his past kept him in this world of the living, and he said he didn't have a clue why or what. He'd told her he had no memories of any conflict or unfulfilled mission that needed resolution.

"Hello, George. Hello, Francois," she greeted and crossed to find a nearby chair as the men stood.

"Jeanne! I'm glad you are here," George exclaimed.

"Where have you been today?"

"I have so much news, I hardly know where to begin," she replied. "I have made quite a number of discoveries today."

"You look happy," Francois commented as he and George returned to their seats.

"I am. First of all, I had a few breakthrough memories overnight using Francois' advice. Then, when I met Etienne today, we left the Louvre and went to the apartment of his friend, Gaston, who is a painter. You shall never believe it. He could see me as well."

George and Francois shared a glance before turning their gazes to her.

"How is that possible?" George sat and leaned forward at the edge of his seat.

"I must admit, I am amazed," Francois said.

"There is a compelling reason, I believe," she said. "You see, for years, Gaston has been collecting paintings of an unknown artist. They had small value in the market, but he loved the works. He has the paintings hung on walls all over his apartment. It turns out I am the artist."

"That is incredible," her friend exclaimed, leaning back in his chair.

"It proves there is fate at work here," Francois stated, his expression somber. "This encounter with Etienne fits with some grand purpose."

She nodded. "I feel the same way. And that is not all. Francois, I found out my mother is a famous artist who painted portraits of Marie Antoinette and many other nobles."

The wise ghost was silent, staring at her for several seconds before his eyes widened. "Elizabeth," he stated. "Vigee Le Brun."

"Yes." She was pleased he'd remembered and hoped he could tell her about her mother. "I saw pictures of paintings she had done of you, and Gabrielle, as well as Marie Antoinette."

"Of course, she painted a portrait of me. I knew of her and her paintings back then. Elizabeth was closer to Gabrielle than anyone. She was even the god-mother of Gabrielle's oldest daughter." Francois looked over her head, gaze unfocused.

"What was she like?" She laid a hand on his arm.

Francois brought his attention to her. "I knew her here in

Paris, before the revolution. She was talented, smart, and dedicated to her work. It was not easy for her, trying to be a recognized artist in a world of men who dominated the field. But she did it. She persevered until her talent was recognized. She painted nobility and famous people all over Europe."

George sat forward. "I know of her, too. She was very famous."

Francois paused in his recital of the virtues of Elizabeth Vigee Le Brun. He glanced away.

"Come with me. I want to show you both something." He headed down the corridor with Jeanne and George close behind. He glided along halls and upstairs heading for a far section of Sully on the second floor.

She glanced at George who shrugged. What did Francois have to reveal that involved her mother? Mystified she floated along in his wake, tension rising in her chest.

"I had forgotten about this place for a long time." He paused at the entrance to a chamber and gestured to numerous paintings lining the walls. "I rarely leave the first floor. It's been many years since I wandered up here. I must admit there are also painful memories, making it an easy place to avoid."

She followed him into the room, silently viewing the works of art. Francois went off by himself.

"These are her paintings." She searched the pictures for some sign of familiarity. "Why can't I remember this?"

"Yes, this *salle* is devoted to Vigee Le Brun, finally recognized as a favored daughter of France." Francois came to her. "It is only a small sample of the vast number of portraits she painted."

Jeanne followed George along the walls, inspecting the fine portraits until she reached one that made her gasp.

The painting showed a woman holding a small girl. They both smiled. The woman had her arms around the girl in a joyous celebration of motherhood, and the beautiful little girl looked secure and happy in her mother's embrace.

"Madam Vigee Le Brun and her daughter," George read the inscription. "But this must be you, Jeanne."

She stood before the painting and studied it for deeper meaning in the expressions.

She glanced at George. "I am sure I have seen this painting hundreds of times in my wanderings, and I never knew it was me with my mother. We look...happy."

"Yes, you do," her friend replied, smiling. "The girl looks a lot like you, Jeanne, even now. How interesting."

"She's pretty, too, my mother," she commented. This painting imparted a sense of peace. What a nice vision of Elizabeth smiling in delight, her arms protectively encircling Jeanne. She remembered the spirit who had appeared in the hall. That woman had been much older with gray hair and an angry countenance marked by glaring eyes. She had looked nothing like this younger version full of love and life. Surely she mistook the resemblance. This reminder of the past stirred a sense of familiarity, but no concrete images emerged.

"Does anyone else think this is a peculiar set of coincidences?" George asked, glancing from her to Francois.

"What do you mean?" the wise ghost asked, coming toward him.

"I mean, Jeanne learning of this connection between you, Gabrielle, Marie, and her mother," George pointed out. "It seems odd the way this comes together after Jeanne interacted with Etienne."

Francois scratched his chin then nodded. "Yes, I believe you may be right. There's more to this grand mission of Jeanne's than just helping Etienne succeed in his fashion show."

The older ghost paced along the hall with his head down. "This is perplexing," he murmured. "The last few days have brought back the past in a vivid manner I have not experienced in hundreds of years." He stopped and glanced at her. "What is happening? Every time I look at you I see Gabrielle, but you're Elizabeth's daughter." He shook his head and resumed pacing.

"It is baffling." Jeanne mused. "You said Marie escaped to Switzerland and took the identity of Gabrielle. My mother took me and left Paris at just the right time to avoid the rage of the mob. She went to Italy and many other places until it was safe to return. She never went to Switzerland where her dearest friend was supposed to be? It was as if she knew Gabrielle was not really there."

Francois stopped in his tracks, enlightenment dawning in

his features. "You are right," he exclaimed. "I never thought of it. I was too consumed by my despair and heartbreak. I could not have gone to Marie under any circumstances after she had allowed Gabrielle to die in her place. I might have strangled her, queen or not."

"If Elizabeth did not know the truth, she would have gone to her dear friend at once. Gabrielle must have shared her secret with my mother."

Francois hung his head. Sadness crept into his voice. "She trusted Elizabeth, but not me."

"That is not true," she declared. "It is not the reason. She knew you would try to stop her."

Francois gazed into her eyes then nodded. "Yes. I would have moved the earth to prevent such a tragedy."

"I think whatever the purpose, it concerns you as much as Jeanne." George said, pointing a finger at him.

"Really?" Francois's brows shot up.

"He is right. I came to the same conclusion today," she added.

"Yes. So we need to get more information about that time and each person. Other than memories, how can we do that?" George crossed his arms.

"I know," she said. "We Google them."

Francois and George sent her questioning looks.

"What is that? Google?" George asked hesitantly.

"It is a way to obtain information. We need a computer though, so we will get Etienne and Gaston to help us," she replied.

"Computer?" Francois asked, his expression blank.

"I will talk to Etienne tomorrow. We need to think of everything we want to know," she said.

Her friend nodded. "All right, we need to know about Francois, of course. And any information about what history says of Gabrielle following the death of Marie Antoinette."

But what about the unknown rich woman who spoke to her in a foreign language when she was a baby? "There is another memory I want to ask you about, Francois. I had a memory of a woman speaking to me, telling me good-bye as if she was sending me away forever. She spoke English."

"What did she say?" Francois asked.

Jeanne repeated the woman's words.

"English." Francois' eyes narrowed. "Interesting."

"She was richly dressed and beautiful. Who could she possibly be?"

"An English noblewoman, I would say," George deduced. "Friend of the family or some such thing."

"There were certainly English nobility who were friends of the French court," Francois agreed. "There were too many. I cannot begin to speculate about what woman might have known you and your mother."

"We shall keep it in mind, Jeanne. This will come together eventually, I'm sure of it," George said, patting her arm. His gentle expression soothed her.

"Yes, of course," she said, and tucked her hand in his. George was always so positive, bless him. I plan to spend more time remembering. Today has revealed a great many new pieces of information. I will see you both tomorrow after I meet Etienne."

She waved and went through the hall. She needed a dark, secluded area where she could concentrate. She craved facts, anything that would help unlock the secrets of her past and reveal the direction of her future. It wasn't until she was far from them that she remembered she had not told them about seeing the woman who looked like her mother. Something in her core told her the woman was dangerous, but why?

***

Margot waved to Lily and joined her at a small outdoor table of a crowded café. Her friend had already ordered glasses of white wine for them, bless her. Conversation buzzed around them, and the aroma of sautéed garlic made her stomach rumble.

"How did it go?" Lily asked as she took a seat.

"I won't know for a few weeks. I only turned it in today." She picked up a menu and perused the daily offerings. "I can't tell my mother or I'll never hear the end of it."

Her friend giggled. "If it's published, she'll know then. Might as well go ahead and tell her."

She shook her head. "No. There's a huge possibility the magazine doesn't want a pictorial essay on The Louvre right now.

If they reject it, no one will ever know. Especially my Mom."

"Just because it was her idea doesn't make it a bad one." Lily smirked.

"Yes, it does," Margot said and laughed. Still if she could make use of the photos she'd done for Professor Galen by putting together her own piece on the museum, why not? Better than letting the great shots go to waste. Besides, being published might enhance her chances of landing a fashion gig. It was worth a shot.

"What's next? The weddings?" Her friend sipped her wine and waved to a waiter.

She nodded. "Yes. One of them is having their reception at the Louvre. That ought to be fun."

"Yum. I hope they have good food catered."

"Don't worry. Sounds like the bride is going all out. Should be great." She leaned her chin on her fist and stared at the busy street in front of the café. Another wedding. A sigh escaped her lips, and Lily gave her a sharp glance.

"What's wrong?" her friend asked.

"Nothing." She waved a dismissive hand and picked up her wine glass. She should be grateful to have a job. Dreams didn't always come true, but a person had to eat and have a roof over their head.

Chapter 12

Etienne worked steadily through the morning, pinning muslin representatives of his designs around the fitting model, Claudette. She chewed gum and blew bubbles to pass the time as he moved the fabric to create the perfect form of his vision.

Her body was perfection for a designer, but her face had a sallow, pitted complexion and irregular features that barred her from runways or ads. She focused on being the best fitting model in the industry. She could stand still for hours and instinctively moved as creators molded their dreams to her figure. Her only vice was the constant bubblegum popping, which had led to her break-up fight with Gaultier this season. When he demanded she not chew while he worked, she quit. She had her standards, much to Etienne's good fortune. He didn't care if she chewed grass.

Jazz blasted from the stereo, punctuated by pops from Claudette's bubbles. Chloe hovered, intuitively handing pins, tape and marking pens based on his grunts and murmurs. She was on her sixth cup of coffee, and her jitteriness was beginning to get on his nerves.

"Raise your arm, please," he mumbled with several pins between his lips. He pulled the bodice more snugly under Claudette's arm and pinned the seam.

"Has your friend in London called back?" Chloe asked for the tenth time.

"No. I'll contact Paul again later. Don't worry," he replied. "It was late last night when I called. I left a message on his machine."

"Versailles is booked, right?" She shifted from foot to foot and clicked her pen repeatedly.

He pulled the pins from his mouth. "Yes, I told you five times already. The Opera Room for the show and the Hall of Mirrors for the ball." He stood and motioned for Claudette to slowly turn.

"That's it. That's the last one. Are the fabrics ready?" He rubbed his neck and rolled his shoulders to release stress and tension.

"Yes, everything is ready. What about celebrities? Do you know who's coming?" Chloe helped the model from the pedestal and removed the muslin pattern so as not to stick her with the hundreds of pins.

"Thanks, Claudette. Sorry for the long stretch, but we're behind the eight ball here." He smiled at the tall, thin girl.

She postured in her underwear while casting longing glances in his direction. "Don't worry. It's worth it if you kick some butt with this show. Some of these designers have turned into monsters. They deserve to have their faces shoved in it. So when do you want me back for the fabric fittings?" She pulled on her jeans and T-shirt.

"Tomorrow," he said.

Chloe rolled her eyes, but nodded.

Claudette popped another large bubble. "Wow. You are in a hurry." She picked up her huge sack-like pocketbook and slung it over one shoulder. She blew a kiss in his direction. "Okay, see you then."

As Chloe started to pour another cup of coffee, he demanded, "Put that down."

She paused. "Why?"

"You're jumping out of your skin and driving me crazy. No more caffeine."

"Oh." She placed her cup on the table and gathered the muslin pieces.

"Stop worrying." He pointed a finger at her.

"Okay, okay," she conceded.

"So, get the fabrics cut and basted, and I'll be back in the morning for fittings. Then we'll work on accessories." He pulled on his jacket.

She grabbed his arm. "Wait, where are you going?"

"More details to work out. I want to complete the ambiance of a period ball by having attendees park at the large stable area outside the gate, board horse-drawn carriages, and arrive at the entrance to the palace as they would have when the palace was a royal residence."

"Wow, that's an awesome idea."

"I don't think another couture show will provide such a

novelty."

"Absolutely not. It should be a big hit if you can arrange it."

"I have Vivienne working on it, too. Call me if you have problems. And stop worrying." He patted her hand and she released him.

He arrived at The Louvre and hurried down the corridor to the Venus statue. He found Jeanne there wearing a big grin.

"Etienne, how good to see you. Is everything going well with your collection?" she asked as he neared her.

"So far," he said, returning her grin. "How about you?" Every time he saw her he experienced the gut wrenching shock of her beauty followed by the sinking sense of loss as reality intruded, reminding him he couldn't touch her.

"I am fine. I have had some more memories and I have to tell you about my discussion with my friends last night."

"I want to hear all about it, but I have an important idea I want to explore with Gaston. Can you go with me to see him?"

Her smile became curious. "Of course. I will help in any way I can."

He led her out to a taxi. This time, she jumped in without hesitating. At Gaston's place, they climbed the stairs and found him in his studio on the top floor.

"Gaston," he called as they entered.

"Ah, there you are. Did you bring any wine?" The large man crushed a cigarillo in an ashtray.

"No, but I'll buy you a case of your favorite burgundy if you do something for me," he promised.

Gaston's eyes narrowed. "What do you want?"

"I want you to paint a portrait of Jeanne," he replied, motioning to the woman at his side.

"Jeanne, my dear, how are you?" Gaston gave her a flourishing bow. "You know you're my very favorite ghost."

"Fine. How are you?" She smiled and leaned toward him. "And you are one of my favorite living people."

"Well, I'd be much better if my dear comrade here had brought me some wine." The artist shot him an evil look. "So, you want me to paint Jeanne? What for?"

"Well, I've been trapped thinking we can't portray her as I

85

originally envisioned as the face of House Etienne because no one
can see her. But you can see her, and you can paint her as no one
else could. If you paint her face from different angles and moods,
we could use your paintings as if they are photographs and
digitally place the clothes on her. What do you think?" If Gaston
would give it his best effort and paint with passion as he used to, it
would succeed.

He wanted to place ads showing her face and small, teasing
portions of his designs on billboards and print ads the week prior to
the show. Then he would use detailed, full versions revealing the
designs after the show. He hoped this preliminary campaign would
increase interest and thus attendance for the big night at Versailles.

He hoped Gaston agreed to do it. His friend had said he'd
lost his edge, but underneath the complaining and posturing, a
genius painter waited. Maybe Jeanne was the right subject to ignite
his spark of creativity.

"Hmm." Gaston scratched his chin and stared at her. "I
must admit, that idea is very appealing. I want to do it as a
testament to you as an artist. You never received your due for the
work you did. That's a shame. I'd hate it if my talent didn't do you
justice. I'm not the artist I was years ago." He bit the end of his
paintbrush and looked at the floor.

Jeanne went to his side. "I am sure you could do it properly
if you only paint from your heart."

The big guy raised his head, and hope lit his eyes. "You
really believe that?"

She nodded. "I do."

Gaston slapped his knee. "Okay, I'll do it."

"All right," Etienne said. "That's what I wanted to hear. I
agree with Jeanne. If you care and paint from your heart, the magic
will happen."

"If you had kept painting, I think you would be
remembered as a great painter yourself, Jeanne," Gaston said.

"I am starting to understand why I stopped," she replied. "I
have captured more memories. There was a man in my past, a dark
angry figure. He is becoming more distinct. I believe he was my
husband, the man I married in Russia, of whom my mother
disapproved."

"Really?" he asked. "How was he involved?"

86

"It seems he felt it was inappropriate for a woman to have a career as an artist. That was the source of friction between him and my mother. I had painted until I married him, but he demanded I stop. That remembrance is still vague, but surely his displeasure would have deterred my pursuit of painting and thus recognition," she explained. "Although, as much as I love them, I do not think they were good enough to sell."

"Bastard," Gaston exclaimed. "To rob the world of talent such as that. It's a crime."

"But history says you returned to Paris to join your mother, and though he came with you, eventually left to return to Russia." Etienne couldn't imagine forcing someone to give up a dream. "Did you return to painting then?"

"I am not sure." She twirled a curl around her finger. "That part of my memory is still developing. All I can determine is that I was very sad for a long time before my death."

Gaston lit another cigarillo and paced the room, examining blank canvases. He chose one four feet tall and three feet wide. He placed it on an easel and motioned decisively to her. "I'm ready. I want to do this. Will you sit here?" He indicated a blue velvet cushioned chaise. He showed her how he wanted her to drape one arm over the rolled armrest of the chaise and turn her head slightly away from him. Light from the skylight fell softly across her features.

"Think about your past, that's the expression I want," he instructed. He squeezed tubes of different colored paint on his palette.

A wave of determination and absorption crossed Gaston's face. It was a look Etienne hadn't seen in many years. It reminded him of school when Gaston had kept him up by painting all night, a prisoner of his passion. A rush of warm gratitude for Jeanne filled him. He hoped her magic would create as much inspiration for his friend as it had for him.

"Look, you two are going to be busy with this. I need to make a number of arrangements for the show. I'll come back in a few hours," he said.

Gaston dismissively waved a paintbrush at him, already focused on his project. Jeanne remained staring into the past without acknowledging his farewell.

He returned to his office and his first task of calling his friend in London about their need for models. Chloe busily oversaw the cutting of fabrics, which would become his fantastic new collection. Other employees feverishly toiled at their prospective tasks and barely noticed his entrance. His assistant waved when he entered then returned to her scrutiny.

Fortunately, his friend Paul was in a position to help them. His new agency hadn't built up customers in the Paris *haute couture* world yet, so most of his runway models were available for Paris Fashion Week.

Etienne described the look he needed, and Paul promised to overnight a package of model photos and resumes to him so he would have them tomorrow. His friend expressed excitement at the prospect and vowed to accompany the girls to Paris to make sure everything went smoothly. Etienne smiled.

He sat back in his chair and took a deep breath. That completed two of the major items on his list. They now had the hope of obtaining enough models for the show to be successful. He could still use the same production company to prepare the Opera Room with the runway and all the other sound and light equipment for the show. He would have to speak to them about changing the design from ultra-modern to fit in with the element of history embodied in his collection. He also needed an orchestra.

Auspiciously, Vivienne agreed to handle all the arrangements for the food, beverages and serving staff. They'd transform the Hall of Mirrors into an eighteen hundred's ballroom full of candles and romance. He had already given her a huge advance to make sure she was able to secure the best of everything.

He took another breath and began making phone calls and writing notes. He was spending a great deal more on this show than he'd intended, but he had to create a sensation or he was finished. He'd already dipped into his private funds, but if all went as he hoped, the return would be well worth the depletion of his bank account.

Late in the afternoon, he reached the end of his list. A rush of satisfaction enveloped him. The plans were coming together. A glance at his watch told him he'd worked at it for four hours, much more time than he'd meant to be away from Jeanne. He quickly organized his notes and hurried to the door. Chloe gave him another wave, still intent on the production of the fabrics.

When Etienne made his way to Gaston's studio, he didn't detect any noise and wondered if Gaston and Jeanne were still there. When he entered, it appeared as if they hadn't moved in his absence. The only dramatic change was that Gaston had covered most of the canvas with paint. He whistled through his teeth as he approached the easel. The image of Jeanne was spellbinding. Gaston looked at him with an amazed look on his face as though he could not believe he had produced such a wondrous creation.

"*Mon Dieu*," he murmured.

Jeanne glanced up, her trance broken. "Etienne? What is it?"

"It, it's beautiful. It's beyond words. Gaston, you're a genius. You've done it," he shouted, laughing like crazy. He slapped the big man on the back.

"It is good, isn't it?" Gaston planted his hands on his hips and stood back to admire his work. "I can't believe I did this."

Jeanne came slowly around the easel to stand beside him and gaze at the painting.

"Gaston, it is a masterpiece, but is that really me? Do I look like that? Why, this is a graceful beauty with the smolder of distant memories in her eyes."

"Jeanne, that is exactly how you look," Etienne assured her. It was how he always thought of her.

Vivienne quietly entered the studio and said, "Wow, that's really good, Gaston. Who is she?"

Gaston and Etienne jumped.

"Vivienne!" Gaston exclaimed. "Ah, uh, this, this is a painting of Etienne's friend," he stammered. A flush tinged his cheeks.

"Oh?" She stared at him.

"Yes, her name is Jeanne," Etienne replied, amused at his friend's discomfort. The redhead had truly ensnared the big guy for him to react in this guilty manner.

"She's really beautiful," Vivienne commented. "Gaston, this is incredible work. Where have you been hiding this talent? Why are you wasting time with these copies when you can paint like that?" She pointed to the canvas on the easel.

He stuttered an attempt at forming a reply, but a grin spread his lips.

"My friend's been having inspiration trouble, but I think he's about to surprise us with his work from now on," Etienne said. He winked at Jeanne.

"So, Vivienne, tell us about your progress on the ball, and I'll fill you in on what I accomplished today. I think Gaston wants to continue painting, right, Gaston? I need more poses, remember?" Etienne gave his friend a meaningful glance. He led Vivienne to chairs so they could sit and chat.

"Oh, ah, right, right." His friend returned to the canvas, and Jeanne resumed her place on the chaise.

He watched them from the corner of his eyes. Jeanne clamped a hand over her mouth, the skin beside her eyes crinkled in mirth. Gaston tossed a threatening glare her way, but it took several minutes for her to return to her recollections of the past and compose her features. He kept glancing at Vivienne over his shoulder then making subtle motions to direct Jeanne's pose.

Oblivious to this comedic pantomime, the redhead reported she had secured a source for the ingredients she would need to prepare food for the ball, and she had also hired a company to provide the tableware and servers. There was an area in the palace that could be set aside for food preparation in the ground-floor kitchen gallery.

"Tomorrow, I'm going to meet with palace management to discuss your wish for horse-drawn carriages," she stated. "I have to tell you, I'm really becoming excited about this. I think it can be really big."

"I can't believe everything is coming together." A lightness invaded him as if he could float. It was about time for events to turn in his direction. Today the cloud of failure had lifted.

"Oh, also, I have some friends from culinary school that will be able to help me prepare the food. I wasn't able to meet with the wine dealer today, but I should be able to fit it in tomorrow," she continued.

"Vivienne, are you sure you don't mind helping me with this?" he asked. "I hate to pull you away from your search for a job, but I can't tell you how much I appreciate your taking on this project."

"Are you kidding?" she exclaimed. "If I make fabulous

food for your party, my success is secured. I'll be able to pick and choose between offers instead of begging someone to give me a chance as a chef."

"Then you better make fabulous food," he said with a chuckle.

He told her of his progress today with the models, and how the designs were coming along. Tomorrow would begin fittings of actual pieces, and that was likely to take several days. He held the secret of Jeanne, and his mission to place her face in his ads. If it became vital for her to know, he would do it. For now, he had too many other concerns, which demanded his attention and efforts.

"Seems like everything is coming together then," Vivienne said.

"I hope so," he said. "I have all my money and career riding on this."

"What about celebrities? Do we know who will attend yet? It's not too soon to be dropping names," she commented.

"I'm still working on that," he replied, averting his gaze. He didn't have a clue how to convince A-list stars and fashionistas to attend the show. He couldn't count on the novelty of the ball alone to entice them. Guests would need to perceive a benefit in attending, and he had to determine what benefit would attract the right people.

"If I'm going to keep working, I really need some red wine," Gaston complained, interrupting their discussion.

Don't worry, I know where to find some," Vivienne said, rising from her chair. "I'll make some snacks, too. How does that sound?"

"You're an angel." He blew her a kiss.

When she left, Etienne strolled to his friend. Gaston had started on a new canvas showing Jeanne, face raised with a hopeful expression and faraway gaze. It promised to be as magnificent as the first painting.

"Are you going to tell her?" Gaston jerked his head toward the door where the redhead had departed.

"Vivienne? No, not now anyway," he replied, distracted, still engrossed in the realistic glory of the painting.

"You're going to have to, you know," his friend insisted.

"Why?"

"Because, this is going to cause me a big problem." Gaston threw his hands in the air.

"I don't see how," Etienne planted his hands on his hips.

His friend gave a huge sigh. "I told you, you know nothing of women." He tossed his brush on the palette. "Pretend you're a woman and you see that I keep painting Jeanne in all kinds of different poses, and the paintings are the best thing I've ever done. What does that mean to you?"

"What does it mean to me if I'm a woman?" He was completely lost.

"Yes, yes. It's obvious," Gaston exclaimed.

He shook his head. "Not to me."

"A woman would think I've become obsessed with the person I'm painting, and since that person is also a woman, there's going to be jealousy. Jealousy means trouble."

"He is right," Jeanne added from the chaise.

Etienne shook his head then said, "You mean Vivienne will be jealous, thinking you are infatuated with Jeanne."

"Ex-actly," Gaston said with an emphatic bounce of his head.

"Well, can't you tell her you're painting Jeanne for me?" Irritation gnawed at him. He had enough to worry about. Why couldn't Gaston deal with this?

"That doesn't explain the miraculous change in my ability," his friend stated. "It doesn't make sense for me to be that inspired by someone I'm not involved with romantically. Only the explanation of Jeanne being the artist of my paintings would convince her."

He looked to Jeanne who nodded in confirmation, and ran his fingers through his hair. "Okay, if you feel that strongly, we'll tell Vivienne. But it's not going to be easy."

"Tell me what?" Vivienne stood at the doorway carrying a tray containing food and wine. "What's going on?"

Chapter 13

Etienne lost his breath as if a fist had punched him in the gut. Damn. Now they had to tell her for sure. He hated this sort of drama. He thrust his hands in his pockets and stared at the ceiling. Damn.

Vivienne advanced into the room and set her tray on the small table by the window. Then she turned and faced them, hands on her hips with an expectant expression. She tapped one foot. "Well?"

"Ahh, well, there's something we, uh, need to tell you." Gaston looked at Etienne pleadingly. "So, tell her."

"Me?" he exclaimed, backing away from her.

"Yes, you," his friend said firmly.

"Somebody better tell me something." The redhead shifted her weight and began tapping her other foot.

"Okay, okay. Vivienne, we need to explain about Jeanne," he said. Might as well get this over with.

"Oh?" She raised one eyebrow and glared at Gaston.

Gaston glanced back and forth between them and blurted out, "She's a ghost."

"Do you think I'm stupid?" she shouted.

"Very nicely phrased, imbecile." Etienne rolled his eyes, exasperated by his friend. Could he have done a worse job at telling their secret? He didn't think so. Now the drama began. He lowered his head to his hand.

"But, it's true. Jeanne is a ghost, and, and, that's not all. She's the artist who painted my collection," Gaston said, hands spread wide in entreaty.

Vivienne glanced at the two men, her face flushed. "Do you think I'm going to buy that?" She waved her arms over her head. "You're trying to cover up something. You expect me to accept some crazy story about a ghost? I can't believe I spent this day running around Paris to help you two, and you play this ridiculous trick. Well, that's it for me. You can find another caterer."

She started for the door, but Etienne ran to pull her back. Fear now clutched his gut in its cold grip. He couldn't lose his caterer at this late notice. It would ruin the show. Leave it to Gaston to break the news in an abrupt way. Now she thought they were making fun of her. Fool!

"Please, Vivienne, it's not like that. We would never play such a joke on you. Please listen," he pleaded. How could he make her understand?

Jeanne joined him and spoke into Vivienne's ear. "Vivienne, please stay."

The redhead jumped. "What's this? What the hell?"

"It is true, Vivienne," Jeanne's gentle voice continued. "It is true. I am Jeanne, and I really am a ghost. Please forgive Gaston's unfortunate tongue. I know this cannot be easy to comprehend."

The redhead wildly scanned the room as her eyes became tinged with fear. Etienne tugged her by the arm to a chair and gently urged her into it.

Gaston crossed the room to kneel before her. "It's my fault. I shouldn't have blurted it out," he said, tears forming in his eyes. "I'm sorry, *cherie*. I'm sorry!" He took her hand.

Etienne hovered behind them, praying his friend could calm her.

She snatched her hand away, glaring at her neighbor. "Where's that voice coming from?"

"It really is Jeanne," he replied. "Just listen for a minute. Let us explain."

"Please, stay Vivienne. We really need you," Jeanne added. She paused then said, "I know what I can do. When a ghost passes through someone who is living, they feel a chill. What if I do that to you? Would that help you believe?"

"Is there a microphone in the ceiling?" The redhead searched overhead.

"Just do it." Etienne motioned to Jeanne.

She shrugged then very slowly walked through Vivienne. Goose bumps rose on the redhead's arms and she crossed them over her chest. Breath from her lips emerged as a white fog. Her eyes grew round.

Jeanne motioned to the two men. "Etienne, you and Gaston go down to the apartment, you have botched this enough. Let me have time with her to explain."

"You're not leaving me with a … a ghost." Vivienne half-rose from her chair.

"You will be okay. I swear. I am not going to hurt you. I shall explain everything, and then you will understand why Gaston and Etienne have kept this from you." Jeanne's calm voice seemed to make the other girl relax somewhat, but Vivienne stared askance in the direction of her voice.

Etienne stumbled behind his friend down the stairs in his haste to escape.

"Oh, *merde*," Gaston exclaimed and fell into an armchair in his apartment.

"You can say that again." Etienne paced the room, one hand on his forehead. "You really have a way with words, my friend."

"Well, you weren't doing so great, so I just got it out there."

"Oh, you got it out there all right." He shook his head. "What if she refuses to do the catering now? I'm ruined." He paused in his pacing and glanced around the room. "Where's that brandy?"

"I finished it." His friend ducked.

"Fabulous! Is there anything else here to drink?"

"There's some vodka in the freezer."

"Vodka." He stared at his friend in disbelief.

"It's the only thing left. Really, Etienne, you have been so wrapped up in your show and this ghost business, you never make time to bring me wine anymore."

Etienne stared at him for a minute and then started laughing.

***

An hour later, Jeanne followed Vivienne into the apartment. The men downed shots of chilled vodka with tears streaming down their faces from laughter.

"Come on, Vivienne. Have some vodka." Etienne gestured her to the sofa, his words slurred.

"We'd offer you some, Jeanne, but we can't because..." Gaston began.

"You're a ghost!" Gaston and Etienne chorused together before collapsing in laughter.

"Well, Vivienne, I hope you recognize this for what it is," Jeanne said, shaking her head.

"The joyous sound of men relieved of a difficult task," the redhead said.

"They will be useless the rest of the night."

"I'm afraid you're right," Vivienne agreed. "What shall we do?"

"If you do not mind, I need help recovering my past."

The redhead turned to the direction of her voice and nodded. "Of course I'll help if I can. What do you need?"

She'd spent the past hour calming this woman, and then describing her meeting with Etienne and the eventual contact with Gaston, which led to her discovery of her precious paintings. She revealed some of her conversations with her ghost friends and the need to recover her past. Once Vivienne had settled and been convinced she was indeed a benevolent spirit, she became interested in her tales of fading and how some souls were hindered by unresolved issues from their past. Despite her initial shock, she handled the situation rather well.

They went to Vivienne's apartment where the redhead had a laptop on a desk. She typed entries in the search box.

"Francois is all you know?" she asked Jeanne.

"That is the only name. He said he was captain of the guard, and he frequently escorted Marie Antoinette and her entourage. Also, he had an affair with Gabrielle de Polignac, who was a lady in waiting to the queen." She looked over Vivienne's shoulder. "My mother painted a portrait of him."

"Ah, look, here it says that it was rumored Gabrielle had an affair with the Captain of the Guard, a Comte de Vaudreuil. His full name was, Joseph Hyacinth *Francois* de Paule de Rigaud. That has to be him. It says he ended up in Austria and tried to raise loyalist forces to free the royals." Vivienne continued to scroll down the page and then stopped. "Here it says that he had his portrait painted by Vigee le Brun. That's him."

She nodded, smiling. Yes. That had to be Francois. The description was much as he had detailed his life to her.

"I have a memory of an English noblewoman that does not

fit with the rest of my memories. She is saying good-bye to me. Is there any mention of a particular person of that description who was close to my mother?" she asked.

The redhead typed and scrolled, but shook her head. "It seems your mother spent most of her time on the continent until after you were grown. You were married when she made her trip to London and painted the nobility there. Now, Gabrielle is another matter. She and Marie had many friends in the English court. One particular friend to Gabrielle is mentioned, the Duchess of Devonshire."

"Hmm, I do not see how that could be related. Gabrielle died shortly after my birth. By that time, my mother and I were headed to Italy." She searched her memory for more information, but nothing emerged.

"Do you really believe this story that Gabrielle took Marie Antoinette's place?" Vivienne leaned back in her chair.

"I have no reason to doubt Francois. You must admit there is scant notice of Gabrielle in history after the execution of Marie. The queen would have kept a low profile in Switzerland to avoid discovery. Any hint she lived would have resulted in plots to murder her," she answered.

"True," Vivienne said. "But imagine, all these years and no one knew."

"Yes, what a sad story for everyone concerned," Jeanne added. "You know I told you about my friend, George? He thinks this is tied together in some way."

"You mean you, Etienne, Francois, Gabrielle..."

"Yes. He says when the puzzle is solved there will be resolution for each of us."

"Do you believe that?" the redhead asked.

"I am not sure. It does seem a tremendous coincidence though. On top of this, both Etienne and I have seen a woman in the Louvre who looks like me. I cannot help thinking she is part of this as well. Why would she appear *now*, and both of us see her?"

Vivienne nodded. "That is bizarre. He wasn't able to find out who she was?"

"No, she always slipped away before he could confront her. Of course, she couldn't see me, so contact was impossible."

"Wait." Vivienne scrolled through pages of information

and stopped at one entry. She pointed toward the screen.

"What is it?" Jeanne leaned over her shoulder.

"Your mother's brother. His name was Etienne."

"Etienne," she whispered. She pictured his face, and a pain shot through her heart.

Chapter 14

Etienne awoke on Gaston's sofa after unreasonably numerous shots of vodka. The empty bottle of the offending liquid lay on its side upon the coffee table. His friend snored in the armchair, oblivious.

He rubbed his head and stood. His first course of action was a large glass of water and some aspirin. Jeanne sat on a barstool, staring at him. *Merde*! He had forgotten about taking her back to the Louvre. He was a jerk.

"I'm so sorry. Have you been there all night?" He moved to her side, heart wrenched with remorse.

"No, Vivienne and I researched the past on her computer. Then I came here to wait for you to wake. I like your face." She smiled endearingly.

"Please forgive me. Gaston and I started drinking and letting off steam. The next thing I knew, I woke on his couch. I think the pressure of this show, meeting you, and the other issues have caught up with me." How could he have forgotten her? He blamed it on the vodka, an evil drink.

"Do not worry. I understand," she said. "You do not need to explain. I was glad to spend time with Vivienne. It seems we uncovered some important information last night."

"You did?" He went to the sink and poured a glass of water. He rummaged through Gaston's cabinets and found a bottle of aspirin.

"Yes, and now more pieces of the mystery are falling into place."

"What did you discover?"

"My mother had a brother named Etienne."

He stopped and stared at her, a strange shiver of apprehension running through him . "Really? Is he someone you remember?"

"Until last night. I did not remember him. I had only a few memories of a man who encouraged me in my painting and was very kind to me, but I could not clearly see his face. Last night when Vivienne made the discovery, the face instantly became clear. Etienne, you have his face," Jeanne exclaimed.

He stood holding the glass of water trying to make sense of this revelation. What did it mean? He was some sort of reincarnation of Jeanne's uncle? But that didn't fit. He loved her. If she was living, he would have already kissed her and held her and told her of his feelings. He turned to hide his expression.

"Etienne?" she asked with concern shading her tone.

He stalled by refilling his glass. Did she see him as a benevolent uncle who had encouraged her artistic endeavors? This was wrong, wrong, wrong.

"Etienne?"

"That's really interesting." He turned around, his features schooled in what he hoped was an open smile. "You had an uncle named Etienne."

She studied him for a moment then replied, "Yes. It is very interesting, don't you think?"

"Do you want to go back to the Louvre?" He moved to the sofa and stared across at the sleeping Gaston whose snores rumbled on.

"No, I want to stay here. I will tell Gaston to make more paintings of me when he wakes. That is what you want, right?" She watched him closely.

"Yes, that would be great. Thanks." He avoided meeting her gaze.

"I have an idea that would help you encourage celebrities to attend the show," she said after a minute.

"Oh?" He faced her. "I desperately need help with that."

"Yes. After you decide who would be the most important people to attend, I think you should design period costumes for them individually. Deliver each costume with an invitation. Make the costume so attractive, they cannot resist appearing in it."

"Jeanne, do you realize how much we have going on right now?" He raked his fingers through his hair. "It's a great idea, but how will I find the time to do it? My staff is already on the edge of quitting or having a nervous breakdown."

She floated up close, inches away. "Now listen, this is important. If the celebrities come, so will everyone else. You have to find time to do it. Limit it to four women most followed for their fashion. You can do it."

He saw the determination in her eyes. Yes, it would mean a lot of work on top of the new collection, but it held promise. He could set up a special photo shoot to create publicity for his House. The celebrities would be unable to resist. If the show turned into the success he anticipated, one of the major fashion magazines would jump through hoops for the photos and story. Since Vogue had indicated they wouldn't attend, he would have Chloe call her contact at "W" for the scoop. When Vogue heard about it, they wouldn't dare allow him to exclude them.

"Okay. Damn it. You're right. I'll find a way to work it into my schedule," he said, filled with warm gratitude for her coming into his life, he gazed at her beautiful, earnest face. "You're really amazing. Do you know that? I want you with me forever."

He gazed into the depth of her blue-green eyes. How he wanted to hold her. He ached to pull her against his chest and run his fingers through her glorious curls. "Are you sure about this *fading* business? Is that really what you want?"

"I wish I knew. I only see it as the natural order. Surely that must mean it is the best for me in some way, just as death comes eventually for the living." Her eyes drooped in sadness. "I am in the clutch of destiny for now, so I will follow that path until more is revealed. In any event, at least I am happy since I met you, and I am enjoying the challenges of making your show a success. Let us not worry about anything else right now."

"All right." He nodded. "But I want to sincerely thank you, Jeanne. Thank you for all your help." He retreated a step, hoping distance would quench his desires.

Her lips curved in a halfway smile, and she averted her gaze.

"Well, I really need to go to the office. I'll drop by here this afternoon." he said.

"I shall be here." She cast a longing glance in his direction.

Etienne stopped by his apartment to shower and change clothes, and then returned to his atelier. Chloe was in her office, talking with some of the staff, so he traversed the spiral stairs to his own workplace. He flipped through messages on his desk and noticed an overnight package. Eagerly he opened the folder from his friend Paul and pulled out photos and resumes of models.

He'd sorted them into *yes* and *no* piles when Chloe appeared. Fatigue formed dark circles under her eyes, but she grinned, letting him know the collection progressed well.

"Claudette will be here at ten," she said as she crossed the room to sit in the chair before his desk.

"Good. We have a lot of work to do. Look at these photos and see if you agree with my assessment," he said, pushing the two piles across the desk. "Any crisis I should know about?"

"Not yet, but it's early," she said, half-serious as she leafed through the pictures.

"Chloe, if you had to pick four celebrities most vital to our show, who would they be?"

She glanced up from her perusal of the models' faces, head tilted to one side. "Hmm. I would say a mix from different areas would probably be best. For instance, actresses like Penelope Von Klef and Sara Barker. Singers like Cara or Miranda. Then there are the fashionistas like Evelyn Barrister or Princess Giada."

"Of those, who would we be able to most easily obtain current measurements?"

She glanced at the ceiling then back to him. "I'm not sure. I'd have to do some research. Why?"

"I want to design period costumes for four people who we most need at the show. We'll have the invitations delivered with the costumes and hope the publicity element will assure their attendance." He went on to explain his plan for the photo shoot and luring big magazines, then he sat back.

"That's genius, Etienne. But do we really need more work at this point?" She pressed her fingertips to her temples.

"I'll handle making them myself. I still know how to sew. Just help me with finding measurements and obtaining the fabrics."

She sighed. "All right. It really is brilliant. I can't think of a better way to entice them. Where do you keep coming up with these ideas? Something has truly inspired you recently. Is there anything you want to tell me?"

"No. There will be no explaining," he said. "Just take it and be thankful, as I am."

"Okay, if you say so. Just keep the ideas coming." She rose and headed for the stairs.

He grinned at the thought of trying to explain about Jeanne to Chloe. After the disaster they made of telling Vivienne last night, he wasn't about to bring up the subject to anyone else unless it became an absolute necessity. He pulled the phone to him. He had seemingly endless calls to make and then a grueling day of fittings ahead of him.

***

Jeanne stared at Gaston until he finally opened his bloodshot eyes a couple of hours after Etienne left. He jumped when he saw her and then put a hand to his head and groaned. "Vodka is an evil drink," he mumbled.

"Wake up, Gaston. You need to make more paintings," Jeanne said. She rose and floated to the chair to stare at him with a stern expression, her hands on her hips.

"Aaaaaa, my head, keep it quiet, please?" He put both hands over his ears. "You make a lot of noise for a ghost."

"Well you better get up and make some coffee then or you will see just how much noise a ghost can make." She gave him her best evil glare.

His eyes popped open. "Look, I don't want any horrific moans and rattling chains, okay?" He got up and ambled into the kitchen and set the coffeemaker to brew. Then she nagged until he stumbled into the shower.

"Hurry up. You've been in there too long," she called after ten minutes.

Gaston grumbled, "I should have a longer shower. My head is killing me."

Jeanne threatened, "Come out now or I'll glide through the shower curtain and join you."

The spray of water immediately ceased and she smiled.

It was a testimony to her persistence that she had him in the studio only an hour later after two cups of strong coffee and the quick douse in the shower.

He positioned her again on the blue velvet chaise, and as minutes passed she became lost in her memory world and, given her recent discovery, she found her uncle Etienne.

***

His face was a perfect version of what the current Etienne's would be in five or six years' time: a handsome, striking figure dressed in the latest Parisian fashion. She employed a brush to paint the garden from the window of her father's house in Paris. She and her husband had just returned to France from Russia.

"That is coming along very well," her uncle commented. "I really wish you would allow me or your father to sell some for you. You deserve to be recognized. You could become independent, like your mother."

She paused in her work and cast him a wistful look then shook her head. "You know Bernard will not stand for it. I paint in secret when he is away as it is. Selling my work would only bring to the open what we have fought about for so many years," she replied and returned to her painting. "Besides, I fear you are the only one who sees value in them. Mother certainly never did. I do not think they are very good. I paint for the joy of it."

"Then we shall agree to disagree, for I see they are very fine." Etienne fingered the lapel of his jacket. "You will not recognize your husband is at fault in his demands?"

"What can I do? Mother was so angry at my marriage she left me in Russia and refuses to support me in any way. Father is not rich, and despite their divorce, he is supported by my mother. So, I keep the peace with Bernard."

"He does not like it here," Etienne commented. He walked to the open window to inspect the outside scene she reproduced on the canvas.

"Bernard? No, I do not think he does. But I came to hate the never ending cold of Russia, and I want to see if I can make peace with my mother." She shrugged. "I can never go back there or I will become so depressed I would kill myself."

"But, what about your daughter?"

"Etienne, you are so full of hard questions today. I meant to enjoy Bernard's absence and paint this garden while the sun shines." She closed her eyes and sighed, her heart heavy. Why couldn't he understand? If she didn't think about her problems, they seemed less real. Painting was one way she escaped from her dreary reality. "He will never let her leave Russia. She is with his mother. When she is older, she will go into the convent school and there she will remain until she comes of age. I have no say in the matter. Bernard is very old-fashioned."

"Will you tell Elizabeth?" He moved from the window and faced her.

"About my daughter?" She turned to him. "Of course not. Not as things stand anyway. When she returns from England, we shall see if she still harbors her paranoid thought that we tried to discredit her in Russia. I am hoping her anger has mellowed and we can renew our relationship, but you know what she is like."

"My dear Julie." He sighed and shook his head.

"Do not call me that," she demanded, hot with anger. "That is *her* name for me. Julie or Juliette. I want to be called Jeanne. I want to forget all those days when she controlled my life. I hate those names."

"Very well, let us change the subject to something more pleasant," Etienne said. "There is a ball at Versailles this Saturday. Napoleon is celebrating some new victory. I am invited to read one of my poems in celebration of the new empire. Suzanne does not like that sort of thing, so I want you to go with me."

A hot flush of true pleasure rushed to her cheeks replacing the heat of her ire. It was the first break in her gloomy existence since her arrival in Paris. How she used to love attending balls and parties. "Oh, Etienne, how lovely. I would love to go. Bernard will not be back for two more weeks. Are you sure your wife would not like it?"

"I am positive. I am afraid she finds my poetry dull. She is more content in her sitting room with her embroidery these days. That's why I spend so much time here with you."

"But I have nothing to wear fine enough for such an occasion." Gloom returned like a heavy blanket dampening her spirits.

"Do not worry." Etienne laughed. "I want to see that pretty smile on your face again. I will take care of the details. Just say you will go."

"Of course, of course. Darling Etienne!" She ran to him and enveloped him in a grateful embrace. "You are the only one in my dismal family who understands me and cares for me."

He returned her hug and kissed her cheek.

105

"Then it is settled." His gaze met hers. "I am very pleased to see the old sparkle of youth back in your eyes. I worry about you, you know." He flicked a finger under her chin. "I have to go now. You keep painting and enjoy your brief freedom. I want to see a masterpiece when I return."

She laughed and tucked her hand in his arm as she walked him to the front door. The idea of the ball had lifted her spirits as nothing had in many years. She dearly loved her uncle, he seemed more of a friend than relative, always encouraging her and never condemning.

She returned to her easel and stared out at the garden. Had it been worth it - her marriage, defying her mother? She'd truly loved Bernard in the beginning. Given different circumstances, they might have been very happy together. He was not a bad man, but he was old-fashioned and from a culture so different from her own. She'd grown up traveling with her mother through the great courts of Europe, socializing with the free and easy manners of the nobility and those in the art world. The restrictions of the less socially advanced Russian society had drained the life from her.

Etienne was perceptive. Bernard would not like it for very long in Paris, just as she had not been able to tolerate Russia. She faced that fact. She hoped over time she could reunite with her mother, and then her dependence on Bernard would not force her to return when he finally found France intolerable.

Dear Etienne. He'd always encouraged her painting and kept her supplied in paint and canvas. He even took the finished pieces away to store so Bernard would not find them. But painting was just a way for her to engross her mind in a fleeting pleasure and escape the worries of her reality. She could never aspire to sell any. Her own mother had judged them worthless, and she was a great artist.

She put away those disturbing thoughts and turned her attention to the garden and painting, which soothed her soul. Time enough to sink in worry when Bernard returned.

***

"Jeanne? Jeanne, are you all right?" Gaston's voice broke through her revere and she returned to the present.

"Y, y, yes," she managed. Actually, she remained in turmoil. The brief biography she had read of her mother's life had not mentioned details revealed in this memory. She and her mother had been estranged? All the warm feelings from her mother must have been memories when she was much younger, before the fateful trip to Russia. She began to see how pieces of sadness had come to shade her life. An unsuccessful marriage. A child she'd left behind. Arguments with her mother. How could she not be sad?

"Are you sure?" Gaston walked around the easel and stood before her, concern etched in his eyes. "It's been two hours. I need a break even if you don't. Okay?"

"Two hours?" Jeanne asked, amazed. It seemed seconds since she sat,

"Yes, take a look." He motioned to the canvas.

She went to the painting. He had used this canvas to paint multiple versions of her head and neck. Gaston was painting at a ferocious pace. She could trace the story of her recent memory with Etienne in the changing expressions on the painted faces. Sadness, hopefulness, elation, and pensive thought were all depicted.

"They are very good, Gaston. Very good," she said, wishing she could be more enthusiastic, but the recently uncovered memory weighed heavy on her soul. "Etienne will be so happy."

"What about you? Are you happy? You suddenly seem sad."

"I had a memory that renewed a painful issue. No need to worry. I will be fine." She gave him a reassuring smile.

"Okay, I'm going to get something to eat. I'm starving. I hope Etienne brings some red wine when he comes back this afternoon," he said as he left the garret.

Jeanne hurried to the chaise. She wanted to recapture her memory with Etienne. She had to see what had happened. She replayed the recent images she had experienced and closed her eyes, returning to the past.

Chapter 15

"It is so beautiful, Etienne." Jeanne swirled before a mirror. The elegant gown was the latest French fashion; white silk organza trimmed in gold ribbons, cut low across the chest and falling in layers to her ankles. A golden silk ribbon tied under her breasts, and bunches of white and gold ribbons were gathered at the shoulders with tendrils falling down her bare arms. She had piled her unruly brown curls on top of her head and threaded a red satin ribbon through them. She pulled up the hem of her skirt to admire the delightful white kid slippers with kitten heels and diamond buckles on the toes.

"*You* are beautiful," he said. He handed her a red silk shawl with fringe to drape over her arms. "Shall we go?"

To giddy to speak, her glowing smile was her only answer. She took his arm and they went out to the street where his hired coach waited.

"Bernard would never approve of this dress," she said, giggling as she ascended the folding steps. She could imagine his frown of disapproval.

Her uncle followed her in and took the seat across from her, then tapped the roof of the coach with his cane. The driver started on the drive to Versailles.

"Then it is a good thing he is not here," he replied, giving her a conspiratorial wink.

"I am sure it would finalize the already imminent demise of our marriage," she agreed. "But I refuse to think about that tonight. I am going to pretend I am a young girl again without any mistakes behind me."

He winced but quickly turned his attention out the window. "We have a bit of a drive ahead of us, so settle in and try not to use up all your enthusiasm before we arrive," he warned, bestowing an indulgent smile on her.

She returned his smile, knowing he worried about her. She was fully aware that ever since her return to Paris, he'd tried to make up for the neglect his sister had shown her after the ill-fated marriage in Russia. Unfortunately, some sorrow could not be overcome.

How dearly she would love to return to the young, carefree girl she had been before her mother escaped with her during the revolution. Now, she had a husband who insisted on drab, conservative clothes and declined offers of meaningless frivolity such as balls. This evening was a step back into a happier, more distant time. Perhaps she could be the old Jeanne for a few hours.

She forced her attention out the coach window as a diversion from her thoughts, pointing to remembered landmarks and changes since her last trip down this road. Along the way to Versailles they encountered other coaches and she exclaimed at the splendid sight of shiny carriages and prancing pairs of horses. As they approached the palace, the stunning array of lamps and candles gleaming in the darkness made her gasp in appreciation.

"You're so beautiful tonight, Jeanne." Etienne's gaze fixed on her. "I wish this animation could last. When you're happy, every gesture, every expression, everything you say is a work of art, elegant and flowing. I want to write a poem about you in this mood."

She smiled. "You flatter me, dear Etienne. But tonight I will allow it. A few hours of pleasure is not too much for one to have. Is it?"

"Not at all," he said softly and escorted her from the coach.

Inside the fabulous Hall of Mirrors, thousands of candles reflected light in a fantasyland of sparkles. Red, white and blue flowers, and bunting declared the joyous victory of the French people with Napoleon at their head. Jeanne stared around her with lips parted at all the wondrous sights. And then there were the people. Gowns and jewels worth a fortune, accented by the decorated uniforms of the invited officers, and noblemen in formal attire.

Etienne led her directly to the dance floor and they joined in a waltz, which had just begun. They both grinned as they swirled joyously around the room. Jeanne's heart glowed with the happiness that might have been hers had she been able to stay in Paris and grow up in a more conventional lifestyle, marrying someone from their social circle. But unfortunately, the revolution had forced them out of France and in another direction.

The waltz ended and they strolled to an upper chamber off of the Hall where refreshments were laid out. He took glasses of champagne from a passing waiter and handed one to her. She took a sip of the heavenly liquid, which her husband never allowed, and then swallowed the whole contents, a mischievous smile curling her lips. He laughed and went to fetch another one. It pleased her immeasurably to have a man treat her in this pampered manner again.

"This is the most wonderful time I have ever had," she exclaimed when he returned. "Thank you so much for inviting me."

"The pleasure is mine, *cheri*. I would not have this much fun with anyone else."

"Have you ever seen such beautiful people?"

"Well, not since the last time I was here." He laughed and she joined in.

The rest of the evening was magical. They danced and drank more champagne. Then, when Napoleon and Josephine made their entrance, Etienne was called forth to recite his poem of victory. She told him she was so proud of him and his talent. He was a very successful playwright and poet and was given much acclaim for tonight's poem by the attendees. His spark of success surrounded her.

"I am so honored to be on the arm of such a handsome, talented man, adored by everyone at the ball." She teased. "Even the emperor loves you."

He coughed and lowered his head. "It's nothing. Just a poem."

She laughed at his depreciating comment and pinched his cheek. "I love you, too."

He gave an odd stare but didn't answer.

By the end of the evening she declared she was dizzy from the champagne, and the joy of being back in her element after so long. In the carriage she chatted for a while of the spectacle and then fell asleep on his shoulder. Before she succumbed to oblivion, she felt his arm curl around her waist to steady her in the rolling movement of the coach. She luxuriated in the warmth and security of his embrace.

When they reached her home, he gently shook her awake.

110

"Jeanne, time to rise. We are back at your house."

She yawned, still a bit fuzzy from the alcohol. It seemed only seconds had passed since they left the ball.

Etienne's face hovered over hers and he tucked an errant curl behind her ear and kissed her cheek. He whispered against her ear, "My sweet, darling, Jeanne."

A shiver of pleasure engulfed her body and she clung to him. Once he left the magical night would be over and she would have to return to her drab, sorry existence. "Please do not leave me yet. Dear Etienne, I am so afraid to go back in that house and resume my life."

"Shh." He placed a fingertip on her lips. He studied her face and pressed his mouth in a firm line. "Come, let me take you inside."

He told the driver to go ahead and he would make his way home shortly on his own. She nearly cried from relief. The house had become a tomb. Hers. Once inside she would begin dying again. Maybe if Etienne were with her they could charm the future and make it better. They walked arm and arm together up the stairs and through the front door, still under the enchantment of the evening.

Jeanne wobbled on her feet from all the champagne. She accepted Etienne's strong arm around her waist to help her up the staircase to her bedroom so she didn't fall.

A sob shook her. It had been a mistake to go to the ball. Now she was reminded of all she'd lost, all she didn't have. How could she pretend to go on living with a man she didn't love and who didn't love her?

"Oh god, I want to die." She sagged against him, hopelessness draining her of strength.

"No. No. Jeanne. Don't say that. I can't bear it." He held her close and kissed her cheeks and then her wet eyelids. "Please don't cry. Everything will be fine."

"No, you don't understand. I can't live like this anymore. I'd rather be dead than cut off from love and the joys of life." Her sobs shook her as despair welled in her chest. "Maybe I'm being selfish, but I can't believe it is too much to ask for a little happiness."

"There must be a way." He brushed a damp curl from her

cheek. "I'll talk to Elizabeth. If she will support you, you can paint and do all that you desire here in Paris. Bernard can return to Russia and you will be happy."

She shook her head, her heart breaking. "My mother has turned evil. She will not forgive me."

"Let me try." He pleaded.

"You are so good to me." She gazed up at him beneath wet clumped lashes. His tender gaze sent a surge of desire through her that made her gasp. Here was the man she wanted. A man full of love and refinement. He'd always been there for her.

When they reached her room, she turned to him and put a hand on his chest. Her eyes searched his and found an answering passion there. Her arms crept around his neck and his head lowered to hers until their foreheads touched. His breath came faster, and she lost all sense of reason swept up in lust. "I love you, Etienne. I want you."

"Are you sure?" he whispered, a catch in his voice. He stroked her hair tenderly.

She nodded, her eyes never leaving his. Her heart swelled to bursting with love for him. In one movement, he lifted her in his arms and carried her into the bedroom.

Her skin prickled with a rush of passion when Etienne swept her into his arms. Her heart thudded. Despite the lingering flush of champagne, she knew exactly what she was doing. The evening had blossomed into a fantasy sparked by the light of love in Etienne's eyes. That illumination broke through the despair drenching her soul and shone on the love she'd always had for him. She saw it now for what it was. The truest passionate love between a man and a woman. He could save her.

He carried her to the bed and gently set her on her feet. His fingers worked the fastenings of her gown, and she removed his coat and shirt. She moaned as his lips traveled over her throat and along her shoulder.

Her dress fell to a ripple of organza at her feet like a white cloud. She trembled as she removed her undergarments. He sat on the bed to pull off his boots then removed his pants. They stood naked, facing each other, only an inch apart.

"Jeanne, you are so lovely," he whispered then took her face between his hands and kissed her deeply.

She circled her arms around his waist and pressed her hands to the small of his back, bringing him tight against her. The hard warmth of his body touching hers forced the breath from her lungs. Never had Bernard brought this response from her with his clumsy attempts at sex.

Etienne's fingers moved from her face to her nape, stroking the tender flesh there. She shivered and murmured into his ear, "I love you."

"I love you, too, my darling. Always have I loved you. But tonight it became real."

She nodded, on the verge of tears at the force of her emotions. Why had she made such a mess of her life? She swallowed a sob, unwilling to allow the curse of her mistakes to ruin this perfect evening. Even if it ended after tonight, at least she would have this memory to cherish for the rest of her life.

They settled on the bed, and he covered her body with his. She gasped at the sweet feel of his flesh pressed to hers. He kissed her, gently at first, trailing his lips over her face, neck, breasts, and abdomen. She arched her back in ecstasy, tremors shaking her.

"My sweet love." He returned to her lips, ravishing them with greater intensity as his hands cupped her breasts, kneading the soft flesh until her nipples peaked and grew harder.

"Darling Etienne," she managed between soft groans. "Make love to me. I need you."

He ran his tongue past her lips, entering her mouth. She twined her tongue to his, warm and soft. With one hand, he parted her legs. She gasped as he entered her. Her hips moved involuntarily, loving him inside her, stroking slowly.

Tingles spread from her groin to her legs and grew as his rhythm increased. His torso rose and he balanced on his hands. He stared at her as she exploded in a torrent of passion. Both panted, and he groaned as he lowered his body to hers, spent. A thin sheen of sweat covered his skin.

"So perfect," he said softly. "My sweet love."

She ran her hands up and down his back, wishing this moment could last an eternity. She had no wish to return to reality. This is where she was meant to be, in Etienne's arms. Yet, it was impossible.

***

The soft glow of morning light awakened her. They lay tangled in the sheets, her head on his chest and his arm around her shoulders. She gazed at him in wonder. It had never been like this with Bernard. Last night had been the most extraordinary event in her life. They were meant to be together, and only time and circumstance had kept them apart. She had no guilt or regrets.

"Darling, Jeanne, my one and only love," he said softly, looking into her eyes.

"Oh, Etienne, I never knew. I never..." she stammered.

He smiled and kissed her forehead.

"Are you sorry?" he asked, suddenly serious.

"No, no, no. Never," she declared. She touched his face with her fingertips. "How can I be sorry for something so perfect?" All her life she'd wanted this kind of love, this feeling of abandon and freedom tied into the rush of passion. Why had she made such horrible choices?

He pulled her to him then and kissed her lips, the urge to love rising like a flood between them. He ran his hand from her neck down to her stomach, and she pressed her body to his, meeting his desire with her own.

***

"Jeanne?" Etienne's voice broke into her thoughts.

She opened her eyes and found him staring at her with concern evident in his eyes. For a moment, she had trouble distinguishing him from the man who just carried her to the pinnacle of ecstasy.

"Are you okay?" He sat beside her on the blue velvet chaise.

Fog filled her head after the abrupt removal from her memory, and disappointment crashed upon her. She'd wanted to stay in that memory forever.

"Yes, I am okay," she said finally, pressing a hand to her heart. "I just had a very intense memory."

"It must have been a good memory from your expression."

If he only knew. This new aspect of her past left her

spinning. Given her feelings for the current Etienne, how could she be surprised? It made sense. It made more sense than his being her benevolent uncle. They were lovers, but what had been the outcome? She still didn't know.

"I do not really want to talk about it yet," she replied. "Did you see what Gaston has accomplished today?"

"No, I just walked in and found you in some kind of a trance. I wanted to make sure you were well."

"Come and look." She motioned him to follow as she rose and moved to the front of the easel.

"Wow. Gaston has really made a comeback." He stared at the canvas.

"Talking about me?" Gaston entered the room, munching on a sandwich. "I hope you brought some wine this time."

"It's in my briefcase." Etienne motioned to a heavily loaded leather satchel by the door.

Gaston immediately rummaged through and brought forth a burgundy, which he speedily corked and poured into two glasses. "So, what do you think?" he asked, joining them at the canvas.

"Genius, my friend. I think two cases of wine are in order instead of one." Etienne pounded the big man on the back. His friend smiled broadly, with a glass of wine in one hand.

Gaston said, "Well, there are some finishing touches, but it won't take long. And then...."

"And then what?" Etienne asked.

"And then I can have Jeanne pose so I can make a painting for me."

"Well, that's up to Jeanne," Etienne replied.

"Of course. If it would make you happy," she said.

"Beyond anything."

"Then it is settled. So, what is happening with the collection?" She glanced at Etienne.

"Actually everything seems to be on target. I'm shocked we haven't had a major block to our plans so far. We'll see what Vivienne accomplished when she arrives. We have models now, and the clothes are coming along nicely. Chloe is working on finding measurements for the celebrities so we can make costumes for them, and she's throwing out enticing lures of exclusive photos to the competitors of Vogue. I have to say that, for the first time in

115

a long time, I'm feeling very hopeful."

"That is wonderful news," she exclaimed.

"Drinking without me?" Vivienne's voice interrupted.

"Absolutely not." Gaston poured another glass and handed it to her as she strolled into the room.

"Well, I see you two have recovered from your male bonding with vodka experience," she said, glancing between them.

"Not our finest hour," Etienne said. "Sorry about that."

"*Really* sorry," Gaston added.

"Well, due to the fact that I got to meet such a wonderful person as Jeanne as a result, I'm willing to forgive you both," she said magnanimously. "Is she here?"

"Yes, Vivienne, right here," she replied.

The redhead gave a wave in the direction of her voice.

"Good, so we're all here. Then I'll bring you up-to-date on what happened today." She launched into a report of her success at arranging the horse-drawn carriages, and on her meeting with the wine merchant who, despite his other commitments during the frantic fashion week, was going to be able to provide what they needed for the ball.

Etienne relayed his accomplishments, and they discussed ideas for invitations and Vivienne's proposed menu.

Jeanne drifted to the memory of making love with her uncle, and a shiver filled her. This was a remembrance she could return to over and over with great pleasure. If only she could be with *this* Etienne in the same way, but it was impossible. By meeting him, she was certain the past had reached out to her. The reason was still unclear. Unfortunately, she had much of her history yet to discover. In any event, this illicit affair had greatly impacted her remaining years before her death. She needed to return to the Louvre and spend time alone with her emerging memories. Then she needed to talk with Francois.

Chapter 16

When Jeanne returned to the Louvre, darkness fought against flickering city lights. The museum had closed, and she floated through empty halls, occasionally passing another soul. She hadn't seen Blonde Hair in quite a while and assumed she had completed her fading. There was no sign of George or Francois in the corridors. Most likely they were in one of the salon areas. She wasn't ready to see them yet, so she made her way to the café where she and Etienne had their first "date."

Silence filled the deserted café except for a ticking clock. Souls rarely frequented this area, keeping to the more visually stimulating displays of art. She settled in a seat and tried to calm herself. Images of her previous memory kept intruding into her thoughts. An uneasy sense of anticipation urged her to learn how her life had progressed after this revelation of her love for Etienne. She closed her eyes and was immediately back in that bedroom.

***

Etienne dressed, and Jeanne lay against the pillows, memorizing every inch of him to cherish after he left. Contentment glowed in every part of her body. His touch had worked a miracle, bringing her back to life.

"You look happier than I have seen you in a long time," he commented. He kept glancing at her as he fastened his clothes.

"I am deliriously happy. When will you come to me again?" She wished he could stay forever.

"Tomorrow. I will bring you more paints if you like." He pulled on his jacket.

"Just bring yourself. You are what I need." She stretched in the bed like a cat in a warm patch of sun, luxuriating in the sweet afterglow of lovemaking.

Etienne came to the bed and sat on its edge. He pulled a tendril of her hair loose and wrapped it around a finger. "My beautiful Jeanne," he murmured.

"My darling Etienne." She took his hand in hers and kissed his knuckles.

"We really need to talk about what we will do, you know," he said softly.

"Shhhh." She placed a finger on his lips "Not today. Today is perfect. Let me have today and I will talk to you tomorrow."

He nodded. "Very well, as you wish." He kissed her hand as he gazed into her eyes, then rose from the bed and started for the door.

"Wait," she called.

He turned.

"Take the gown, Etienne, and the shoes. I could never explain them. You must find a way to keep them for me." She pointed to the floor where her lovely ball gown had landed last night.

He took the gown and shoes and returned them to their box. He gave her a final kiss and then hurried down the steps.

The vision became dim and then a new scene emerged.

She was in the sitting room of the house her father let her use. She looked slightly different, as though time had passed since that night with Etienne. Coldness filled her, and she sank into the memory.

A knock sounded on the door, and she jumped to her feet. Trepidation caused her hands to shake as she reached for the knob. Her mother stood on the stoop, her expression guarded. Gray tinged her straw colored hair, but her face remained unlined. She wore an expensive green velvet pelisse and matching hat with a feather in it.

"Mama, it is so good to see you again," Jeanne said. "Papa told me you had returned two days ago. So you got my message?"

"Yes, Julie," Elizabeth said, her eyes taking in every detail of Jeanne's appearance. "I understand you have been back in Paris a year now."

She showed her mother into the sitting room. Elizabeth looked about as if the room held clues. She didn't dare ask her mother not to use the name Julie. This was the first time she had seen her since the wedding in Russia five years ago. Her brusque manner indicated Elizabeth would not make a reunion easy. She had made no move to hug her daughter after their long separation, which boded ill for reconciliation. Elizabeth handed Jeanne her coat and removed her gloves, but kept them gripped in one hand.

"You look well, Mother," she commented as they sat in armchairs before the fireplace.

"Thank you. I am worked to death as usual, but my health is good," her mother replied. Her eyes continued to dart about the room.

"Your trip to England went well?"

"Yes, very. I prodigiously painted royals as well as members of the nobility. Lord Byron was one of my sitters."

"Lord Byron? How fascinating. Was he as interesting as the rumors say?" She hoped she could keep her mother discussing her art. That always pleased her.

"He assumes a brooding air, which he thinks makes him romantic, I believe," her mother replied. "But enough about me. Tell me what you have been doing in Paris since your return. Where is your husband?" Elizabeth asked, her voice cold and impersonal.

"Ah, well, Bernard is out of town on business. He is frequently away. I am trying to keep busy. I am painting some in my spare time," she said, a nervous flitter invading her stomach. This meeting was not going as well as she'd hoped.

"Yes, I have heard that your husband is not much about. Some say he is not happy in France." Her mother's eyes held a disturbed, feverish light.

So, that was it. Her mother had heard rumors and, suspecting her marriage was in trouble, came to dig for details. Given her previous displeasure at the wedding, it surprised her this would upset her mother.

"Well, you may want to ask Bernard that question. He has not mentioned any unhappiness to me. We have only been here a year," she replied, not willing to confirm any rumors, no matter how true. Why did they have to talk about her marriage? Her mother seemed intent on rehashing the past.

"Hmm, well, we shall see. I never thought it was a good match in the first place, as you well know, so if the union falls apart I would not be surprised in the least."

"Mama, would you like some tea?" Jeanne asked

Elizabeth ignored her offer of refreshment. She nervously

fidgeted with the gloves in her hands, and her eyes constantly shifted about. "There is another rumor that has reached my ears, Julie. I must say, it is most disturbing."

"What can possibly be more disturbing than the projected demise of my marriage?"

Elizabeth eyed her with speculation. "That you are spending a great deal of time with Etienne," her mother stated flatly, eyes sharp and accusatory.

It seemed the blood suddenly drained from her body and a haze covered her eyes causing her to sway. She had never expected this.

"More time than is considered proper for a niece and uncle," Elizabeth added, glaring at her.

"Wh-what are you suggesting, Mama? Etienne encourages me in my painting, that is all," she stammered. "He's been very kind to me."

Her mother stood, fury in her eyes. "I need no words from you. The truth is written in your guilty face. Have you lost all reason? It must stop. Have you not hurt me enough with your foolish behavior? I tried to forget what you did to me in Russia, but it is evident you are still bent on my downfall. What a hateful child you turned out to be."

"Mama, please," she pleaded.

"No, that is the end between us. I can never forgive you. Stop seeing Etienne or I will go to your husband and father. I will not have such scandal, do you understand? Although you deserve to be ruined, I will not have my brother and his family involved in such sordidness." Her mother turned, grabbed her coat and stormed out without waiting for a word from her.

Painful sobs made her clutch her chest. It was as though her life ended. Hope for the future gone.

She ran to the window. Horror filled her as Etienne pulled up in his coach and descended to the sidewalk. His happy expression crashed into a frown as Elizabeth grabbed his arm and shouted at him. She pushed him into the coach and followed him inside. The driver whipped at the horses, and Jeanne stayed at the window until the carriage vanished down the road.

In despair, she wheeled around, staggering. Tears streamed down her face and sobs uncontrollably shook her. After several minutes, she managed to crawl upstairs to her bedroom and throw herself on top of the covers. She cried herself to sleep and mercifully did not awaken until the following morning.

She waited three days for Etienne to come to her. She could not go to him. Finally, on the evening of the third day, a post arrived. She cried out when she recognized his handwriting on the letter. She tore it open with shaking fingers and read:

My dearest and only love,
By now you know that your mother has, by some means, learned of our affair. She has threatened me in every possible way so that I dare not come to you. I fear she has even paid my servants to report my whereabouts to her. I can only hope her vigilance will tire in time, and the heart which has hardened against you will soon yearn for her daughter's love. For now, she is quite mad with this idea of a scandal, and she is daily at my door with further threats.
Stay strong, my dear one. When possible, I will be back at your side.
Always yours,
Etienne

She fought a new onslaught of tears. How could her mother be so unforgiving? Had she truly gone mad as Etienne had hinted in his letter? This was not the woman who had doted on her and petted her as a child. Yet, as she reflected on those early years, her mother's love had a feverish, clinging quality, which was one of the reasons Jeanne had made a stand on getting married in Russia. Her mother had become so fanatically controlling that she had been eager to escape into marriage when a likely man presented her the opportunity.

After that unfortunate episode with her mother, the lonely time in Paris passed with unbearable slowness. She sank deeper and deeper into a listless depression. Bernard returned to Russia a few years later, unable to assimilate into the more liberal society of France and frustrated by her gloom. She waited, but Etienne didn't come. He had her paintings stored somewhere, but she had lost interest in painting amidst the haze of despair in which she dwelled.

***

Jeanne opened her eyes to the dim lighting of the empty café. What terrible sadness had prevailed at the end of her life. The entry she had read on Gaston's computer said that she had died at age thirty-nine, many years before her mother's death. She assumed her mother had never forgiven her and had never come to see her again. Etienne had never returned either. Her memory could not tell her why. So many bits and pieces still floated around unconnected.

One clue to his care at the end had not escaped her. The dress she wore now was the one she had worn to Versailles that fateful night when their passion had been realized. Etienne had taken it with him to keep for her, and obviously she'd been buried in it. Although an inappropriate dress for a dead woman's final attire, Etienne must have insisted. She thanked him for that final act. Perhaps it was he who'd saved her paintings. No one else cared so much for her or her work.

After the dramatic memories she'd experienced today, she needed to confer with Francois and George. She headed for the Richelieu Wing, the burden of her past weighing on her soul. The two men lounged in the Napoleon Salon in deep discussion as usual.

They stood, smiling when she arrived.

George's grin faded as she came closer. "Jeanne, what has happened? You look sad again."

She relayed her activities over the past two days and the memories she had recovered. Sorrow filled George's eyes as she recounted the final memory. Francois lowered his head, and covered his eyes with one hand.

"I do not understand why this has happened, my meeting Etienne and everything else. I do not think my helping him is the only mission for me." She glanced at the older soul. "What do you think, Francois?"

He did not speak for several minutes. His head remained bowed and his forehead wrinkled. Finally, he raised his head and gazed into her eyes, grief radiating from his expression. "My poor Jeanne. It seems your past is as tragic as mine. I wish I knew the answer to your questions, but I do not. I can only suggest that you continue the path you have begun and all will be revealed in time." He covered her hand with his.

"What if there is more pain involved? I thought this process might bring relief and resolution, but so far it has raised only turmoil," she said. "I almost wish I did not know of my sad past."

"But you have been happy helping Etienne. Do not forget that. Then there was the rediscovery of your paintings, which gave you pleasure. So there has been some good," George, the eternal optimist, pointed out.

Yes, meeting Etienne and helping him had added so much happiness to her existence. When she was with that group, discussing the show and sharing ideas, she was carefree and content. How did that figure into the grand purpose?

"That is true, George. Thank you for reminding me. I also met Vivienne, who Gaston has made his girlfriend. She is living and cannot see me, but we have talked and I like her very much."

"How did you become acquainted if she could not see you?" George asked, excited.

She explained the fiasco of Gaston blurting out her presence and how she had passed through the other woman to convince her.

"That is incredible," George commented.

"You must be careful with passing through the living, Jeanne," Francois cautioned.

"Why? Is there a danger?" Concern filled her that she had put Vivienne at risk.

"If you pass into them and do not depart within a certain small amount of time, you can become locked in the body of the living," Francois said. "I have seen it happen."

George leaned forward in his chair. "That is something I have never heard. Why are the souls not warned about this?"

"I was told to avoid walking through them, but I thought it was because the chill might raise questions," Jeanne added.

"Most souls do not know about the possibility. Since passing through the living is generally avoided, it rarely happens." Francois shrugged.

"What happens if a spirit gets stuck in a living person? Do they know? Do you take over the body?"

"Yes, is that possession?" George questioned.

"I am afraid I cannot answer that." Francois laughed. "To know, one would have to be stuck, and to be stuck means one cannot return to report."

George grinned. She smiled as well, but she continued to return to her past.

"Have you heard that souls can influence decisions of the living?" George asked. "I have heard that rumor, but how can it be? Would that be related to being stuck?"

"No, it is not the same. Influencing the living is something a soul should not take lightly. Changing the course of history or causing harm to the living can have dire consequences," Francois warned. "You once asked me about souls who crossed boundaries and the possibility of evil consequences. This is one such example."

A chill of fear enveloped her at his words, but George appeared thrilled at this new discovery.

"You mean a soul with evil intent could have a living person do something wicked?" George asked. "The souls I know of are so focused on fading, it would never occur to them to cause mischief."

Francois nodded. "But we are speaking of aberrations, not what is normal."

"I do not understand." George's brow crinkled.

"Influencing is done merely by speaking in the ear of the living in the way that souls speak to each other. It is not usually audible to the living and is taken as a thought that has simply occurred. So, consider a soul who whispers in the ear of a loved one that they are fine and shares thoughts of love. That soul is doing nothing wrong. His intent is to comfort. But an evil soul who plants a thought to have someone killed, that is an aberration."

"Really?" George grinned at Jeanne. "How interesting. You know, Francois, souls should receive a handbook when they die so they know all this. Would that not be a great idea?"

She couldn't agree. Better the souls didn't know such wickedness could exist among them. It was a disturbing thought.

"George, you are incorrigible." Francois shook his head. "I wish I had known you when we were alive, my friend."

Amusement bubbled in her breast at their banter, a relief

after the tragic memory with her mother. But other thoughts intruded. She still needed more information, and she needed to discuss this with someone other than Etienne who lived. She suspected he would be hurt by her pain, and she wanted to spare him that. She had to work this destiny out by herself. Vivienne! She could talk to Vivienne. Another woman would understand as a man could not, and give her advice. Tomorrow, when Etienne came to pick her up, she would have to find a way to be alone with Vivienne and share her secrets.

Chapter 17

When Etienne picked her up the next day, she was determined he should not notice any change in her mood. They rode in the taxi not speaking. She focused on the passing sights to help compose her thoughts.

When they reached Gaston's building she followed him from the car and floated to the door. She smiled at him. "What if Gaston and Vivienne are making love? We should not interrupt."

He let out a bark of laughter. "Why would you think that?"

"It's obvious they care about each other. I'm sure they are lovers."

"Really?" He motioned her inside when he opened the door. "I don't know how I miss this stuff."

"You're a man." She grinned. "How did the morning go?"

"I spent the most of it working on fitting the new garments to Claudette's perfect model body. I'm nearly deaf from all the gum popping. There are still many days of fittings ahead, but we're on schedule."

"That's good news. I'm so excited to see the finished pieces."

"I hope Gaston has completed his final touches to your portraits. I've asked Claudette to model the clothes for a photo shoot as soon as the garments are done. I explained we would only be using her body, not her head, but she was so excited to finally be in a photo shoot she gladly signed the contract," Etienne said, climbing the stairs to Gaston's studio. "She thinks it will be a great joke on the fashion world. Of course the contract swears her to silence on what we're doing."

"That is fabulous," she replied. "How much longer until the clothes will be ready?"

"Probably a week. In the meantime, I can take the portraits, make digital photos, and begin the process of preparing them to merge with Claudette's body."

She shook her head and laughed. "That makes no sense to

me, of course."

"You're right. I forget you come from another era. You're so smart and savvy when it comes to marketing ideas." He stopped on the stairs beside her and spoke in a low, husky voice. "Some nights when I lie in bed unable to sleep, I envision you as living. Can you imagine? We would be the hottest team in fashion design. Then I think about holding you and conjure up what it would be like to make love with you. But that dream ends painfully and frustrating."

She wished she could put her arms around him and comfort him—tell him she had experienced making love to one who looked like him and how wonderful it had been. She couldn't share that with him now. "I know, Etienne. I feel the same way. I feel guilty I cannot give you what you want and need."

He put up a hand. "No, don't say that. I didn't mean to make you feel bad. I just wanted you to know how much I care for you, how much I appreciate you."

"I understand," she said. "Thank you, from the bottom of my heart. You have given me so much happiness, something I never had in my living life."

"I wish I could give you more."

"When your show is a success, I will feel complete."

They continued up the steps and entered the studio to find Vivienne supervising Gaston who made final touches to the portraits he'd painted yesterday. They were amazingly lifelike. Etienne slapped him on the back and promised delivery of his wine that afternoon. The big man gave the redhead a high-five then crushed her in one of his near fatal bear hugs.

Jeanne shot Etienne a meaningful glance at this interaction.

"So what are the plans for today?" Vivienne inquired after escaping. Her cheeks flushed and she fanned herself.

"I have to go back for more fittings," Etienne replied. "Jeanne has agreed to pose for Gaston's personal portrait, so I'll return this evening for her."

"The food, wine and servers are all arranged, so that gives me a day off," she said.

"Why don't you stay and watch Gaston paint?" Jeanne asked. She hoped to get her alone later. "I'd like your company."

Vivienne turned to her voice and smiled. "That's not a bad

idea. I'd love to see the big genius at work."

Gaston blushed and shuffled his feet in pleased embarrassment.

"Good. Then I'll see you all back here tonight." Etienne waved as he headed out the door.

Jeanne gazed wistfully after him. She missed every second not being with him, but she knew it was important to help Gaston, and she looked forward to talking with Vivienne later.

"How do you want me to pose, Gaston?" She might as well have fun, so she struck an exaggerated stance and giggled.

The painter raised one eyebrow at her antics and waved a hand." Behave, ghost! Now try standing, three-quarter profile with your gaze over to that corner, expression of your choice." He gestured to the corner over his right shoulder. "I'll make up the background."

She moved to the position he had directed. "What shall I do with my hands?"

"Hmm, let's see." He studied her, his gaze going from her head to her toes, and then said, "Hold your hands in front of you as if you are holding flowers gathered from a garden. Yes, that's it. I'll paint in the flowers, or something, later." He began squeezing tubes of paint enthusiastically onto a palate. Soon his brush swooshed over the canvas in rapid strokes.

Vivienne watched, expression rapt. "You know, you are such a goof sometimes, but there's no denying you have talent. I hope this renewed inspiration lasts so you can realize your full potential instead of painting those damned copies."

"Humph." He glanced over his shoulder, gave her a wink, and then returned focus to his canvas.

Silence reigned in the garret as he painted intensely. After a couple hours, Vivienne departed to prepare lunch. He was so absorbed he never acknowledged she'd left. When she returned and touched his arm, he jumped.

"I've brought lunch, Gaston. You have to eat, you know," she said. "Jeanne, come and look."

She went to the canvas. Vivienne stared at the painting, her lips slightly parted.

"Hey, it's not finished yet." Gaston waved a paint brush at them.

She studied the progress he'd made. He'd started on her face. She imagined he probably could paint that in his sleep by now. He'd also begun on her gown, which was only partially blocked in. She could tell he drove his passion into this work. "It doesn't matter, Gaston. I can tell it will be great."

He gave her a pleased smile then took one of the sandwiches from Vivienne and bit off a hunk.

"Jeanne, how are you doing?" Vivienne asked. "Do you need a break?"

"I'm fine. How do you like the painting?"

"Brilliant," she replied. "Truly brilliant."

"Are you going to take a break, Gaston?" Jeanne asked.

"I have to eat these sandwiches or Vivienne's feelings will be hurt," he replied.

"Good, then she and I will go to her apartment. There is something I want to discuss with her."

He stopped chewing, eyes narrowed. "Women talking together usually means trouble for me." But he nodded in between bites and waved them away.

As they went down the steps, the redhead said, "I've wanted to talk to you as well, but I wasn't sure you'd welcome the news. I've been researching your mother. I found something disturbing."

Jeanne explained about her recent memories. "So, I really will not be too surprised at anything you have to tell me. Please go ahead."

The other woman nodded. "After our first meeting, I became interested in your past and spent time digging deeper into your family story. There is more information on your mother than anyone else since she was so famous. You already know your return to Paris for reconciliation was not successful. It seems your mother never helped you in any way after that. What I read said that you became destitute, reduced to selling your sheets and petticoats to survive. On your deathbed, your mother came to you, but too late. You died the next day. Even more interesting, Etienne died a year later."

What a tragic ending. Her mother had never forgiven her and had left her to die a pauper. No wonder she'd been so sad. Etienne died so soon after her. Perhaps he had been ill and that was the reason he never came for her. She could not remember.

"How did I die?"

"From all accounts, it was pneumonia. There are indications you'd sunk into a major depression and could not take care of yourself. Back then, with no money for medical care and no support from your mother, an illness like pneumonia could be fatal."

"And my father?"

"He died years before, leaving you his house and his debts."

The weight of that miserable, final existence bore down on her. What a shame.

"I'm sorry, Jeanne, so sorry," Vivienne said quietly. "You know there was some speculation about your mother's mental health in her later years. Maybe that accounts for her treatment of you," the redhead added hopefully. "Surely no one sane could be that nasty to her own child."

"It is possible, I suppose," she replied. "I never thought she was the same after we went to Russia. She had a paranoid delusion about a plot to discredit her. I just do not know."

"Are you going to tell Etienne about this?" Vivienne pushed the laptop back.

"I need to understand why this is happening. Originally I thought this encounter would lead to a resolution that would allow me to fade and find rest. If fading is supposed to bring peace, I do not see how that works for me. I do not want to fade and be with those people who made me unhappy. I want to stay here with this Etienne. The old Etienne disappointed me even though I loved him so much. I no longer want to go to Everlasting."

Vivienne nodded in understanding. "I see what you mean. I want you to stay, too. We've become friends."

"Do you think if my mother forgave me, this would turn out right?" she asked.

Her friend shook her head. "I can't say, Jeanne. Anyway, how is that possible? How could you reach her? And if you did, what could change her mind?"

"I am not sure. I am trying to make sense of this situation and what it is I am supposed to do," she said. "But you are right. There is no way to reach her, so it is pointless."

"Unless..." Vivienne said with a thoughtful expression.

"Unless what?"

"There are people who believe they can contact the dead. They have séances and that sort of ceremony. I never thought they were real, but what if they are?"

"Hmm, there used to be gypsies in Paris who claimed such things and that they could read the future. I wonder," she mused. "You know, the other thing I want to find out is what happened to my daughter. She grew up in Russia. I wonder where she ended up. I hope she had a better life than I."

"I can try and do some research on that if you like," Vivienne offered.

"Oh, that would be lovely. I do not have the ability to accomplish much in my present form."

"In any event, I think you should tell Etienne about this." Her friend shifted in her chair. "What if his soul is some continuation of the old Etienne? That would mean he's part of your past and now he's in love with you again. This could be his chance to correct his actions when you were alive."

"Really? You think Etienne is in love with me?" Jeanne asked, a flush of pleasure warming her. He said he did, but it was nice hearing an outside observer comment on it.

"You don't know? Of course he is. Totally besotted. It's obvious."

She placed a hand over her mouth. "But Vivienne, you are suggesting Etienne is the same person as back then? Do you believe that is possible?"

Her friend ran a hand through her spiked red hair. "I didn't believe in ghosts, but here you are, so I guess anything is possible. Is Etienne the same person? Well, he certainly has no memories of a previous life, although you can't deny the resemblance. Regardless, he does love you."

"Are you two coming?" Gaston stood in the doorway, still munching on his lunch.

"Yes, we're on our way." Vivienne shooed him. "So, you'll tell Etienne?"

"Yes, I will tell him. You are right. He should know," she relented. "Now, let us return to the studio before Gaston has a fit."

Vivienne left to run errands while Gaston continued work

on his portrait. By the time her friend returned, Etienne had arrived. He pulled up a chair and relayed tales of his successful day of fittings to Jeanne and his buddy.

"Gaston, I need help making dinner." Vivienne motioned to the big man. "Come downstairs."

Jeanne picked up on Vivienne's ploy to leave her alone with Etienne. She glanced at him from under her lashes, suddenly shy. What if he took this news badly? When their friends had gone, she said, "Etienne, I have had some memories I want to share with you."

"Something's been bothering you, hasn't it?" He studied her. "You haven't acted like yourself since yesterday."

"Yes, I have learned a great deal. Most of it is disturbing." She proceeded to repeat the content of her remembrances about her return to Paris, her unhappy marriage and finally the revelation of the forbidden love between herself and her uncle. She was able to tie-in Vivienne's discoveries about her mother with her own experiences and the sad conclusion of her life.

He kept his head down, staring at the floor until the end of her tale. He did not speak for many minutes after she finished.

"How could he?" he finally muttered.

"What do you mean?"

"How could that Etienne not go to you? I would have. If he loved you the way I do, he wouldn't have let anything stop him." His voice shook.

"I do not understand it either. Things were different back then. That Etienne could have lost everything if my mother had brought the affair into the open. He married into a wealthy family and would have lost their support. If society turned against him, his life as a poet and playwright would have been jeopardized. In part, I believe he was protecting me and my reputation. I think he hoped Mother would lose interest after a time, and he kept waiting for that day. Then it was too late and I died."

He ran his hands through his hair. "It's so frustrating, this ugly view of the past. I can't stand the thought of you dying like that, penniless, depressed and alone. What a tragedy." He shifted in his seat. "I wish you could stay with me forever, Jeanne. I would take care of you." He looked deep into her eyes. "I love you."

A soaring thrill of happiness enveloped her. Yes, he loved

her. "I love you, too, Etienne. I know that now," she replied, looking down. "I would like to stay with you more than anything. I have no reason to fade. My past has shown me the only person who cared about me was Etienne. But that man was a tragedy. You are not."

"Is fading inevitable?"

"Usually," she admitted. Only Francois seemed to be lingering past his time. "But you cannot live your life in love with a ghost, anyway. That would never work."

"I can't bear the thought of losing you," he said. "You're part of my life."

"If it is any comfort, I do not seem to be anywhere near fading. I guess we may continue as we are. Hopefully, I can find more information that will help me decipher the meaning of all this."

She mentioned her idea of trying to seek absolution with her mother as a path to resolution. "But there are so many problems inherent in that endeavor. Vivienne says there are people who believe they can talk to the dead. Do you think that is true?"

"I always thought it was a big joke, but then I thought the same about the existence of ghosts." He shrugged. "Besides, what makes you think she would forgive you now when she didn't back then?"

"Vivienne found an account which said my mother finally visited me the day before I died. Maybe she came to feel remorse for her actions, or shame that she did not try to help me."

"Maybe, but if she was really crazy she may not have been capable of remorse. Wouldn't another rejection upset you more?" His brow wrinkled in concern.

"Not now. Not after all this time and what I have learned. I would take that opportunity to tell her how her own actions led to my demise before my time. It would be a relief to hold her accountable."

"Stay with us, Jeanne. Gaston, Vivienne and I, we love you. Please don't fade."

"I know, Etienne. I know," she said, sadness dimming her voice. "But the choice is not mine."

Chapter 18

That night, Etienne brought Jeanne to his apartment. She'd told him she wanted to accompany him the next day and see the clothes, so he asked her to come home with him. This served him in two ways: first, it would save him a trip to the Louvre, and second, he was suddenly reluctant to be away from her for fear she would fade and he would never see her again. The story she'd relayed this afternoon deeply disturbed him. He didn't want her connecting him to the old Etienne who'd failed her, and yet the suggestion nagged at him.

They entered his place, and Jeanne studied his things. When she lingered over photographs on his mantle of himself, family and friends, he left her to her inspection and went to the kitchen. After grabbing a glass and a bottle of red wine, he returned to the living room and motioned for her to follow him.

"I want to show you something special." He opened a window and climbed the fire escape.

She followed him up, eyes shining in excitement. At the top of the stairs, a half-wall ran around the edges of the roof. He climbed over and waited for her to join him.

Green Astroturf covered most of the roof area, and several chaise lounges and plastic chairs provided seating. Potted plastic palm trees decorated the exterior of the seating area. He flipped a switch on the wall of a utility building, and strings of white lights twinkled. It offered a whimsical, minimalist get-away for the residents of the small apartment building. He loved to come here at night after the hectic environment of the atelier. He could sip wine, look at the stars, and dream. Jeanne was the first woman he'd brought to this special place.

He led her to a chaise and sat in one next to it. He poured a glass of the wine and took a long drink as he gazed at the night sky. "Look at those stars."

She lay back and turned her gaze to the numerous twinkling spots of light. It amazed him that he could see this many stars despite the illumination from the city.

"It is beautiful," she said.

He gazed at her. Her eyes shone like the stars, and she seemed content. He wished he'd lived when she had so he could've taken care of her and made her happy. He would never have left her alone to die in poverty. He would have fought her mother and anyone else.

"The stars last forever, do they not?" Her gaze remained on the sky.

"They last a very long time, but sometimes they age and explode. Why do you ask?"

"I was thinking I may have seen these same stars when I was alive."

"Very likely," he said. "Did you enjoy the stars back then?"

"Oh, yes. I loved to sit in the garden and look at the sky. I kept hoping for a shooting star so I could make a wish."

"What did you wish for?"

"For Etienne to defy my mother and return so he could take me away from my sadness," she whispered.

A lump in his throat choked any words. A hard knot formed in his stomach and he clenched his free hand. How would this end? More tragedy for Jeanne? He hoped not. He silently vowed to do everything he could to ensure her happiness.

They enjoyed the twinkling panorama, and he steadily drank wine until he emptied the bottle and his anger dissipated. He sat on the side of the chaise and yawned, then smiled at Jeanne.

"Well, some of us have to get some sleep," he said. "Come on down. Please lie in the bed beside me so your face is the last thing I see before I go to sleep."

She returned his smile and followed him to his bedroom. She reclined on one side of the bed as he removed his clothes and donned pajamas. He joined her and lay on his side, facing her. With one finger, he traced the outline of where her face appeared. Then he pressed that finger to his lips. His body ached with a need to hold her.

"Good night, dear Etienne," she said softly.

"Good night, Jeanne, my love," he replied and let out a harsh breath. "Don't go anywhere while I sleep," he said and closed his eyes.

The next day, she accompanied him to his atelier. Jeanne stared in amazement at the hustle and bustle inside the fashion house. Etienne's employees worked furiously to pull this collection together in time. He swelled with pride at the way his people had put their hearts into making these new garments. Their hopes rode with his.

He climbed the spiral stairs, and Chloe soon followed. He had explained who the main players were at his business, so Jeanne recognized his hard-working assistant.

"Claudette will be here shortly. I've narrowed the list of celebrities down to four, whose measurements we can definitely obtain," she reported. "I have friends at houses who've made clothes for them recently."

"Okay, who are they?"

"Penelope, Sara, Miranda and Evelyn."

"I was hoping for Princess Giada, given the whole theme of the event," he said and laughed.

"Sorry, no princess," Chloe said.

"I'll start designs for them tonight. I already have preliminary sketches." He flipped through messages on his desk. Chloe saluted and made her way downstairs.

As soon as she departed, he motioned to Jeanne with a grin. He opened the doors of a wardrobe beside his desk and pulled out clothes he'd worked on during the past two days.

Her eyes grew wide as he held up one outfit after another, and ran his hand lovingly over the fabrics. "I know you don't know about history past your own, but these designs are a blend of past and present. For instance, this gown is a blend of what's called art deco and with a touch of flapper influence."

He motioned to the sleek black satin sheath that had inserted panels of a checkered pattern along the lower half of the skirt that only showed when the person walked. The neckline made a V in front and an even deeper V in the back.

"The model will wear a long string of pearls that will hang in the rear to bring attention to the curve of a woman's back."

"It's beautiful," she whispered.

"This coat is similar to the old opera coats of the past." He held up a voluminous black velvet garment with a ruffle around the neck that grew tall in the back to frame the face, and billowing sleeves that gathered at the wrists. Jeweled buttons ran down the front, glittering."

"I'd love to wear something like that." She grinned.

Next, was an empire-waist gown of gold silk with tiny puff sleeves and a deep round neckline.

"I visited the Regency Period of England for this look." He pointed to tiny sparkles on the skirt. "These are hand-sewn crystals in a rainbow of colors that looks fantastic when the skirt moves. It will be worn with elbow length gloves in a darker gold and jeweled bangles.

It continued. Piece after piece, a gorgeous spectacle.

"They are astonishing, really," she said when he held up the last finished piece. "Your show will be a success, never doubt that."

"Thanks. It's because of you, you know. I'm positive. It will come off okay, especially if we can attract the right celebrities."

"I think I can take care of that for you," she said with confidence.

"What do you have in mind, my darling ghost?"

"It is best if you do not know, Etienne, trust me," she replied with a wink.

He laughed. "Okay, but don't expect me to come bail you out of jail."

"Are you talking to someone?" Chloe asked. She suspiciously glanced around.

"No, uh, I'm just talking to myself," he said. He had to be careful. The last thing he needed was having to bring another person into this ghostly secret.

"You worry me. Especially after you asked me if I believe in ghosts. I mean I know you're overworked and stressed out, but..."

"Wait a minute," he said, holding out a hand in a stop gesture.

"What?" Chloe crossed her arms over her chest.

"When we were talking about ghosts a couple weeks ago, you told me you had a friend whose aunt was a medium or something, didn't you?" He stole a quick glance at Jeanne.

"Um, yes, yes, I did. Etienne, you're totally creeping me out," Chloe said, taking a step back.

"Look, I just need you to get me an appointment with her, okay?"

"The aunt?"

"Yes, the aunt. Why would I want to meet with your friend?"

"I wonder why you would want to meet with the aunt, actually."

"Don't worry about it. I just, uh, I want to see if she can predict the success of my show," Etienne improvised.

"Ohhhhh-kaaay," Chloe responded, shooting him a suspicious glance. "And when do you want this appointment?"

"As soon as possible. Hey, Claudette." Etienne welcomed as the tall woman appeared from the stairs.

"Ready for me?" She threw her jacket across the back of a chair, tossed a new piece of bubblegum in her mouth and walked toward him, swinging her hips.

"Yes, Chloe was just going to bring me the clothes we'll be working on today, right Chloe?" He gave her a meaningful stare.

"Right." His assistant shook her head and headed for the stairs.

***

Jeanne spent an enjoyable day. Etienne thrived in his element. The process of creating beautiful garments fascinated her, and Claudette's vigorous gum popping became so humorous she constantly had to stifle giggles. Claudette made obvious ploys to attract him, but he seemed oblivious, totally focused on work.

Today she wore the coup-d-gras of the collection, a wedding gown. It was a fairytale creation with a full skirt of netting and silk gathers spotted with satin rosettes. The bodice was a diamond studded bustier half leather and lace. A twenty foot train of layered tulle swept behind it. Jeanne nearly cried at the majestic beauty. It was a dream dress.

Chloe had an amazing ability to juggle cell phone, pins, and take notes, while drinking cup after cup of black coffee. She almost ran through Jeanne several times as she scurried about.

"That's it for now," Etienne announced at three o'clock. He helped Claudette from the pedestal, and Chloe carefully placed the wonderful gown on a hanger.

"Same time tomorrow?" The model raised an eyebrow, still popping gum.

"Yes, thanks," he answered. He missed her lingering look as she left the loft.

Chloe's phone rang, and she kept glancing at Etienne as she talked in a low voice. When she ended the call, she said, "Okay, you have an appointment at four with, ahem, Madam Renee."

"Madam Renee." He cocked his head to one side.

"Yes, the *medium*. She has an opening at four." His assistant stood with a hand on one hip and staring at him like he'd lost his mind.

"Madam Renee, is it? Then I'd better head over. Do you have the address?" He glanced at her. "I'm surprised we, uh, I could get an appointment so soon. That's great."

Chloe wrote the address on a notepaper and handed it to him. She stared at him as if expecting an explanation.

"So, I'll see you tomorrow, then?" He put the notepaper in his pocket and headed for the stairs.

Out on the sidewalk, Jeanne questioned Etienne. "Why do you want to see this Madam Renee?"

"I thought it would be obvious. We'll see if we can call up your mother and convince her to forgive you. Isn't that what you want?" He raised his arm to flag a taxi.

"Oh." She fell silent. It was exactly what she had thought might be a solution to her problems.

"Well?" He glanced at her as a taxi pulled up beside them.

"Yes, how clever you are." She eagerly followed him into the vehicle.

Madam Renee lived in a townhouse in an area not quite respectable and not quite ghetto. Curtains covered windows facing the street, making it impossible to catch a glimpse of the interior. They climbed stone steps, and Etienne rang a bell beside a large wooden door. The porch had several potted plants, brown from lack of care. An old wooden rocker moved slightly in the breeze, making an eerie squeaking noise.

The door opened to reveal a middle-aged woman with frizzy blonde hair, which hung to her waist. She wore a headband of green velvet with a single onyx stone in the shape of a teardrop hanging on her forehead. Her caftan of muted greens and blues flowed about her like waves as she moved. Her piercing grey eyes raked Etienne up and down. "You're Etienne Armand?"

"Yes. Thank you for seeing me so soon," he replied.

"Well, for a friend of a friend," she said. Finally she motioned. "Come on in then."

She led the way through a living room furnished in faded Queen Anne reproductions, and into a small room whose walls were covered with burgundy velvet curtains. In the center of the room sat a round table with a crystal ball perched in the middle. A gold lamé tablecloth covered the table to the floor. Several chairs sat around the table, and she motioned in their direction.

After they had entered and taken seats, she loosed a tie of the curtain that covered the door so they were surrounded in the heavy velvet fabric.

"So, how may I be of service?" She settled in a chair opposite them. She placed her arms on the table, lacing her fingers together.

"I have a friend who had a disagreement with her mother. The mother is dead. She wants to contact her and see if she can make peace."

"Would that be this lady's mother?" She gestured to Jeanne with one hand.

His jaw dropped. He glanced at her then back to Madam Renee. "You, uh, you can see her?"

"Of course, my dear. I see spirits all the time. It's my job. Or did you think this was a big hoax?" She tilted her head expectantly to one side.

"No, no. I didn't think that. I'm simply surprised when anyone else can see her," he said.

"I'm Jeanne," she said to the medium.

"Very pleased to meet you. So, you want to make contact with your mother, dear?"

"Yes. She was angry with me and broke off contact until the day before I died. I want to try to convince her to forgive me," she answered. "Do you think we can contact her?"

"If she wants to be contacted, yes. Many souls do not wish to be bothered with returning to the living world, especially if they feel guilt. If her heart is pure, she will return and join in your wish for reconciliation," the woman said. She smiled kindly. "We can only try."

Jeanne glanced at Etienne then to Madam Renee and nodded.

The woman rose and lit candles on small tables around the perimeter then turned off the overhead light. She brought three candlesticks to the table and lit them as well.

"We bring candles, for the spirits still seek light and warmth," she said once they flamed. "Now, please place your hands on the table and focus on the crystal ball. Don't be alarmed at anything you see or sounds you hear." She waited until they positioned their hands then placed her own palms on the table and stared into the cloudy crystal ball.

"We come before the spirit world and ask for assistance. Beloved mother of Jeanne, we bring you gifts from life into death. Commune with us and move among us, for your daughter loves you and seeks your love." The older woman paused and stared intently at the ball. Its once cloudy interior swirled with many colors.

Madam Renee repeated her plea. The candles in the room flickered, and a cold breeze swirled gently about the room. The woman repeated the plea a third time, and a glow began to form within the crystal ball. The light shone golden with swirls of blue. After it ascended about three feet above the ball, it twisted like a tornado.

Etienne gasped, and Jeanne stared in amazement.

Madam Renee raised her hands and waved them before her. "Spirit, we beseech you to take shape and speak to us," she intoned.

Slowly the swirling pattern of gold and blue took the shape of a woman's torso. As the vision solidified, Jeanne recognized her face at once from the paintings done by Elizabeth. She swallowed and turned to Madam Renee. "That is not my mother."

"Yes, this is indeed your mother," Madam Renee replied serenely. "The spirits do not lie."

Jeanne gazed at the glowing face smiling at her with a loving, but surprised expression. It was not Elizabeth Vigee Le Brun. It was Gabrielle de Polignac.

Chapter 19

"M-M-Mother?" Jeanne questioned, staring at the apparition of Gabrielle de Polignac.

"My dearest Juliette," the figure said. "I cannot believe this. I never thought I would see you again. You grew to be so beautiful."

"You are truly my mother?" If a ghost could faint, she would surely do it now. What strange happening was this?

"Yes, my love. I hope you will forgive me for abandoning you. I dared not have your birth in France," Gabrielle said, her brow wrinkled and eyes darkened.

"But I thought Elizibeth Vigee Le Brun was my mother," she said. Elizabeth wasn't her mother? Somehow that relieved her.

"It is so complicated. Please believe I only wanted to protect you."

"Tell me what happened then. Tell me how you are my mother and what happened after my birth," she said.

"You were a love child, you see," Gabrielle said. "Your father was not my husband. I served Marie as her lady-in-waiting. When I discovered I was pregnant, I became desperate. First, I could not let it be known that I carried another man's child. And second, I lived in turbulent times. I was concerned about the riots and my safety, being of noble birth.

"The queen and I were so close, but she was also selfish. She would not allow me to leave her without good reason, so I allowed an argument to come between us. It was easy with court jealousies and threats of uprising. I went to England for a year and stayed with my dear friend, Georgiana, the Duchess of Devonshire. She agreed to keep you after the birth. Her husband could not forbid it since he had foisted his mistress's children on their household for years. She hid me in one their many summer homes in the country. I gave birth there and named you Juliette. Then I had to return to France to be with the queen."

"But I grew up with the Le Bruns," Jeanne said.

"Yes, I arranged it with Elizabeth before I left. I could never leave the queen during those troubling times, but I had to provide for your safety. Elizabeth was my best friend. She agreed to take you as her own daughter. She went to England to retrieve you not too long after I had returned to Paris. The revolution was about to sweep the nation, so she took you and fled to Italy. She kept you safe. My destiny lay along another path." She stared off, as if lost in a view of the past.

"Your lover, he was Francois." The realization occurred to her. A second cold wave of surprise flooded her.

"Yes. How do you know?"

"Francois is my father." She had to say it to fully believe it.

"Yes, he is your father," Gabrielle replied. "You seem to know him. How is that possible?"

"He is a soul who has not been able to fade to Everlasting. I met him. We have talked many times. He told us the details of how you died for Marie Antoinette and left him heartbroken."

"Ah, Francois. My beloved. Did he ever forgive me?" her mother asked, eyes pleading.

"For taking the place of the queen?"

"For leaving him. For choosing death."

"He understood your choice, if that is what you mean. He still loves you after all this time," she replied. "He wants to fade and be with you, but he has not been able to."

"Poor Francois. I dared not hope he could understand. It was the most difficult decision of my life. Perhaps he would be at peace if he knew about you, our daughter," Gabrielle suggested.

That could be part of this puzzle. Francois must be told that he had a daughter, and that she had survived. George always said their fates were intertwined. He would be delighted with this discovery.

"My darling, I am so happy to see you grew up so beautiful and happy. It gives my soul such peace to see you thus," Gabrielle smiled, love gleaming from her eyes.

"Yes, Mother, thank you. I am so glad to know the truth. I love you," she said, wishing she could have lived with this woman, and that Gabrielle had not committed to dying for Marie Antoinette. How different her life might have been.

"I love you too, my dear. Give Francois my love. I must go.

Souls cannot linger in the world of the living once they fade. Good-bye." The image of the lady swirled and dissipated.

"Thank you for gifting us with your presence, gentle spirit. Go in peace." Madam Renee waved her hands then lowered them to the table. She bowed her head and took a deep shuddering breath.

Etienne sat spellbound. The spirit of Gabrielle had not seemed to notice him. She had eyes only for Jeanne. "Well, I never would've thought it possible to recall spirits like that. Ghosts walk among the living. Spirits returned from the afterlife. What else is out there?"

"You'd be surprised," the medium murmured.

"Francois was right," Jeanne whispered, dazed. "Gabrielle went straight to Everlasting. She has no idea what happened to me in the end. I am glad she did not linger. It is fortunate she found peace so quickly after her tragic end."

Madam Renee raised her head, her face pale. The interaction had clearly drained her, but she smiled. "Are you satisfied, my dear?"

"Yes. Thank you so much for your help. This begins to make sense of my past. Oh, my," she exclaimed as memories took on new meaning.

"What," Etienne asked, concerned.

"This means Etienne was not my uncle. Elizabeth knew that all along. Her forbidding our affair was more horrific than I realized. I truly think she had gone mad."

Etienne nodded. "You must be right."

"I'm glad I was able to help you, dear," Madam Renee said, rising from her chair. "If you need further consultation with the spirit world, just let me know."

Etienne pulled out his wallet to pay her for the session.

The psychic waved him away. "I do not charge souls, only the living. This was for Jeanne."

She thanked her again, and the medium escorted them to the door and waved goodbye. "Take care, children," she said before closing the door.

"That was amazing," Etienne said, squinting in bright sunlight after the darkness of the séance room.

"Yes, amazing and revealing. I must return to the Louvre. I

have an obligation to tell Francois of this development," she replied.

He found them a taxi and, after dropping her at the Louvre, was pressed to return to his workshop to continue production of the unfinished collection pieces. "I'll come for you tomorrow so we can visit with Gaston and Vivienne, and update them on the show's progress. I'm sure Gaston will want to continue his personal portrait then."

She blew him a kiss. "Good-bye, my love."

She hurried along museum corridors in search of Francois. Instinctively, she headed for Sully and was rewarded to find her two friends talking in the Salle Grog-Carven.

"Francois," she called as she neared.

He glanced up, and his face brightened.

George smiled and waved a cheery hello. He motioned her forward. "What news, Jeanne?"

"You are never going to believe," she exclaimed. "I have the most exciting and interesting information to tell you."

"Come, my dear, and join us." Francois made an inviting gesture to the settee beside him. George sat in an armchair across from them.

First, she relayed what Vivienne had uncovered in her more detailed research of her adoptive-mother. Francois and George both shook their heads over her sad, destitute death. Then she recounted her day with Etienne, ending in the trip to Madam Renee's.

"Did your mother return from the dead to speak with you?" George stared at her eagerly, clearly fascinated.

"Yes, yes, Madam Renee called for my mother to return and her image appeared to us," she replied.

"Amazing," Francois murmured. "I cannot believe it."

"Francois, the most amazing part is that the person who appeared was not Elizabeth Vigee Le Brun. It was Gabrielle. Gabrielle de Polignac. *Your* Gabrielle," she exclaimed, pressing her hands to her cheeks. Her soul welled with emotion, knowing this great man was her real father and she could bring him this wonderful news.

He sat back. His blank expression slowly transitioned from joy to confusion. "There has to be some mistake, I would have known such a thing, surely. My Gabrielle? Pregnant? I don't understand. How can that be?" A flash of hurt shone in his eyes. "I was always with her. She could not have had a child without my knowledge."

"She went to England, remember? She had a disagreement with Marie and went to stay with the Duchess of Devonshire in England, just before the revolution broke out." She recounted Gabrielle's story of hiding the birth and the attempt to save her daughter from the clutches of the revolution by giving her to her best friend, Elizabeth.

Both George and Francois stared and did not speak for several minutes.

"The child was mine," Francois started, his eyes turning to her, shining with realization. "That means you ... you are ... you are my daughter," he exclaimed.

She nodded, smiling with joy, and then fell into his arms.

"My daughter. A child with my beloved Gabrielle. I cannot believe it!" He kissed the top of her head and hugged her tightly. "How happy this makes me. I thought from the beginning that you resembled her. I should have known it at once."

"May I call you Father now? It would make me so pleased."

"Of course, my darling. It will be music to my ears," Francois replied.

George beamed. "Wait. That also means Etienne was not your uncle."

"Yes, that is right," she said, emerging from Francois' embrace.

"And Elizabeth knew all along, yet she used the familial connection in her condemnation of you and would not come near you or help you in your darkest hours." Francois frowned. "Her reaction to the affair went beyond mere moral censure. Everyone in the nobility had affairs during that time, and she was not known for her pious nature."

She shrugged. "It is sad, but it happened. Perhaps it was never meant for me and that Etienne to be together given that he was married. I paid the price for my sin with a lifetime of sorrow. However, I am not going to dwell on tragedies that cannot be changed. I want to have the happiness now I never had in my living existence. I am going to take pleasure in being with you, my father, and continue to help Etienne with his show and enjoy watching his success."

George nodded. "It is obvious a great weight has been lifted from your soul." He stood and floated close to put a hand on her shoulder. "I have been thinking. Is it possible we could go to this ball he is having? That would be quite an experience."

"I do not see why not," she said. "In fact, I think it is a wonderful idea. I am going, and I would love to have both of you there with me."

George glanced at Francois. "I certainly want to go."

"Yes, I want to dance with my daughter at Versailles," Francois announced. "We never had the chance when we were alive."

"What fun." She clapped her hands in delight.

"I wish I could change my suit to something more formal," George said, staring despondently at his brown coat and trousers. "This one is clearly for day wear."

"My friend, it won't be necessary," Francois said.

"Why not?"

"Because no one can see you," her father replied. Then he and Jeanne broke into laughter, soon followed by George, who could never stay gloomy for very long.

She hugged them both. "My dears, three ghosts at a couture fashion show. That is going to be interesting."

Chapter 20

The week before the start of Fashion Week, Etienne and his House breathed a collective sigh of relief. They'd pulled off a major miracle in completing the collection within the last few days. He sank into his desk chair as Chloe carried away the last finished garment.

The frantic pace did not end there. He now had to enter into a flurry of publicity to assure the show was well attended. He flipped through his notes, making sure he hadn't forgotten any vital piece.

He couldn't help stopping to admire the digital melding of Jeanne's head and Claudette's body. The pictures were perfect. Teasing billboards and magazine ads had Paris humming with conjecture about the identity of the beautiful new figure in fashion.

He'd told his staff the woman's face was just a concept Gaston had made up and painted. Claudette had laughed so hard after reading one speculative article in the newspaper the gum had fallen right out of her mouth. Everyone tried to guess the identity of the mystery woman, and Claudette had the time of her life at the center of the conspiracy.

Gaston completed his full-length portrait of Jeanne on a nearly life-sized canvas. He would reveal it to the world, displayed on the red carpet at Versailles in place of the real Jeanne's attendance. Every time they visited him he made them sit before the huge picture and listen to his tale of finding his mojo again. His jolly mood even allowed Vivienne to convince him to attend in costume as Henry the Eighth.

Etienne sighed. His friends had been his salvation in this crisis. Vivienne had the arrangements completed for the ball. She was poised to present her culinary talent to the *haute monde*. He smiled at how inseparable she and Gaston had become. The redhead had surely tamed the big man. He mercilessly teased his friend, as only a best friend could.

In a few days, the fashion world would flock to Paris. A

twinge of uneasiness invaded his gut. It was make or break time. Either this collection propelled him to the pinnacle with the world's top designers, or he would likely never be heard from again.

***

On Monday, five days before the show, Jeanne sat in Etienne's office as he reviewed the list of invitations he had sent out. Occasionally he'd break off and run last minute ideas by her.

"Are you sure I made the right choices on the costumes for the celebrities?" he asked for the tenth time.

"Yes, Etienne. I am positive," she assured, also for the tenth time.

Penelope Von Klef, the famous British actress, stood to win an Oscar this year. She would make a glamorous Duchess of Devonshire. Sara Barker, the most fashion-conscious American actress, would be Queen Elizabeth due to her fiery red hair. The pop singer, Miranda, would attend as Empress Josephine. And the acknowledged queen of the fashion world, the heiress Evelyn Barrister, would be Marie-Antoinette.

Chloe had made certain the characters chosen would appeal to each woman individually based on their backgrounds and interests. Etienne had done a superb job of designing the costumes in a way that best suited the contemporary women who would wear them. He told Jeanne that all four had such intense interests in fashion they had arrived in Paris over the weekend to attend parties and publicity sessions with their favorite designers. They would receive their invitation and costumes, specially boxed, by personal courier today.

"Calm down. Everything is going to be fine," she assured him.

"I think I need to get out of here. Want to go to Gaston's? We can see how Vivienne's doing with her menu," he suggested.

"That is a good idea. You need to have a breath of fresh air. Chloe is busy preparing the packing for the clothes, and the models will not arrive until tomorrow."

"You're right. Let's go." He headed down the steps.

When they arrived, Vivienne had prepared samples of a

few of the items she'd serve at the ball. Pate foie gras en croute with roasted pistachios, and canapés of blue cheese and roasted walnuts with caramelized onions and tart apple relish all positioned on a tray sitting on the round table in Gaston's studio. She recited details of the ingredients as she worked, photographing from different angles.

"Okay, okay," she said, finally putting aside her camera and motioning Gaston to eat.

"Me too," Etienne said as he entered the room. He crossed to the table and groaned in culinary pleasure as he savored the tasty treats.

"Vivienne," Jeanne whispered in her ear. "Let us go to your apartment."

With a last look at the happy men and rapidly disappearing food, Vivienne slipped out of the room and down the stairs to her apartment.

"What's up?" She turned around.

"Over here, Vivienne," Jeanne said.

The other woman moved toward her voice. "Is something wrong?"

"No. Everything is fine. At least I want to make sure it is. I need your help," she said. "Can you help me make some late-night deliveries? I have to take the costumes to the celebrities and convince them to attend the show."

Vivienne shrugged. "Sure."

The food had disappeared when they returned to the garret.

Gaston brought out the inevitable bottle of red wine. "Purely to help Etienne relax. Come have some. Er, or at least Vivienne. Sorry, Jeanne."

"Do not worry. I enjoy watching you drink more than I could ever enjoy drinking myself." She smiled and settled on the blue settee to observe her friends. Her heart soared with happiness.

Finally, Etienne yawned and stood to leave. "I have to be at the office early tomorrow, so I'd better head home for some sleep," he said. "Ready, Jeanne?"

"I thought I would stay with Vivienne tonight, if you do not mind," she said.

He paused then glanced at the redhead and back to Jeanne. "Okay. If that's what you want."

"You know, girl talk time." Vivienne smiled.

"I see." He studied Jeanne a second then shrugged. "I guess I'll see you tomorrow evening then. I have a full day at the office tomorrow."

"Good night, Etienne." She blew him a kiss.

He blew one back and left.

Once she made certain Etienne had gone, she said to her friend, "Chloe wrote where the celebrities are staying. I memorized the addresses. Let us go."

"Hey, what's going on here?" Gaston interrupted, his eyes narrowed.

"Don't worry, sweetheart." Vivienne kissed the top of his head. "We have some, um, shopping to do. Don't wait up." She waved as they headed out.

Vivienne whistled to a taxi and gave the address of the first hotel. Fortunately, three of the four celebrities were staying there.

They picked up four vases of roses along the way at an all-night florist. When they reached the hotel, Vivienne paid the driver to wait and left one of the vases on the back seat.

Inside the hotel, Jeanne approached the desk with Vivienne.

"I have deliveries here," she said. She gave the names of Penelope Von Klef, Sara Barker and Evelyn Barrister.

The agent at the desk looked up the rooms and wrote the numbers on tags for each vase. Jeanne moved beside him and read the room numbers for each of the famous women.

"We'll call the rooms and let them know," he said with a dismissive flick of his hand.

The redhead smiled and thanked him.

Jeanne went with her to the elevator and then to the door of the first room. "Are you sure you do not think this is evil?"

Vivienne emphatically shook her head. "No way. You're helping Etienne. There's nothing harmful in convincing these women they should go to his show. They get to wear a beautiful dress and have people make a big deal about them. How evil is that?"

"Okay. I just want to make sure. I would never want to do something that would cause someone harm." She nodded, relieved. She'd struggled with this idea but couldn't devise another plan to assure the fashion divas attended the show. She was determined to help Etienne. "Wish me luck," she said and vanished through the door.

Penelope Von Klef wore an elaborate dressing gown and talked on the phone. She strolled about the room as she chatted then stopped to stare out a window. The call ended, and Jeanne waited for her to approach a large golden box sitting on a table. The lid already sat askew, revealing the fabulous costume wrapped in silver tissue paper within. The famous woman hesitated then pulled the dress from the box and held it up by the shoulders as her gaze swept over it approvingly. Yet after a few seconds, she frowned, fingering the luscious fabric.

Jeanne moved to her side. She leaned close and whispered, "This dress will complement you beautifully, and the world will be at your feet."

Penelope smiled.

It was true. Everything about this design would complement her face and figure. Photographs of her wearing it would be fabulous.

"You will go to the show, and the ball will be so much fun," Jeanne whispered.

Penelope's eyes narrowed and she folded the dress carefully into the box. "For God's sake," she exclaimed. "I'm Penelope Von Klef. If I want to go to this second rate show for my own amusement, who would dare question me?" She tossed the invitation into the box as well. "To hell with what anyone says." She made a note on a hotel note pad by the phone. "Remember to accept invitation to House Etienne show" she wrote. Then, smiling in anticipation, she headed to bed.

Jeanne rushed to the hall. "It worked," she said in Vivienne's ear.

The other woman let out a soft squeal. "Don't do that. You scared me."

The other celebrities were as easy to entice with her whispers and Etienne's beautiful designs. Excitement bubbled like champagne inside her as she rode to Vivienne's apartment. She described each encounter, and the redhead chuckled, slapping her knee.

Vivienne grinned. "I must say, I'm extremely pleased with our interesting and exciting evening. I felt like some sort of spy on a secret mission. That was so much fun."

The taxi dropped them at the curb, and they climbed out, giggling.

"Thank you for your help, Vivienne. You were magnificent."

"Are you going to tell Etienne what we did?"

"No. I want him to think it was his dresses alone that made them decide. He needs the confidence. He is nervous about how much is riding on this show."

The redhead nodded.

"Jeanne. I have some more news for you," Vivienne said as they entered her apartment.

Upstairs, opera wafted from Gaston's studio. "What is it?"

"I found information about your daughter."

She'd almost forgotten about Vivienne's promise to research what had happened to her child in the flurry of activity involved in the show.

"What did you find?" Her interest piqued.

The redhead went to her desk and sat before the computer. She pulled papers from a folder and flipped through them then extracted one.

"Your daughter was named Catherine, after Catherine the Great it seems. She married a minor Russian noble and had three children: two daughters and a son. The son and one of the daughters stayed in Russia, but the other daughter came to France."

"Is there any trace of descendants alive today?" she asked, intrigued.

"Yes. I was so excited to be able to trace the line to a family here in Paris. Their name is Rousseau. The woman is the descendant, her name is Charlotte. She has a daughter named Margot, who is thirty-two years old. Margot is a photographer. She does freelance work for newspapers as well as private events such as weddings."

"That is very interesting," Jeanne said. "So, I have family still, right here in Paris. I would love to see this Charlotte and her daughter. I wonder what they look like."

"Wait until you see this," Vivienne said. She pulled the laptop closer, typed and then pointed to the screen. "This is Margot's web site for her photography company. That's a picture of her."

"*Mon dieu*," she exclaimed. She couldn't believe her eyes.

"Yes. There is a strong resemblance." Vivienne smiled. "I thought you would like that."

"No, you do not understand. It is not just the resemblance. I have seen her before. She was in the Louvre. Even more bizarre, Etienne saw her there, too. He saw her twice."

"You're kidding. What are the chances of something like that happening out of the blue?"

She leaned forward for a better look at the picture. "Yes, really, this is amazing. I mean, when you look closely there are certainly differences, but I do see the overall similarity." She tilted her head to one side. "She looks confident and happy, I must say. Well, I am very glad to know who she is now. That solves a big mystery, but it does not explain her appearing now when she never did before. I would really like to know more about her and see if I can ascertain what part she may play in our lives. Thank you for looking into this, Vivienne. You have given me a gift."

Vivienne turned pink. "I just wanted you to know something nice resulted from your life. I didn't know you'd already seen her. I also checked into something else that was very interesting," She picked up another folder and pulled out a few sheets of paper. "I'm intrigued by this meeting with Etienne. How you've connected, and why he looks like the Etienne of the past. I thought he must have been a distant ancestor or something."

"I am not sure," she said. Apprehension gripped her at mention of the question she least wanted to explore. She'd tried to keep the two men separate, and she wasn't ready to have them merge.

"You don't want to know?" Vivienne tilted her head.

"I have thought about it since we talked before, but I am not sure I want him be the same Etienne. I think it is better if he is a different Etienne. Then it is possible we can have a different destiny. A happy one. I cannot bear the thought of another tragedy," she replied. "Do you understand?"

"Yes, I do, but I think you will want to know this."

She paused, considering the possibilities. In truth, she didn't want to know. The old Etienne should remain buried with the past and her other hurtful memories. She'd learned so much from this encounter, and despite her death, she'd grown spiritually over the last few weeks. She knew what was important now. She would never give up hope of a happy life to redeem her previous one.

"Keep your paper. I appreciate your interest and I know you are trying to help, but I do not want to know. Not now. If I change my mind in the future, I will come and ask for that information."

"Okay, I understand. I'll keep this for you if you ever want it. I want you to be happy. That's the most important thing. That's what I want."

"Thank you, my dear friend. Thank you," she said.

Gaston opened the door to Vivienne's apartment and poked his head in. "Where the hell have you girls been? You know I don't like to drink by myself."

"I am sorry, my friend." she laughed. "I had to borrow Vivienne for a while."

"Poor baby," the redhead said. She went and put her arms around the big man. "My big teddy bear."

Gaston grinned, and hugged her back then planted a big kiss on her lips.

"That food was exceptional tonight, *cherie*," he said, looking into her upturned face. "You're going to be a huge success."

"I hope we all will be," Vivienne replied. "No more sadness or problems."

Chapter 21

The next day, Vivienne started making phone calls as soon as she woke. She smiled, satisfied, as she ended the last call. She made a few notes and then climbed the stairs to see Gaston.

The artist brewed a pot of coffee, dressed in his habitual jeans and T-shirt. His grizzled face lit up when she entered.

"Good morning, *cheri*." He motioned her to take a seat while he finished with the coffeemaker.

"Good morning, yourself." She went to one of Jeanne's paintings and studied it, humming a lively tune.

"You're in a happy mood," Gaston commented as he joined her beside the small canvas, which depicted a spring meadow in full bloom.

"I have a plan."

"Oh, what kind of plan?" He paled. "The plans of women always terrify me."

"I want to do something for Jeanne. Because of her, we're about to launch new hopes in our careers."

Color returned to his cheeks and he smiled. "I agree. What are you thinking?"

She explained how she'd investigated Jeanne's descendants and found the local Rousseau family. Then she told him about Jeanne and Etienne seeing Margot at the Louvre, and that Jeanne wanted to know more about her. "Margot's a photographer. I need someone to photograph my food so I can put together a portfolio. Why not engage her for the job? Then it may be possible for Jeanne to see her. Jeanne would love to know the bleakness of her previous life produced some valuable legacy. Plus, we can try to figure out if she is part of this strange encounter with ghosts we're experiencing."

Gaston rubbed his chin and nodded. "Sounds like a good idea. I would love to meet her, also. I wonder if she paints."

Vivienne laughed. "That's my sweetheart, one-track mind." She gave him a kiss on the lips, wrinkling her nose at the scratchy growth of hair on his face. "I'm glad you approve. I have a meeting set up with Margot for later this morning. I'll let you know what happens."

"I have an idea also." He gave her a sheepish grin.

"Oh?"

"I have to admit, I feel the same about Jeanne and have been thinking of a way to show my appreciation." He glanced sideways at her. "I mean I owe her a debt for bringing me back to real painting."

Vivienne stared at him in amazement. Who knew the big goof had such sentimentality. "What's your idea?"

"I want to have a gallery showing of Jeanne's paintings. I feel she deserves to be recognized for her work after all this time."

"Hmm, that's not a bad idea. I could help and make some hors d'oeuvres for the opening night."

He grinned. "That would be great. I hated to ask you since you're already doing so much helping Etienne."

"You big oaf. Of course I'll help you. We'll plan it after Etienne's show."

Gaston grabbed her and enveloped her in one of his bear hugs and then issued a pat on the butt as a sendoff. "Report back after you meet Margot, okay?"

She gave him a mock glare and pushed him. "I will." She looked at her watch. "Oh, I'd better hurry. And please shave before I get back."

She'd arranged to meet Margot at a café to discuss the job. Excitement coursed through her at the thought of meeting Jeanne's descendant. She couldn't wait to see if an element of her ghost friend's character remained in this distant relative. She was also eager to determine if the resemblance to Jeanne from Gaston's paintings was as marked in person.

A taxi brought her to Rue Recamier to the Café Recamier. She scanned the terrace tables until she saw a young woman in sunglasses, head bent over a notebook. There was no mistaking her as Margot from the recognizable features. She wore a blue sweater, black jeans and black patent loafers. Comfortable but chic, Vivienne admitted.

"Hello." She approached the table and greeted the other woman.

"Hello. Vivienne, right?" Margot stretched out her hand in greeting. A genuine smile lit her face.

She froze and her knees grew weak. Here was Jeanne with a fresh younger appearance, untainted by the tragedy of her past life. Her hair was darker and her eyes a true green. She'd pulled her long, straight brown hair back and tied it with a silver scarf at the nape of her neck.

She recovered her composure and sat across the table from the younger woman. "Yes, I'm Vivienne. I'm pleased to meet you." She scanned her face, fascinated at the resemblance. "Thanks for agreeing to meet me so soon."

"You said you needed some food photography?" Margot inquired.

"Yes. I'm catering a *couture* show and I want to have the items photographed."

Margot's eyebrows rose. "A *couture* show? Which one?"

"House Etienne. It will be held at Versailles to coincide with a period masquerade ball following the show."

"What an interesting idea. Seems House Etienne is trying for a big come-back."

"Not just trying. It will be. His new collection is fabulous, and this will be a fantastic event. The food has to be exquisite. I want pictures made beforehand to use as a standard so the food produced at the show will be exactly right. I also want photos done at the venue, which I can use in my portfolio."

"Sounds like an exciting assignment. I'd love to participate." Margot waved to her waiter to take Vivienne's order.

After she decided on a classic *boeuf bourgignon* and a glass of red wine, she wrote her address and phone number on a slip of paper. "Can you come to my apartment tomorrow? I'll prepare the food that will be served, and then we can take photos there." She passed the paper with her information to Margot.

The other woman took the paper, glanced at it then nodded. "Yes, that's fine with me. I don't have any engagements. What time?"

"Let's say at eleven. That will give me the opportunity to have everything prepared."

"Excellent. How do you want the digital prints sent?"

"Can you send them to me by e-mail?"

"Yes, and if you need any enhancement, I can provide that service as well. I do a lot of work with photo enhancement for other clients."

She nodded, pleased. Margot seemed very pleasant as well as knowledgeable about her business. Jeanne would be delighted with her. They finished lunch, discussing superficial subjects, and agreed to meet again for the photo shoot the next day.

Vivienne restrained from leaping in the air after the meeting. Margot was all she'd hoped she would be. She was confident Jeanne would adore her. Perhaps they'd be able to learn more about her tomorrow while they worked. She couldn't wait to tell Gaston about this meeting and how delightful she'd found Margot.

***

Etienne ran up the steps to Gaston's garret that evening, fighting a huge grin. He found Gaston, Vivienne and Jeanne gathered around the small table. His friend and the redhead shared more samples of her cuisine, and the obligatory bottle of red wine.

"Etienne," Gaston roared, raising his wine glass high. "Join the feast."

They exchanged happy greetings, and Etienne settled into a chair with his glass full of the ruby liquid. Jeanne sat beside him, a glow of satisfaction consuming her features.

"I have the most exciting news," he proclaimed. "*All* of the celebrities have accepted my invitation. *All* of them!"

Cheers and shouts arose from his three friends at this welcome information. Vivienne looked smugly delighted. Now that the celebrities had RSVP'd, the show was sure to be a success. This put everything on a different level. The people he needed would attend, that was assured. So, now he had to rely on the designs to reclaim the honor of House Etienne.

He pulled a bottle of champagne from his briefcase, and the redhead rushed to her apartment for flutes. Gaston went to his portrait of Jeanne, currently covered in a sheet, and drew off the cover. He pulled the easel, holding it forward so it stood only three or four feet from the table.

Vivienne returned and Etienne popped the cork and poured

the bubbly liquid into tall crystal glasses.

His friend raised his champagne, looking toward the portrait he'd painted with such intensity. "To Jeanne."

Etienne stood and raised his own glass. "Yes. We owe all of this to Jeanne. To Jeanne."

Vivienne came to her feet. They clinked glasses and drank deeply, followed by unbridled laughter filled with relief that everything had finally worked out.

Jeanne put her hands over her face, but smiled. "What wonderful friends you are. I cannot imagine being happier than I am right this minute."

Gaston and the redhead shared a glance, and his friend cleared his throat. "Ahem. Well, Jeanne, actually we have another idea in mind that might please you. I hope you don't feel I'm being presumptuous, but after Etienne's affair, I want to have a gallery showing of your paintings. You deserve to have recognition for your work."

***

It was as though a hand had punched Jeanne in the stomach, pushing out the substance of her soul. Speechless, she looked from one of them to the other. She could not imagine such a tribute.

"What a great idea." Etienne slapped him on the back. "What a clever guy you are. I never thought of that, but it's perfect. Jeanne?" His gaze went to her and his grin faded. "Jeanne, don't you like the idea?"

"I do not know what to say. I am overwhelmed. Of course I love my paintings, but I never saw them as very good. Elizabeth telling me so reinforced my opinion."

"But Jeanne, now you know she wasn't your mother and how little she cared for you in the end. Don't you think her intent was malicious?" Vivienne punched Gaston's arm and shot him a sideways glance. "You must respect Gaston's opinion if no one else's."

"That's right. She probably didn't want any competition." He rubbed his arm. "Also, think about this. Maybe since you weren't her real daughter, she didn't like you having talent that didn't come from her."

Jeanne considered this. "You know, maybe you are right. I had not thought about it in that way until now. It would certainly coincide with her general paranoia."

"You have to admit, Gaston should know about art. He's a talented artist. If he says your work is good, you can feel confident in that," Etienne said.

She experienced lightness, as if her soul soared in the clouds. "I am so flattered. I never thought to have my work presented to the public. If you think so, then yes, it would make me very happy."

Etienne smiled indulgently. "That's good. We want you to be happy." He reached out to touch her shoulder, and then dropped his hand as he remembered. He seemed to force a bright expression. "The rest of the week is going to be busy. I need to focus on the models, fitting the clothes to them, and going through the runway program rehearsal. I may not see much of you until the show Saturday night. I want you all to know how much the help you have provided means to me. I could not have done this by myself. When it's over, I'll help with the gallery showing."

"My friend," Gaston said. "It has been a great journey of discovery. Now, after all these years, we have our passion back."

The two men touched glasses and, with solemn expressions, drank to the return of passion. Etienne punched his friend's other arm. We've been together through many turns of fortune over the years, and we never gave up on each other. Thanks, my friend."

"Just keep the wine coming to show your appreciation," Gaston said, punching him back." There's still the show to do before we announce true success."

The big man was right. They couldn't count their fortunes until the *haute monde* saw the collection and approved. She prayed the fashion world would see Etienne and his genius as she did. If they disapproved, his life as a designer would be over.

Chapter 22

Etienne and Jeanne arrived at Gaston's place a little after
ten-thirty. He opened the door to the building and allowed her to
enter before him.

"Why are you being mysterious?" she asked, pausing on
the landing.

He glanced at her. "Vivienne has a surprise for you."

She grinned. "Oh, my. That is exciting. I love surprises as
long as they are nice."

"You'll like this one, I'm sure."

He preceded her upstairs, led by a heady aroma of garlic
and butter. Vivienne carried completed food trays to the garret
where the light was better and set them on the table. Gaston
hovered over the plates, and his girlfriend continually reminded
him he couldn't sample until after the photo session. He grumbled
but complied.

"Good morning, everyone," Etienne said.

"Vivienne, these look wonderful." Jeanne went to the table
admiring the display. "You're an artist as well as a chef."

"Thank you," the other woman said to the direction of
Jeanne's voice. "Also, we have a surprise for you today."

"Really? What is it?"

"Remember I showed you the picture of your great, great,
great granddaughter on her website?"

"Yes, I remember."

"I've hired her to come today and photograph my food.
You'll have a chance to see her like you wanted."

Jeanne's eyes grew round. "What a wonderful idea.
Vivienne, you are so clever. I cannot wait. When is she coming?"
She glanced at the doorway.

"She should be here soon. I told her to come at eleven, so
any minute."

"How about that, Etienne? Are you excited?" Jeanne turned
to him, eyes twinkling. "She may be your mystery woman from the
museum."

"Yes, of course I'm excited for you. It should be a great pleasure to see how your descendants have fared. I understand from Vivienne this Margot is someone to make you proud."

Her brow wrinkled. "But you don't want to meet her?"

He exhaled and ran a hand through his hair. "Sure, sure, I want to meet her."

"I wish she would hurry," Gaston grumbled. "I'm hungry."

Vivienne rolled her eyes and pushed him from the table. Footsteps sounded on the stairs. She grinned and pointed toward the door.

Margot entered, paused in the doorway and then took a step back. "Uh, hello, Vivienne. Am I interrupting anything?"

"Oh, no, no, no. Not at all. These are friends of mine. This is Etienne Armand, the designer. The food is for his show." She gestured in his direction. "This is Gaston, my sweetie. We're in his garret."

Something like an electric shock crackled through Etienne. It was as if Jeanne had walked out, changed clothes and hairstyle and walked back in. The urge to rush forward and take her in his arms almost overpowered him. He realized he held his breath and slowly let it out. His knees wobbled like rubber, but he forced them in a locked position.

After a few seconds, he managed to move forward and shook her hand in greeting. The feel of her skin was like a drug, and he struggled to break contact, his heart thudding. Margot stared at him quizzically, but he gave her his best charming smile. She visibly relaxed.

She placed her backpack on the seat of a chair and pulled out her camera and other equipment. "I brought some small table lights I thought would be perfect for food shots." She began setting up the stands and conversing with Vivienne how best to position the plates.

He backed away and went with Jeanne and Gaston to the other side of the room. Jeanne's smile in observing the young woman relieved him. He hoped she didn't notice his discomfort. Margot filled him with confusion.

"She's very pretty," Jeanne whispered.

He nodded. She was indeed. Gorgeous. Today she wore jeans, a black pullover knit top, and a pink hoodie jacket. She had black boots with medium-high heels, which made her a bit taller than Jeanne. Occasionally she shot a glance in his direction, but he couldn't read her expression.

Gaston shot a 'thumbs up' in Jeanne's direction then wandered to the table where the women worked.

"You should get to know her," Jeanne said. "Then you can tell me what she is really like. Maybe you can offer her a job photographing something." She motioned him to the group.

He frowned but went to observe the progress. Although Margot captured his interest, he didn't totally understand Jeanne's need for such in-depth information. Sure, it was great to see her and know that a part of Jeanne's life had survived and thrived past her own tragedy, but he had a sense that digging for information was much too intrusive. He no longer wanted to delve into the mystery of this woman's visits to the Louvre or why she looked so much like Jeanne. He didn't want to think she would become more involved in their lives than this photography session. Maybe, just maybe, his discomfort came from how much she looked like Jeanne and his attraction to that. It really bugged him.

Vivienne and Margot moved the food in different positions and adjusted the lighting. The redhead had also brought a variety of drapes and props for accent. His friend critically appraised the layouts and nodded his approval. Margot pulled bottles out of her bag and began to spray a dish of raw Ahi tuna.

"Aaa, what is that?" Gaston's eyes popped in alarm.

"Glycerin," Margot replied. "It makes food look moist and delicious."

"But..." He cast a frantic glance at his girlfriend.

Vivienne pushed him from the table and gently laid a white orchid beside the tuna. "Don't worry. I have more in my apartment. You can't eat these samples. They'll be destroyed by the time we finish messing with them."

Etienne had to chuckle at his friend's downcast countenance brightening at the prospect of more food. Once reassured, the big man returned to his unofficial "artist in residence" critiquing. Vivienne rolled her eyes, and Margot smiled at the banter.

"We should have music," Gaston suggested. "What types of music do you like, Margot?"

"I like a variety, but I'm partial to jazz." She held a light meter beside the first dish.

Etienne glanced at his friend. They both loved jazz. Why did she have to be so perfect?

Gaston raised an eyebrow and nodded in appreciation. "All right then. Let's have some jazz." He located his iPod in the mass of jars and tubes he'd removed from the table Vivienne used. He placed it in its speaker holder and made a selection. He smiled and closed his eyes as the smooth sounds of a saxophone wafted across the room. "Ah, that's nice. All we need now is wine."

Etienne held up one finger and headed to the bag he'd brought. Alcohol might help him deal with this situation. Great idea. He withdrew several bottles of burgundy. The big man hurried down to his apartment for glasses.

***

The morning moved smoothly into afternoon as the process of photographing the food continued. Gaston cracked jokes, Vivienne and Margot laughed. Jeanne beamed as happiness blossomed to bursting inside her. Here were her friends, and one who could replace her daughter, all laughing and having fun. This life she wanted. Not the gloom and depression of her past.

Her glow of contentment continued as Margot talked, revealing more about herself. Jeanne had to prod Etienne, but finally he started talking to her relative and seemed to enjoy the interaction. They looked so nice together. She wondered if that was how she and Etienne would look as a couple—like they belonged together.

"Okay, that's the last photo." Vivienne dumped her display samples in the trash. "I have more samples downstairs, if my dear Gaston will help me, I'll bring them up."

Margot packed her bags. "Everything looked delicious. I think your food will be a big hit."

The redhead and Gaston returned after a few minutes with trays of food. They placed them on the table and she began pointing to each type. "Now some of these you haven't tried before. So be honest and tell me what you think. This one is squares of layered pressed chicken and fois gras with black truffle on toasted country finger bread. Here is the raw ahi tuna bites with a ginger soy sauce. Finally, a marinated salmon topped with herbed goat cheese and a dollop of caviar sorrel sauce on a white cracker. Enjoy."

"Oh my, this is wonderful," Margot said holding a sample of two different items in each hand.

"My sweetheart is a genius." Gaston planted a kiss on the top of his lover's head.

Jeanne stood beside Etienne as he tasted the delicacies. Her joy overflowed to see her friends enjoying Vivienne's unique recipes. "Are they good?" she whispered to him.

He nodded emphatically, mouth full.

"Wow, I didn't expect this," Margot said as she accepted a glass of wine. "My mouth was watering the whole time I was shooting. Thank you.'

Vivienne motioned her to eat more. Gaston turned up the music and grabbed Vivienne for a dance.

"I'm looking forward to seeing your collection," Margot stepped closer to Etienne. She took a bite of the pressed chicken concoction, chewed and closed her eyes. "Oh my God, that's good."

Etienne grinned and appeared to relax a bit. "Vivienne's food is awesome. We're lucky to have frequent opportunities to sample."

"I love fashion. I remember your first show. That black velvet evening gown will stay in my memory forever," she said.

"Thank you. I'm impressed you remember it. But I have to tell you, it was my favorite, too. Do you do any photography for designers?"

She shook her head. "No, I wish. It's my dream. If you ever need anyone...I'm not the most experienced, but I work hard and I'm good at what I do."

"I'll keep it in mind." He took a drink of wine.

Jeanne retreated to the side of the room content to watch, glad Etienne had struck up a conversation with her relative. A shining sense of love and pride flooded Jeanne's spirit.

Suddenly, blackness exploded around her. No light. No shadows. Only darkness. Out of the gloom rang laughter. Maniacal laughter echoing in her head. It grew louder, radiating to the depth of her being. She flung her arms wide and twisted, fighting a mental haze that enveloped her. *No, no no!*

In a second, the strange sensation disappeared. She returned to the happy room with jazz blasting, and her friends talking and laughing. She trembled and wrapped her arms around her shivering torso. Had she been about to fade? No. That couldn't be the cause. Why the crazy laughter? Why had she come back? That was not fading. The others appeared unaware of her momentary distress. She looked down and gasped in fear. She floated three feet above the floor.

Chapter 23

Jeanne hurried through the first floor rooms of Richelieu until she reached the Salle d' Napoleon. She'd said nothing of her eerie experience to her living friends, but when Etienne dropped her at the Louvre, she immediately rushed to consult her father and George on the matter.

The two souls talked with a young woman. As she approached, the woman smiled and faded away. Her friend and Francois shared a look of fulfillment.

"Father," she called as she approached.

He glanced at her and smiled. His smile melted to concern. "What is wrong, my dear?" he asked as he and George rose to meet her.

"I have had the most disturbing experience." She put her hands to her cheeks.

"What happened?" her friend asked.

She relayed the incident to them and how it had horrified her. She looked to her father. "At first I thought I was fading. But it was a violent experience, not peaceful at all. Have you ever heard of anything like this?"

He placed a hand at his throat and bowed his head. George floated closer and wrapped an arm around her. Gratitude for his comforting presence filled her heart.

Finally, Francois said, "Yes, I have heard of something of this nature. It is one of those aberrations we have talked about when souls step outside their boundaries. I am very disturbed such an event has occurred with you, my daughter."

"What happened?" Fear sliced through her like an icy knife.

"It is not common, but I am afraid it means some entity from Everlasting is attempting to make you lose your soul."

"What?" she and George exclaimed together, sharing shocked stares.

"If a soul is forced into Everlasting before their time, the

168

soul is lost, reduced to a meaningless specter, void of memories or any sense of who they were. It means an eternity of mindless agony."

"How do you know this?" George's jaw dropped.

Francois' gaze moved to the distance. He remained silent for a long minute. "I had an interaction with two souls many years ago. They were from Everlasting. They had faded and were content. Then they witnessed something there which troubled them so much, they slipped back into this reality."

"Souls can return from Everlasting?" If that was true, then maybe she need not fear fading so much.

"Only for a few moments. Remember how Gabrielle returned to speak to you? She was called back by the medium, Madam Renee, but she could not stay forever."

She nodded, remembering Gabrielle saying she could not linger.

"Most souls do not want to return. Everlasting is the place of eternal rest for us. As in the case of the two souls I mentioned, however, they were so disturbed they returned for only the brief time it took to warn me."

"They warned you specifically?" George asked.

Francois nodded. "Yes, the threat was to me. These two souls were among those I had helped in the revolution and again many years later when they were new souls in search of answers. They felt indebted to me for helping them.

"The threat came from the soul of a madman who had delighted in the deaths of aristocrats during the revolution. He somehow found me after death. His warped mind still hated me for helping the nobility escape. It further enraged him that I helped souls after death. I was quite relieved when he faded soon after arriving, as he made a point of disrupting my meetings with his mad, evil ravings."

"So he wanted to pull you into Everlasting before your time? How is that possible?" George rubbed his chin.

"The souls explained this particular soul bragged about how he would return, meld his spirit with mine, and force me to Everlasting. They had witnessed this before and watched that tortured soul roam while wailing the grief of his nothingness."

She could only imagine such horror. What a fate to suffer

for eternity.

"It seems there is knowledge in Everlasting we do not have here," George said. "It is appalling how a soul in Everlasting who suffered from mental illness during life can seek to wreak revenge on a soul left behind. To create an aberration against nature and return to the living world to exact vengeance is reprehensible."

"So a soul from my past is trying to do such a thing to me?" Chilling terror filled her.

"I am afraid so, my dear. There can be no other explanation." Francois' eyes reflected his fear for her.

"But who? Who can be so determined to create further sadness for me?" she cried. "Did I not suffer enough during my life?"

"You must understand, this is not based on a sane thought process. Insanity would negate the ability to reason through such considerations. For centuries, this soul thinks of nothing but revenge." Francois placed a hand over hers.

"The person most likely to make such an attempt can only be Elizabeth," George said, his lips in a grim line. "You learned she exhibited patterns of paranoia and mental instability when you lived. Who else could it be?"

"The woman who raised me and acted as mother to me?" Bitter revulsion rose in her throat.

"Who, other than her?" George threw up his hands. "Nothing else makes sense."

"I am afraid George could be right in his deduction. Think of what you have discovered recently." Francois stood and paced. "She showed signs of imbalance in life, which increased with age. Consider her paranoid delusion of persecution in Russia and her harsh treatment of you when you returned to France. These are not the actions of a mentally stable individual."

The maniacal laughter still rang in her head, unforgettable and chilling. It was unmistakably female and certainly conveyed an element of madness. She'd fought desperately to keep the voice out of her head then discovered she drifted high above the floor. Had Elizabeth been trying to drag her to Everlasting? Dear God!

George turned his worried gaze from Jeanne to Francois. "But how did you avoid the insane soul?"

"At first, I doubted the ability of this madman to carry out his threat. He did make an attempt shortly after the two souls had warned me. I saw him, fortunately. I raced through the halls of the Louvre, giving him no chance to catch me and attempt the bond. With the limited time he was allowed in this world, he was forced to depart.

"I left the Louvre for a while. I told none of the souls here where I planned to go. I left no trail of information and stayed in a place unfamiliar to me from the past. After a year, I was compelled to return here, to the place most dear to me. I remained in a vigilant state for many months, but never heard or saw him again. I can only hope his madness left him unable to maintain the discipline of carrying out his plan. Who knows?" He shrugged.

She floated up and down as she digested the implications of his story. Then she asked, "What should I do?"

"You must leave. At once."

"Where can I go to be safe? Somewhere she would not think to look?"

"It must be a place Elizabeth does not know." George turned to her father. "We should go with her. We can help keep watch."

Francois rubbed his chin then nodded. "Yes. I will not let this happen to my daughter. Where will she be safe?"

"Wait, I know a place. Come on." She turned and headed into the hall.

Francois and George shared a worried look then followed.

She emerged from the darkened halls of the Louvre into the flashing brightness of Paris at night. George, who had not previously come outside as a soul, froze and stared. Jeanne and her father urged him to hurry. Even after he refocused and started moving, he continually lagged as he paused to investigate sight after sight. She kept stopping and retracing her steps to remind him of their need for haste. She almost regretted bringing him, but knew he'd never have consented to stay behind.

Finally, she arrived in front of Etienne's atelier, deserted at this time of night. She floated inside and led her father and friend upstairs to Etienne's office.

"You think this place is safe?" George asked, scanning clothes hanging on hangers, numerous bolts of fabric, and several trays of sparkly jewelry and accessories.

"I hope so. How could Elizabeth know of this place?" The aura of Etienne remained here and imparted a sense of safety, but she couldn't be completely confident.

"How did she find you at Gaston's?" George responded.

"I think she saw me and Etienne taking a taxi there one day. She surely followed us."

"What?" Francois exploded.

She nodded. "I saw a woman on the street that resembled the pictures and my memories of her, only much older. She was far away then disappeared, so I was convinced it was simply a coincidence."

"And now you think otherwise." George settled in a chair.

"Yes. I am afraid so. You see, I saw the same woman again in the Louvre after that. She glared at me then was gone. Now that I consider it, especially after what my father told us, I must assume she was Elizabeth. I suppose she looked as she did when she died, much older than my memories."

"Why did you not inform me? I warned you to tell me if anything disturbing occurred." Francois paced the room, hands clasped behind his back.

"I am sorry. I never thought anything bad could happen because of my meeting with Etienne." She sank onto another chair. "I certainly never dreamed the woman who raised me would now seek to destroy me."

"I do not think this is because of Etienne." Her father shook his head.

"Really?" Jeanne looked up, hope brimming inside her. "I never meant to cause any disruption of the spirit world or put anyone in danger."

His expression softened. "I know, my dear. I am not angry with you. I am upset something could happen to you. You must promise to let me know if anything unusual happens in the future."

"I will," she promised.

"So what do you think has brought Elizabeth back?" George asked.

Francois settled on a chair. "I do not think there is any way we can know. I doubt it is because Jeanne talks to Etienne." He gazed at her. "Elizabeth could have been returning for brief amounts of time, searching for you since her death. Perhaps she finally happened upon the right time and place. Now that she has some knowledge of your whereabouts, she can be more exact in her search."

"That is frightening." George glanced to her in concern. "But what does she hope to achieve?"

"I suspect she was not content with my suffering while I lived. She wants to inflict more. What else?" Her shoulders drooped. Would she never escape the misery of her past? Had Elizabeth not tortured her enough?

They sat in silence. She didn't want to recover any more memories. She was done with her previous history and had no desire to fade to Everlasting. Only the hope of staying here with the living had any allure for her. But if Elizabeth succeeded, even that would be lost to her.

"In any event, we must be vigilant. If she should appear, Jeanne, you must run. George and I will try to distract and hinder her. That is the only course I can premeditate at this time," Francois stated after a while. "We must be careful not to touch her if she appears, or we too could be forced into Everlasting." He motioned to George.

Her friend nodded. "It is a good plan. Running away worked for you."

"Yes, thank God I was forewarned and saw him manifest. Had he caught me unaware, he might have overpowered me."

"We should discuss specific details. If Jeanne runs and we stay behind to provide protection, where shall we meet later?" George asked.

Francois nodded. "A good idea. Let us have several plans based upon our location should Elizabeth come."

"Agreed," she and George said, but shared worried looks.

Chapter 24

The next morning, Etienne climbed the stairs to his office. He paused at the top, surprised to find his ghostly love present. What the hell was going on?

Jeanne sat on a chair, rubbing her arms and glancing about.

"What's wrong?" He dropped his brief case and hurried to her side.

She rose quickly. "Etienne, I am so glad you have arrived."

"How long have you been here?"

She relayed her experiences yesterday. "My friends came with me to help keep watch."

"*Merde.*" He sat, running fingers through his hair. What a crazy complication. "So Francois and George are here?" He searched the room for evidence of their presence.

"Yes. Very pleased to finally make your acquaintance, *monsieur*," Francois answered, a deep cultured voice.

"We have heard so much about you. It is a pleasure to meet you in person," George added. His English-accented French distinguished him from the older spirit.

"Thank you both for coming with Jeanne," he said in their direction. "This situation is unexpected, to say the least. What can I do to help?"

"Let us stay here for a while, if that is possible," she replied.

"Are you kidding? Stay as long as you want. I'd do anything to help you, Jeanne."

"Etienne?" Chloe emerged from the spiral stairs. "Oh, I thought you had guests. I heard voices."

"I was just talking to myself." He moved to the chair behind his desk. "What's up? Anything going on yet?"

"We're taking the rest of the garments to Versailles so the models can practice." After a suspicious scan of the room, she gathered the hanging clothes. "I have a photo shoot set up with "W" preceding the show."

"Sounds good. Way to go, Chloe." He glanced nervously at

Jeanne.

"What are you working on today?" She draped the last garment gently over her arm.

"Last minute details, interviews, that sort of thing." He started fanning through his message slips, hoping she would leave.

"Okay. See you later then." She hurried toward the steps with one last look behind her.

He put a finger to his lips and went to the landing. When Chloe had gone, he returned. "What are you going to do now?" he asked.

"I am not sure, but we do have plans in case Elizabeth shows up," Jeanne replied.

He hit his forehead. "Damn, Margot is coming by this morning. Did you remember? You wanted me to find a way to hire her and help her in her career. Are you sure that's a good idea now?"

"Yes. With what happened yesterday after the photo shoot, I forgot. But I still want you to help her and find out more about her."

"If you insist. I have some promotional events over the next few nights until the show. I thought I could use her for publicity shots. She told me her dream was to work in the fashion industry. What do you think?"

"That is so kind of you, Etienne. Thank you. What a wonderful idea."

"She'll be here any minute."

"Do whatever you need. We will stay out of the way." Jeanne moved to stand next to a chair.

His phone rang, and he answered call after call from different newspapers and fashion publications regarding his upcoming show. Fortunately, the media had become intrigued with the idea of a period ball and the mysterious model on his billboards and ads.

While he talked on the phone, one of his seamstresses escorted Margot to his office. He gestured her forward. She wore a narrow, ankle-length black skirt with a gold knit top and matching jacket. Today her dark, silky hair hung loose, almost to her waist. She carried a soft briefcase with a strap over one shoulder. He swallowed as she moved gracefully across the floor. A knot formed in his stomach. This was a mistake. But he'd promised Jeanne.

"Hey, thanks for coming," he said when he hung up. He reached across his desk to shake her hand. Her fresh eager face was such a contrast to the despair which currently resided on Jeanne's that it pained him. Margot's beauty was unsullied and pure. Somehow, the appreciation of that shot a bolt of molten guilt into his gut. He averted his gaze, afraid he'd stare.

"I'm happy to be here. I enjoyed meeting you and your friends yesterday. What can I do to help you?" She shook his hand and took the chair he indicated in front of his desk.

"I brought my portfolio, if you'd like to see some of my work." She produced a hard-bound notebook from her briefcase and handed it across the desk.

He flipped through the pages. Most of them were wedding pictures, but her talent was evident, and she showed a flair for positioning her subjects. Her shots of the bride and groom up close, staring lovingly into each other eyes, made him jealous. Why couldn't he and Jeanne have that? "I have a series of publicity engagements over the next few days before my show Sunday night. I need a photographer to travel with me and record the appearances so I can have photos for my website and to use for future ads. I'd like you to be that photographer."

"Of course, I'd love to. Do you have a schedule of events?" Her features glowed with her bright smile.

"I'll send you my agenda by e-mail. Basically, there's an event every night from tonight through Saturday then my show is on Sunday. I know you'll be at the show to shoot Vivienne's food, but I'd like to have you take pictures of the general festivities at the ball as well."

"That shouldn't be a problem. Vivienne's photography will have to be done before the crowd arrives, so I can do her photography first and switch to the ball."

"Excellent. I'll email you a contract. If the terms are acceptable, we'll start right away. The first event is tonight, a cocktail reception sponsored by reporters of fashion magazines. A chance for designers to talk about their upcoming shows. It's at Alcazar Mezzanine. Do you know that place?"

"Yes, I know of it. I've never been there though."

"You'll like it. It has two levels and is open in the middle of the second floor. Great for photo ops. The whole place is rented for the party, so it should be fun. I can send a car for you at seven. Then it can swing by and pick me up at my place. Give me your address and e-mail."

She bent to retrieve a paper from her briefcase and the curtain of her brown hair cascaded around her. His gut tightened thinking of spending the evening with her. It should be Jeanne. How would he endure Margo's proximity when her appearance was a constant reminder of what he couldn't have?

"Everything's here on my resume." Margot handed him the sheet of paper. "What about dress? Is it black-tie?"

"No, it's casual cocktail attire. Designers tend to dress eclectically anyway, so anything goes except very casual."

"Would you like a CD with the images?" She made notes in a separate notebook.

"Yes, definitely." The strain of maintaining his composure around her was about to crack his façade of professionalism. Every part of him wanted to crush her in his arms.

"Okay. I guess those are all the questions I have." She picked up her purse and briefcase and stretched her hand to him. "Thanks so much for the job. I look forward to working with you."

"Of course. Thank you. I'll see you tonight." He forced his gaze to his desk.

"Good-bye." Margot hesitated, but turned and went down the spiral stairs.

"Etienne," Jeanne said after Margot left.

"Yes?" He looked up.

"Do you not like her?" She tilted her head to one side.

"What do you mean?" His heart pounded. He knew exactly what she meant.

"You seemed very dry and short with her. It is not how you usually are with people. I thought maybe you had taken a dislike to her."

"She seemed very nice to me," George commented.

"And very beautiful. There is a strong family resemblance." Francois said, thrusting out his chest.

"I like her okay. Yes, she's nice. Yes, she's pretty. But she's not—" He slapped his desk, frustrated.

"She is not what?" Jeanne looked at him, head tilted.

He crossed the room and ran a hand through his hair. How could he explain? Margot made him uncomfortable. She looked too much like Jeanne, yet was warm and real. In different circumstances, he'd show interest. Her involvement was becoming complicated.

"She's not you," he said and crossed his arms, staring at her.

"Oh." Jeanne retreated a few steps, blinking. "I never thought of that. I had an overwhelming desire to find goodness from my previous life. I wanted to help Margot. I am sorry. I did not mean to cause you difficulty. If you do not wish to help her, that is fine. I understand." She came to his side, her expression full of contrition.

He shook his head, ashamed of his insensitivity. "No, it's okay. I know you want to do something for her and you can't do it yourself. I really do understand that."

"Are you sure?" She didn't look convinced.

"Yeah, sure. No problem." He turned to his desk to avoid her scrutiny. "I need to get some errands done before tonight. Are you three going to be okay here?"

"Yes. I do not think Elizabeth will find us," Francois responded. "Thank you for helping Jeanne and Margot."

He relaxed. "Hey, like I said, it's not a problem. I want to do it if it pleases Jeanne. I'll be back tomorrow morning."

"Good-bye, Etienne." She blew him a kiss.

"Good-bye," George called.

He waved and headed downstairs. Why had he let Jeanne talk him into this? How was he going to deal with Margot and his feeling of attraction over the next few days? He gritted his teeth. He'd do it. He'd do it for her.

Chapter 25

Margot squealed as soon as she got in the taxi. The driver shot her a speculative glance in his rearview mirror. She couldn't believe how easy that had been. Almost *too* easy, but she was too excited to dwell on that. This could be her big break. She finally had a job in fashion photography. Of course, Etienne wanted a project more like her wedding gigs, but he still opened a door for actual fashion shoots down the road. Her stomach flipped in excitement.

When she returned to her apartment she took a deep breath. She pulled clothes from her closet and tossed them on her bed. What would she wear? She had to look *chic*, but effortlessly so. What she wore to wedding jobs would not do for a party with the world's top French designers. Her hands shook as she discarded one outfit after another. She seriously needed to spend some money on clothes.

She settled on a pair of black leggings with a black sequined tunic and matching jacket. She could wear her new peep-toe black patent pumps. Then she remembered she had a black sequined beret that went with the tunic. That would to have to be *chic* enough.

Her phone rang. Her mother. Great. "Hello?"

"Hello, darling. I wanted to see how your interview went."

"It was great. I got the job. I'll be working with the famous Etienne Armand shooting publicity photos for his new collection." The words still sounded like a fantasy to her.

"I hope he's paying you well. I've heard those designers are cheap." Her mother sniffed.

She clenched a fist, forcing herself not to scream. "Mom. This is my big break. I'd do it for free if it gave me a chance to work in fashion."

"You're too good for that. Free? What are you thinking? You can always get more work from Professor Galen. You're father said he was very pleased with the photos you did."

It took a strong surge of control not to fling the cell phone at the wall. "I have to go, Mom. I need to have time to get ready. I'll call you tomorrow and let you know how it went." She hung up quickly before her mother had a chance to respond. After tossing the phone on the bed, she jumped up and down, hand above her head. "Yes, I'm on my way up!"

Heaving a sigh of relief, she settled to work on Vivienne's photos from yesterday. She'd already gone through most of them, cropping and adjusting brightness and contrast. Now she copied the finished pictures into one file and e-mailed it.

She smiled. Vivienne was fun to work with and was a very talented chef. Gaston had provided comic relief.

Then there was Etienne. He was killer handsome. When his macho guard was down, she detected a sensitive, humorous personality. He was difficult to read, though. He offered her a chance of a lifetime without even calling her references. He'd barely glanced at her portfolio before he made her an offer. And yet, he remained distant most of the time, unwilling to connect on a personal level. A bit strange. Maybe he had a girlfriend or was gay and didn't want to open up too much.

She shrugged. It didn't matter as long as he hired her. She determined to do a good job so he would continue hiring her. Who knew? Maybe his professional veneer would crack once he realized she would be an asset.

She grinned and headed into the bathroom to shower and begin the primping process for tonight.

  ***

Francois took a chair beside Jeanne, his countenance troubled. "My dear, are you sure it is wise for you to attend this event at Versailles? I am concerned Elizabeth can find you there."

She looked down then met his gaze unwavering. "I have to, for Etienne and for myself."

"You think it is possible Elizabeth knows of that place?" George approached. He'd wandered around Etienne's office inspecting different items. His curiosity had already led him downstairs, but he returned soon after.

"I am not certain. I think it may be too big a risk." Francois shook his head.

"I have to see Etienne's show. I simply must," Jeanne protested. "It is not only about how important it is to him. I want a sense of accomplishment for my contributions. I never had that in my life. I am willing to take the risk," she pleaded.

George moved to join them. "You know Versailles, Francois. You can make plans for us to escape like we did here last night. We will keep a lookout and then Jeanne can flee."

She gave him a grateful smile and turned to her father, grasping his hands in hers. "Please."

"Very well," Francois relented, his expression softening. "We will discuss the layout of Versailles. When we get there, you can travel the routes. I am sure it has changed since my day, so we will want to tour it with new eyes when we arrive Sunday."

She laughed in excitement. "Thank you, thank you. You know, Etienne will go to Versailles early that morning. We can go with him, and that will give us time to become familiar with the palace before the show."

"That sounds like a good plan," George agreed. "I wonder if there are souls there like at the Louvre."

"Of course," Francois said. "Souls go straight to Everlasting, stay in the area where they died, or go somewhere holding overwhelming importance to them. There will surely be souls at Versailles given its history."

"How interesting," George exclaimed. "I can hardly wait."

A bubbly excitement filled her with heady anticipation. She'd have her father and her friends together on that special night. A night of triumph for Etienne, and one of satisfaction for her. Margot would be there as well, like the daughter she never had the chance to enjoy. She prayed Elizabeth would not find her and ruin everything.

***

Etienne drew in a quick breath when Margot smiled in greeting. She appeared stunning in her simple ensemble. Lean leggings and high-heels accented her shapely legs. The beret added a jaunty air that fit right in with the flair of the fashion crowd.

She took pictures of him as he entered the restaurant.

Friends in the fashion industry crowded around, slapping him on the shoulder and uttering compliments on his campaign. He had trouble keeping his gaze off of her. He regretted this forced interaction. Nothing good could come of his contact with this gorgeous woman, a living embodiment of his beloved Jeanne.

"Etienne, old friend," a fashion reporter from a newspaper hailed. This fortyish man with dark hair graying at the temples and a big smile handed Etienne a glass of champagne.

"Hello, Evan. How are you?" He accepted the flute and shook the man's hand.

"I'm fabulous. What about you? I'm hearing all kinds of rumors. Some people say you're finished, and some say you're headed for a big come-back. What's with all the mystery?"

"There's no mystery. I'm just doing my job, designing great clothes."

"Come on, what about the model? Nobody knows who she is and everybody wants to. You can tell me. Who is she?" Evan moved closer and leaned his head near in a conspiratorial manner.

"Sorry, can't tell you. You'll have to come to my show like everybody else." He smiled and sipped his champagne.

"So, she'll be at the show?" Evans asked, eyes alight with anticipation.

"In a sense," he said vaguely and moved into the crowd. A glance over his shoulder showed Evan staring after him, brow wrinkled.

***

Margot glanced around between taking pictures. The evening progressed and the crowd thickened. People enjoyed drinks, hors d'oeuvres, and moving between the two floors. They greeted friends and spread gushing remarks on their new collections. Flashes continually sparkled as most of the designers had brought someone to take publicity shots. Also, the media had photographers of their own.

The tented glass ceiling of the second floor revealed the night and stars, adding to the special ambience of the evening. There were famous people, beautiful people, and peculiar people attracting her attention.

Etienne seemed in his element. He moved smoothly from person to person, laughing, spreading publicity about his line, and deflecting advances from gorgeous women. Surely he was gay. If so, why didn't men hit on him? He came off studly, looking sexy in slim black trousers, white linen shirt open at the throat, and a black shantung silk blazer with red handkerchief in the pocket. She swallowed and returned to her camera. *Keep your mind on business, girl.*

She followed him to the second floor and took shots of him greeting several of his famous competitors. One or two acted condescending, but most offered jovial greetings, treating him as an old friend. They, too, pestered him about his mystery model. She was curious. The model in Etienne's recent ads apparently created a great deal of speculation. Everyone wanted to know about her. She'd been so busy lately she couldn't remember seeing any of the ads, or if she had, she'd not paid attention. Too much time buried in The Louvre recently.

"Hey, I haven't seen you at these before," a young man with shaggy blonde hair said as he snapped a photo of one of the designers. "You new in town?"

"No." She punched a button on her camera. "I'm just new to fashion."

"Welcome. My name's Gavin." He let his camera hang around his neck and held out a hand.

She hesitated then shook it. "Thanks. I'm Margot."

"You look familiar. Have we met?" His brow wrinkled as he stared at her, then he grabbed two glasses of champagne from a passing waiter's tray and handed one to her. "Might as well enjoy yourself. These things can go all night."

She took the glass and thanked him. "No, I don't think we've met."

"Hmm, well, I'll think of it sooner or later. You look familiar." He returned to snapping pictures and moved away.

She took a sip then set the glass on a nearby table. If she faced a long night, she refused to become drunk. She followed Etienne as he worked his way around the opening in the middle of the second floor, which looked down on the first.

As they returned to the first floor, people stared at her and whispered behind their hands. She glanced at her clothes. Had

something spilled on her? Her clothing appeared unscathed. She
put a hand to her head to make sure her beret hadn't gone sideways
and found it secure.

Gavin came behind her with another photographer, a black
man in his thirties with shaved head and a goatee.

"Hey, Margot. I know where I saw you," Gavin said,
elbowing the other man.

"She's a dead-ringer." The other man nodded.

"You're Etienne's model for his new line. Why are you here
taking pictures?" Gavin lifted his camera to take a shot of her.

She put a hand over the front of his camera and pushed it
from his face. "What are you talking about? I'm not a model. I'm a
photographer."

"Yeah, right. Is this some publicity stunt? That Etienne is
one sly fox." Gavin retrieved his camera from her hand and
stepped back to take his picture.

A hand took her elbow and eased her around. Etienne stood
at her side. "Time to go," he said and led her by the arm. He
hurried outside while talking on his cell phone to his driver.

Gavin, the black photographer, and a few others pushed
their way through the crowd and onto the street. They took photos
of her and Etienne, flashes blinding her as they waited for the car.
More people rushed out of the restaurant. Etienne pulled her to his
chest, and she hid her face against his jacket lapel. Someone
tugged at her jacket, and it tore. Hands tugged at her arms and
shoulders pulling her backward.

A scream faltered in her throat. What the hell was going
on? Etienne pushed two men aside and his fingers dug into her
shoulders as he grasped her against him. Her heart hammered
against his. Shouts erupted around them and a constellation of
camera flashes blinded her.

People spilled into the street. Yelling and more bursts of
light added to the confusion. When the limo pulled to the curb,
tires squealing, Etienne half dragged her into it.

"Go," he shouted at the driver.

They took off, tires screaming.

She sprawled across the back seat of the limousine where
she'd landed. Her jacket hung from one sleeve, ripped at the
seams. She shivered and struggled to push upright. Those idiots

had attacked her! Why were they taking her picture? A peaceful cocktail party had turned into a mob scene with her at the focus. What the hell?

She glanced at Etienne's grim expression. A muscle twitched in his jaw.

"Do you know anything about what happened back there?" She managed a sitting position and put a trembling hand to her head. She'd lost her beret. Damn it.

He let out a heavy breath and shook his head. "They think you're the model of my clothing line for the season. It's been a secret, and everyone is trying to find out who she is. I didn't realize what a big story it would be to find her. I'm sorry you were put in such a position. I never thought anything like that would happen."

Her shaking increased, and her teeth chattered.

He moved to the seat beside her and put his arm around her. "It's shock, *cheri*. Don't worry, you're safe." He pulled off his jacket and put it about her shoulders then wrapped his arms around her. "My God, those people are insane."

She didn't answer, too muddled to make sense of anything. His model? What did that have to do with her? His strong arm around her provided much needed support, but she still shook in the aftermath of the violence. "I don't understand why they think I'm involved.'

He rubbed her arm. "I know. I'm sorry. I feel horrible you experienced that."

The car stopped at his apartment, and he assisted her from the backseat then sent the driver off. He kept one arm around her and helped her up the steps to his door. Once inside, he placed her on the couch and covered her with a blanket. Then he found a bottle of cognac and sat on the floor beside her. He poured a glass and extended it. "Here, drink this. It will help the shock."

She took the glass in both hands and stared into his eyes, seeking a clue to his sudden solicitude. After barely meeting her gaze, he'd morphed into a warm caring protector. Wary, she swallowed a gulp, which made her gasp. "*Merde.*" Tears started at the bite of the fiery liquid.

He patted her back. "That's it. Take another sip. Really, it's good for you."

She took another big swallow, which went down much

easier. He was right. As warmth spread through her, the swell of emotions and fear eased to a modest rumble. After another sip, she managed to sit up and wipe tears from her face.

Etienne brought her a box of tissues and sat beside her on the couch. "Better?"

She nodded and blew her nose. What a mess. The excitement from earlier disappeared in this bizarre turn of events. The rush of adrenaline to escape dissipated, leaving her limp and slightly nauseated. She sniffed one last time and swiped her hair out of her face.

His smile disappeared. He stood and strode to a side table where he picked up a magazine. After flipping through the pages, he folded back the cover and handed it to her.

An ad for his upcoming spring line filled the page. The face of a model with a faraway stare of unreadable depth topped one of Etienne's evening dresses. A chill ran through her. The model looked almost exactly like her. Granted the hair was a bit lighter and curly, and the eyes were a different shade, but the resemblance was unmistakable.

"Who is she?" She glanced at Etienne, enveloped in an uncanny sense of deja vu .

He sat, clutching the magazine, his jaw working. After a few seconds, he rubbed his chin and stood. "Margot, I really don't know how to tell you about this." He went to his bar and poured cognac in a glass and took a large swig. "I'm just sorry I got you involved. Are you okay?"

"Yes, I'm calming now. Just a touch of shock, as you said. You'd need more than that to take me out, I assure you. I was blind-sided."

He nodded and took another sip of cognac. He returned to the couch. "It was a good party until then, don't you think?"

She smiled and averted her gaze. He really was too charming in his attempt to distract her, but she had to know more about this resemblance to his model.

The ease of procuring this job was not as dismissible as it had been. There was an undercurrent of a mystery that involved her, and she wanted to know why.

She turned toward him and rested a hand on his arm. "You really owe me an explanation, you know. There's something going on here that involves me, and you're keeping me out of it. That's not fair. Why did you hire me? You must have a hundred photographers at your disposal. I'm nobody. I shoot weddings, for God's sake. Why would a famous fashion designer hire someone like me? This is tied to the woman in your ads somehow, I'm certain."

He leaned back and stared at the ceiling. Finally, he turned to her and his expression closed. "Margot, you're too perceptive." He took a drink and his tone became matter-of-fact. "How much do you know about your family history?"

She hesitated. "My family history? Not much past my grandparents I guess, like most people. Why?"

"Tell me about yourself. How did you end up in photography?"

She let out a breath of exasperation, and played along. "It was a hobby. Something I experimented with even when I was young." She pulled her feet under her and leaned against the couch cushions. "I majored in communications at university, and when I graduated, I found jobs few and far between in that sector. I started providing photography for friends' weddings and other events. Pretty soon, I was so busy I didn't think about anything except photography. I set up a web site, and went full-time. My dream has always been to break into fashion, but I've had no luck so far. That's my story."

He nodded. "My father wanted me to go into business. I wanted to be a designer. He tolerated my stint in art school. When I began to work in design houses, he washed his hands of me. I think he was afraid I would become gay or something. You know how that generation thinks. Full of stereotypes."

She laughed. "Well, there are a *few* gay designers."

"Anyway, I stuck with it, worked my way up, created my own line and House Etienne was born. Of course, I now stand in desperate need of a successful season. I'm confident I have one for spring. I only need my show to be well attended."

"I'm a novice at this whole *couture* thing, but I'd say you're well on your way to success in that quarter," she commented dryly. "Especially after the spectacle tonight. You know what they say, 'even bad publicity is good publicity.'"

"Yeah, well, that was unintentional, I assure you."

"Mmm, you better not be using me, Etienne," she said. "And now we come back to the mystery model."

His expression grew serious. He went to his stereo. After fiddling with the controls, a slow melody wafted from the speakers with a lusty female voice accompanying. Edith Piaf sang "*Non, je ne regrette rien*" (No, I regret nothing).

Surprised, Margot glanced at him. It was one of her favorite songs from the past. Her face grew warm remembering the nights she'd sat listening to the great songstress over glasses of wine as she contemplated her life.

He returned to her and held out a hand. His linen shirt, unbuttoned at the neck, showed an expanse of muscular chest. She stared at it until she realized she made a fool of herself and raised her eyes to his. He placed a forefinger on his lips. She hesitated then took his hand. He pulled her to her feet and into his embrace. His firm chest pressed against her breasts and her breath caught in her throat as a hot wave of passion swept through her.

"I love this song," he said, swaying back and forth in a movement more comforting than dance-like. He wrapped his arms around her waist and pulled her close.

She slowly laid her head against his chest almost afraid to move and lose this closeness with him. When he didn't pull away, she rested her arms across his broad shoulders. The contact soothed her after the disturbing events of the evening. His strong muscles beneath her cheek gave her confidence he could protect her from anything. He moved slowly, and the ache of the female voice enveloped her. She closed her eyes.

Part of Margot wanted to protest, force him to tell her what she needed to know. But his charm, his fleeting vulnerability and the feel of his body lulled her, so she settled for the comfort of his warmth.

The song ended and he gently pulled away. He turned down the volume, leaving the sound barely audible. When he faced her, his lips formed a firm line. "Margot, I truly did not mean to have you involved in this mess, but now that you are, I want to make sure you're not harmed in any way."

"What do you mean?" Shaken by the broken spell of intimacy, she ran her hands down her hips and sank to the couch. Disappointment cast a cold splash over her longing.

"The media. They're like vultures. They'll be relentless trying to find your identity. At least they don't know who you are." He glanced at her, brows narrowed. "Did you tell anyone there your name?"

"Well, just my first name. One of the other photographers introduced himself before the craziness started. He was the first one outside who tried to take my picture."

"*Merde*," Etienne exclaimed, putting a hand to his head. "Well, that's it then. They'll have discovered everything about you by morning, mark my words. They'll be camped outside your door and mine as well."

"You can't be serious."

"Have you forgotten what happened tonight? Of course I'm serious." He paced, head down.

"What am I going to do?" Shivering, she pulled the blanket around her shoulders, reality and loss of contact with him sunk in leaving her cold.

"You can't go to your apartment. Reporters will be there for sure. You'll have to stay here tonight. I'll go to the office in the morning and send a press release saying you're not the model and the resemblance is only coincidental – try to throw them off your trail."

"Will that work?" She didn't think they would give up that easily.

"I doubt it, but it's the only course I can think of at this point. Maybe something will occur to me tomorrow."

"But Etienne," she interrupted.

"Yes?"

"Is there really a reason I look like that model?"

He let out a long breath and stared at the ceiling, biting his bottom lip. Then he faced her and held out a hand. "Come on. I'll show you to the guest room. Get some sleep and we'll talk tomorrow."

She hesitated but recognized he wouldn't reveal more. After the mob scene at the restaurant, he was right about the media. Tomorrow was going to be horrible. She sighed and took his hand. Frustration made her want to lash out, but that wouldn't solve anything.

When they had danced she'd thought it could to lead to

more. This situation confounded her in the extreme. She hadn't imagined his body's response, melding to her however briefly. What the hell was going on with him? She'd love to have him make a move. Was he involved with the model? It seemed the only feasible explanation. A woman who bore a striking resemblance to her. Now there was a huge complication.

Chapter 26

Etienne lay in bed for hours, unable to sleep. He kept replaying the scenes of the night. Tension in his body came and went with images of Margot. First, the insanity when those people thought she was the model, then the time with her afterwards, especially the dance. Holding her like that had been a very bad idea. He'd been desperate to keep the subject of her resemblance to Jeanne at bay. He rolled to his side and pounded his pillow with his fist.

With a sigh, he realized he wanted more than just to comfort her. Was it because she looked like Jeanne, or was he developing feelings for Margo? Burning shafts of confusion and guilt tortured him. He couldn't betray Jeanne, but Margot was so much like her in personality as well as body, it was as if they were the same person. The thought drove him crazy.

At this point, he could only try to squash reports of Margot as his model. He'd tell Jeanne they had to leave Margot alone. It wasn't fair to disrupt her life, especially when she wasn't in on the secret of Jeanne's ghostly existence. What had started as an attempt to help had backfired badly. How had he ended up in such a mad situation? He loved a ghost he could never touch, yet developed feelings for her living relative. Complete madness. Somehow, he managed to collapse in sleep sometime after midnight.

The next morning, he left a note for Margot telling her to stay inside and make herself at home. He had to begin the process of sending press releases. He didn't mention it in his letter that he also wanted to learn what the media had concocted overnight.

Sure enough, a few early risers were stationed outside his apartment building. They shouted when he emerged and began taking his picture. He took this good opportunity for an impromptu press conference.

"No, Margot is not the model. She's a photographer who happens to have a striking resemblance, but it is most definitely not her. Please leave her alone since she has nothing whatsoever to do with my line, modeling, or *haute couture* in general. If you continue, you'll be harassing an innocent person." The taxi he had called arrived fortuitously, and he made his escape.

When he reached his office, Chloe waited with a newspaper clutched in one hand and an inquiring, but pissed-off look on her face.

"So what is this?" She pointed to the headline, "Mystery Model Revealed." Beneath was a photo of him with Margot on the sidewalk outside Alcazar Mezzanine. Margot was backed against him, her face a mask of fear, and his expression accurately conveyed the anger he'd felt at the time. "So there really was a model and you didn't tell me?"

He took the paper and shook his head. "No, Chloe. This is the photographer I hired yesterday after you left. She looks like the picture Gaston painted. I would never hire a model and not tell you. You're too important to me. Really, do you think I'd do such a thing?"

Her expression softened. "No, I wouldn't think that, but look at her. It's amazing, you have to admit." She pointed to the picture.

"I know. I made a mistake. I was so wrapped up in details yesterday I barely looked at her. She's a friend of Vivienne's who's doing her food photography, so she referred her to me. Honestly, I never thought about how she looked." It was true. He'd been too intent on the fact that she wasn't Jeanne. What a stupid mistake.

"So what are you going to do now?"

He headed for his office. "I'm going to send out a press release. I'll write it and fax it to the advertising agency. Let's hope the media believes it and everything calms."

"Okay. I'm sorry I jumped on you. Do you need me? I really should go work with the models."

"No, go ahead. I'll take care of it." He continued up the stairs.

Jeanne waited. She came to her feet when he arrived and came toward him. "What happened? I heard you talking to Chloe. Is something wrong with Margo?"

He opened the paper and laid it on his drawing board so she could see it.

"Oh, heavens. Father, George, come look at this." She

scanned the page, her mouth hanging open. "People think she is me."

"Yep. It was a mob scene. You wouldn't believe it. Someone actually tore her jacket before we could get in the limo." Etienne sat behind his desk and started writing a memo to send to the ad agency. Gazing at Jeanne today was hard. Had he betrayed her by merely thinking of his feelings for Margot?

"Poor Margot. That had to be traumatic. Is she all right?" George asked.

"Yes. She's still at my apartment. I made her stay last night because I knew they'd figure out who she is. They're outside her apartment right now, I'd bet."

"Such a tangle," Francois commented. "How do you propose to address this?"

"I'm sending a statement to the press to try and convince them the resemblance is merely a coincidence. I'm hoping they'll leave her alone then."

"What about the other events you have scheduled for the next two nights. Will they bother her again?" Jeanne moved beside his desk.

He finished his press release, went to the fax machine and sent it. He tried to think of the best way to talk to Jeanne about Margot. He sat in one of the chairs in front of his desk and motioned for her to take the other.

"Look, I've been thinking about this all night. I know you wanted to help Margot, but the situation is turned around now. It's not fair to disrupt her life like this. She doesn't know about you, but she's smart enough to suspect there's something to this uncanny resemblance. I think it would be better if she didn't do my photography anymore. I'm sorry."

If a soul could cry, by her look, Jeanne would've had tears in her sad eyes. His heart ached for her.

"I so wanted her to be at your show. I wanted us all there together, with her as my daughter," Jeanne said, wringing her hands.

"I'm sorry to disappoint you. It's not a good idea." He wanted to kick himself, but he couldn't be around Margot anymore.

"She still has to take pictures for Vivienne," George

interjected.

Jeanne's face brightened.

"That's before the show. None of the attendees or media will be there when she's taking pictures. So no one will see her. She can easily slip in and out," he replied. Then maybe he wouldn't have to interact with her.

"Surely there is some way she could see the show and the ball." Jeanne's wistful expression tugged at his heart.

"I have an idea," Francois said.

"Oh?" Jeanne turned eager eyes in his direction.

Etienne grimaced. *Dammit, leave it alone.*

"Well, it is a period dress ball. In my time, there were fabulous masquerades. Could we not disguise her in a costume so she cannot be recognized? A powdered wig to hide her hair and makeup. Maybe a face patch here and there?"

"Father! That is a fabulous idea. Etienne?"

He hesitated, but he didn't have the heart to dash her hopes. He sighed and nodded. "Okay, we'll have Vivienne tell her. We can say it's just in case someone sees her while she's photographing the food."

"Thank you so much. I was not able to help my daughter when I was alive, but now I can help Margot. You do not know what this means to me."

"I do. Really, I do. I hope it works out the way you wish." He smiled, glad to please her. He'd have to deal with his feelings and get over Margot. "With that out of the way, what about our other dilemma? What do we do about Elizabeth? Will it be safe for you at the show?"

She told him about their discussion while he'd been gone, and the plans they'd made for escape if Elizabeth should appear. Francois had schooled them on the general layout of Versailles and some possible routes of escape.

He shook his head. "I don't know. It sounds risky."

"I am going," Jeanne replied. "There is no way I am not going to see your show."

She left no room for discussion, so he raised his hands in surrender. "Okay, it's your decision. Now, I have to call Margot and let her know what's going on. She needs to stay with a friend for a few days until the excitement dies down." He crossed to his desk to use the phone.

Jeanne talked excitedly to the other ghosts about the upcoming show, her expression shining with excitement.

He called her cell phone. "Margot? It's Etienne."

"There are people outside your apartment. Reporters I think." She sounded breathless.

"I know. They were there when I left. Look, I talked to them and just faxed a statement for our ad agency to send to the media. Hang there for a while. I'm hoping they'll get tired and leave after a few hours. They have no way of knowing you're there."

"Then what? They're probably at my apartment, too."

"Count on it. Can you stay with someone? A friend perhaps? Only for a few days until this dies down?"

"Yes, I have a friend. I've already called her. I thought it might be a good idea after I saw the people outside. I can't believe this is happening."

"Good. I'll call you when I know more. As far as the photography goes these next two nights, you understand we should cancel."

She sighed. "Yes, I know. I'll be sorry to miss out, but I understand. It's okay. I still have the job with Vivienne."

"Right, and I have some ideas to make that safer for you. I'll have Vivienne call you on your cell, okay?" Relief that she recognized the hazard of continuing her job with him lifted a huge weight. But he experienced a pang of regret despite his best intentions in the matter.

"Okay, Etienne. I'll talk to you later."

"Good-bye, Margot." He hung up and glanced at Jeanne. She was so beautiful, especially when animated as now. Why couldn't she be alive?

"Is everything all right?" Jeanne asked, facing him.

"Yes. Margot's fine. She's going to stay at my apartment for a few hours then try to make her escape to a friend's place."

"She is still coming for Vivienne's photography, right?" she asked anxiously.

"Yes. She's looking forward to it. I'll have Vivienne call her as we discussed."

"Wonderful! Then it is planned. I cannot wait for Sunday

night," she exclaimed, pressing her hands to her cheeks.

He nodded, but inside, he had to tamp an anxiety that kept forming a knot in his stomach.

Chapter 27

Jeanne, George, and Francois took positions beside the crowded red carpet at the group entrance to the North Wing of the palace. She placed a hand over her mouth, in awe of the fabulously dressed attendees arriving for the show. What a beautiful vision, women in sweeping skirts and satins, glittering with jewels, men in dashing period attire.

Earlier, Etienne fetched them in a limo from his atelier and transported them to Versailles. Jeanne had floated around the palace while he oversaw final preparations. She'd memorized the escape routes and meeting places set up by Francois as the three ghosts wandered the secluded rooms of the palace, ignored by the souls there. Now she could enjoy the show and keep a lookout for Elizabeth.

"The carriages seem to be a hit," she said in a low voice to her father.

He beamed with a faraway glint in his eyes. "It reminds me of the last ball I attended here."

Flashes from cameras sparkled in the darkness, illuminating period costumes parading along the carpet. Everyone laughed, enjoying this departure from the typical *couture* show. Horse-drawn carriages added to the air of delight, and the night remained cool but clear.

After a few minutes, she floated inside the entrance where Gaston displayed his portrait of her. His Henry the Eighth costume was the perfect choice. She whispered in his ear, "You look very regal."

He grinned and executed a courtly bow with a sweep of one arm. "Milady. It is in your honor."

"The picture is wonderful."

"I'm getting a lot of comments. Especially people wanting to know who you are." He chuckled. "I'm having fun making up stories. My favorite is that you are a secret descendant of Marie Antoinette and will soon be asking to become Queen of France again."

She stifled a giggle behind one hand. "No one will believe that."

"Ex-actly."

George flew in from outside. "Come on, Jeanne. The four special guests are arriving wearing Etienne's costumes."

She waved to Gaston and followed her friend outside, eager to see how the women looked in their exclusive garments.

Chloe had arranged for the four divas of fashion, wearing Etienne's specially designed costumes, to appear together. Their carriage arrived to thunderous applause and wildly flashing cameras. Earlier in the afternoon, they had gathered for an exclusive photo shoot with "W" magazine, and they looked fantastic.

George and Francois stared. George declared he'd never seen such an event in his history. Francois spoke of glorious days before the revolution when Marie-Antoinette had held lavish parties in this same palace. He and Gabrielle had been alive then, carefree and in love. At times, his gaze seemed to stray to scenes of the past, although he continually glanced at Jeanne with such a loving gaze, her soul blossomed with contentment.

The divas left their carriage, waving to the onlookers, and led the throng inside. Attendants in red and gold livery guided them toward the Opera Room for Etienne's show. Jeanne weaved her way between the living, and paused at the threshold of the opulent room. Gold and marble box seats lined the walls. Above, a painting of people frolicking among clouds in a blue sky peered down at her. She stared open-mouthed at the lavish decorations from another era.

When she regained her composure, she went beyond the stage curtains to a hectic room where models hurried about in various stages of dress. George and her father followed close behind.

Etienne hand-sewed a loose strap on one of the dresses a model wore. Chloe, clipboard clamped under one arm, checked accessories and hair. Other workers from the House moved among the models, adjusting and tucking.

Paul, head of the London model agency, cracked jokes and spoke encouraging words as he circled through. This was the first major runway show for many of his models, and some appeared edgy, like young thoroughbreds at a first race.

"Etienne," Jeanne whispered.

"My love. How are you doing?" He sidled away from the model.

"Fine. It is really fun for us. We are only observing. How are you?" She looked around. "It seems crazy in here."

"Yeah." He glanced around. "Crazy is a good description. Actually, everything seems to be progressing as planned. I can't believe it, but I think we're going to pull this off."

"I knew you would. I have every confidence in you," she said. "Now we are going outside so we can find a good place to view the show."

"No sign of you-know-who?"

"Not so far." She raised a forefinger to her lips.

"That's good, but be careful." He waved and returned to his task of checking each garment before it headed for the catwalk.

"Let us find Vivienne," she said. Her living friends were fulfilling their dreams. Excitement bubbled in her chest forcing a constant smile. Lightheaded giddiness made her giggle from time to time for no apparent reason. The feeling reminded her of the memory she'd experienced visiting this place for the ball with Etienne of the past.

Vivienne scurried in the ground floor kitchen gallery, overseeing the production of her recipes. She wore a period costume of a cook with a gathered off-shoulder blouse, dark long skirt with a frilly, white, full-length apron. A tiara in her bright red spiked hair added a whimsical touch in harmony with Vivienne's personality. The pictures Margot had taken of her food were posted on the wall, and *sous* chefs glanced at them periodically as they duplicated the presentation in their makeshift kitchen.

"Vivienne," she said close to her ear.

The redhead jumped, but a broad grin spread across her face. "Jeanne," she said, softly. "I'm so glad you're here. What's happening outside? Is Gaston doing well? I hope people aren't pushing too much about the identity of the model."

"It is spectacular. Everyone loves the painting, and Gaston is more than a match for anyone too inquisitive, I assure you. Truly, people are laughing and having a great time. It is packed."

Jeanne replied. "We just visited Etienne, and he says everything is proceeding smoothly."

"That's great," Vivienne said with a sigh of relief. "The food is also going according to plan. As soon as the show is over, we'll have the buffet ready."

"I cannot wait to see your presentation of the food," Jeanne said. "I cannot taste, but my eyes can feast."

Vivienne took a deep breath. "I'm starting to relax now that most of the prep work is over. Soon, I'll know if the elite of the fashion world loves my cooking. Anticipation is eating at my gut like acid."

"I have friends with me tonight. George and my father, Francois. You cannot see them, but they are here," she whispered.

"Oh, how wonderful," Vivienne said in the direction of Jeanne's voice. "I'm so happy you two are here. Etienne told Gaston and me about your concerns with the other spirit. I feel better knowing you are with Jeanne and keeping an eye on her. In the meantime, I hope you have a wonderful time."

"Thank you, Vivienne, we will leave you to your work. We are going to watch the show. We shall hurry back as soon as the show is over so we can see Margot and your food before it is destroyed," Jeanne said. "Good luck."

"Thanks," the redhead whispered. "Have fun, all of you."

Jeanne left the kitchen area and returned to the Opera Room. Music began, and she moved to find a position with a good view. Gaston sat in the front row beside Claudette. Jeanne elected to stay with George and Francois further back where they had a clear view of the room and could detect Elizabeth's presence if she appeared.

A runway protruded into the middle of the room from the stage area bisecting the orchestra pit. Tall screens flanked the stage where photos of clothes from different eras flashed in time to upbeat jazz tunes. It perfectly set the tone for Etienne's merging of fashions from the past.

As the audience settled, sound and video ceased. The room plunged into total darkness. Then a single spotlight focused on the stage. An orchestra played Vivaldi, and models began sauntering along the runway as more lights circled their movements. The music perfectly accented Etienne's clothing.

The audience kept silent. As each outfit made its debut, excitement and anticipation became palpable. The final model exited the runway wearing the glorious billowy white wedding gown, and for a slight pause there was only silence. Applause erupted and the attendees came to their feet.

Etienne emerged from behind the curtains and strode halfway down the runway bowing left and right. He wore a dashing musketeer's outfit, which accentuated his height and muscular build to perfection. He beamed with success and happiness.

His gaze scanned the audience and found Jeanne. He blew her a kiss and waved. The models emerged and made a last turn around the runway then posed behind him as flashes of cameras went off like fireworks. He posed for several minutes, and with a last wave, went behind the curtains.

"Ladies and gentlemen, thank you so much for attending my show," Etienne's voice boomed over the sound system. "Please proceed to the Hall of Mirrors for a ball in your honor."

More applause erupted, and murmurs of conversation rose to a roar. Everyone milled around, slowly moving toward the exits. Museum attendants, hired by Etienne, guided them along the halls from the ground floor to the first floor. Excited chatter flew back and forth among the guests. The tone of their comments let Jeanne know the show had been an enormous success. Now, they moved from an electrifying show to a thrilling ball.

"We have to hurry to see Vivienne's food. Margot should be there by now," she said, and flew along in ghost mode, arriving in the banquet area in seconds. Anticipation bubbled inside her despite her wary lookout for Elizabeth.

201

Chapter 28

The arrangement of food took Jeanne's breath. Candles replaced modern lights and flickered everywhere. Large silver candelabra stands lit the perimeter.

In the center of the Salon of War, which flanked the Hall of Mirrors, an enormous layered construction offered the culinary delights in a fantasy setting. At first glance, it appeared to be one huge round table with center tiers that rose almost to the ceiling. Upon closer examination, she discovered separate elements. The center had a stepped tower of shelves which displayed a mountain of white flowers interlaced with tiny white lights. Platforms at different heights, covered in silver lame and white lace, thrust from the towering floral arrangement. Silver trays of food covered the platforms. Sprays of flowers and an eclectic mix of silver candle holders with white candles of different sizes and shapes interspersed among the platforms.

Aside from the spectacular setting, the food became the star. Beyond what they'd already seen were thinly sliced York ham on toasted brioche with a mango-avocado relish, garlic buttered escargot in individual puff pastries, and skewers of poached Brittany lobster flavored with a celery remoulade and shaved wild apple.

Vivienne had also prepared finger food desserts. Miniature Baba au rhum, tiny tarte au chocolat, lavender crème brulee in puff pastry, bite-sized crepes filled with almond crème and raspberry preserves, and finally, a simple slice of Saint Marcellin cheese topped with sour apple relish tempted the masses.

"It is like a dream," George said, awestruck. "I wish I could eat."

Jeanne and Francois nodded. She focused her gaze on absorbing the beauty of the scene, which was accented by gold on the walls and ceiling.

To one side, the redhead talked to Margot, elegant in her chevalier costume. She wore black velvet pantaloons, vest, and a jacket with a ruffled white linen shirt. A powdered wig covered her dark hair, topped by a black hat and feather. With her face powdered and a couple face patches, she became unrecognizable.

She moved gracefully in her period clothing as she took pictures of the completed masterpiece. Jeanne's heart swelled with pride. This beautiful, confident woman emerged like a phoenix rising from the flames of Jeanne's dark tragic past.

"Vivienne, this is spectacular," she whispered in the chef's ear.

The redhead excused herself from Margot and moved away to converse with Jeanne. "Do you really think so?"

"Yes, absolutely. It is not just food, it is art. George and Francois are nearly speechless, which is quite rare for them. You have created a stunning success. Tomorrow, Paris will be at your feet."

"Well, I think that's it." Margot approached and placed her camera in a bag she carried over one shoulder. "I can have proofs ready by Wednesday, if you like."

"Thank you so much," Vivienne said. "That would be wonderful."

"I'll wrap things up and head out then," Margot said as she zipped her camera bag.

"Tell her to stay," Jeanne whispered urgently, desperate to have a little more time with her despite Etienne's reluctance. "Tell her to stay for the ball at Etienne's request."

"Margot, we would really like you to stay if you can," the redhead said after a puzzled glance in the direction of her voice. "Um, Etienne regrets what happened and said to ask you to at least stay and enjoy the ball. No one will know who you are."

"That's so kind, but Etienne shouldn't feel that way. Really, I understand. I don't want to impose." She glanced at her suit and tugged the hem of her jacket.

"You're not imposing," Vivienne assured. "He made me promise to invite you to stay. No one will recognize you in that costume."

"If you think it would be okay." Margot wistfully glanced into the ballroom.

People filtered into the Hall of Mirrors, and the orchestra began a waltz, lilting music among the flash of jewels and swish of velvet and taffeta.

"Etienne is my friend, not just an employer. He wouldn't tell me that if he didn't mean it." Vivienne snatched two glasses of champagne from a passing waiter's tray and handed one to her. "I absolutely insist. You'll be my guest."

Margot took the flute and gazed at the gathering mass of glamorous people. "If you put it that way," she said and laughed. "Who can resist a ball?"

"Wonderful," the redhead exclaimed. "I'll stow your bag with mine. Have some food and drink champagne. I'll find Etienne."

Margot nodded and tipped her glass to her lips. She glanced at the guests, into her glass, and then went to the mountainous buffet.

"Vivienne, you are a genius," Jeanne said when her friend returned. Her gaze followed Margot as she moved around the display. "I so wanted her to stay and enjoy the ball with us. I may never see her again after tonight. You must find Etienne so he can talk to her. I regret their last meeting ended in drama. I want him to like her. She's part of me."

"If you're sure. Etienne will probably be angry. But I doubt anyone will recognize her." With a last look at her creation before the hordes consumed it, Vivienne heaved a contented sigh then headed through the now crowded ballroom.

George and Francois joined Jeanne, and she motioned to Margot by the buffet. "She is *your* relative, too," she pointed out to Francois.

"I cannot believe it. I have so many new relatives, I do not know what to do. She is a beauty, like you."

"*Very*, like you," George added. "No wonder the reporters thought she was the model."

"There is something oddly comforting about her looking like me," she replied, gazing at Margot. "Why do you suppose that is?"

"It makes us feel some good of us remains even after we are dead," her father said. "I remember Gabrielle. How much you resemble her. Now Margot carries on the legacy."

"Yes, I can see where that would be comforting," George commented, a bit sadly.

***

Etienne entered the ballroom in his rakish musketeer costume. Ahead of him, Vivienne made her way through the crowd. Beside her strode a jovial Gaston dressed as Henry VIII. Etienne's heart pounded at the thought of seeing Margot. At least Vivienne had warned him.

When he reached the beautiful photographer, Gaston took her hand and scanned her face before executing a gallant bow. "I'm very pleased to meet you, *monsieur*," he said with a wink. "I hope you are enjoying the festivities."

Etienne's lips opened and closed. She looked as sexy in men's clothing as she did in women's. He'd hoped his reaction to her would diminish over the past few days. Instead, it seemed to have increased.

Jeanne appeared at his side, smiling. "I knew you would be happy to see her again," she whispered. "Talk to her. I want to know how she is doing since the problem at the restaurant."

"Yes, um, *monsieur*. We are so pleased to have you here," he managed a shaky smile.

"Thank you. You are kind to be so welcoming. I didn't want to impose, but Vivienne insisted," Margot said, breathless. She kept her eyes downcast.

"I had hoped you would stay and enjoy the ball," he lied. "Are you doing okay?"

Her hand trembled where it grasped her champagne glass. "Yes, the paparazzi have disappeared, thankfully.

Out of the corner of his eye, he caught Jeanne watching. She whispered into Vivienne's ear.

"On the opposite end of the Hall of Mirrors is the Salon of Peace where tables and chairs are set up for the guests." Vivienne pointed. "You can talk there away from the noise."

"Don't go too far." Gaston cast a suspicious glance at Vivienne and Jeanne who made shooing motions to encourage Etienne away with Margot.

Etienne went a few steps then hesitated, glancing back at them.

"Oh, go on, Etienne. Tonight I must focus on my darling

kitchen wench, Vivienne. How about a dance, *cheri?*" Gaston turned to the redhead and bowed.

"Of course, my king. It would be a pleasure," she replied and curtsied. "Then I have to attend to the food supply."

They soon disappeared into a mass of dancing bodies. Jeanne took an invisible hand, probably Francois', which led her onto the floor.

Etienne sighed, accepting the inevitable, and escorted Margot through the mass of people in the hall, past shiny mirror panels and gold sculptured cherubs holding crystal candelabra. Friends greeted him and strangers stared at him smiling. But his gaze stayed on her. He gazed into her eyes, trying to come to terms with her remarkable resemblance to his beloved Jeanne. She lowered her gaze, fidgeting with her fake sword.

"Are you having a good time?" He reached the entrance to the Salon and gestured to a corner where a marble bench sat partially hidden by a couple of fake palms brought in for the occasion. Most of the crowd stayed in the Hall with only a few couples gathered at small linen covered tables scattered in the room.

"Yes. I've never experienced anything like this before." She smiled wryly. "This isn't the circle I move in."

"I'm glad you stayed," he said. "Maybe it will help make up for the trouble I caused you."

"Don't worry. In the end, it'll be good publicity for my business. I guess you helped me in a way. Although, I have to admit I was excited about working in the fashion world." She glanced at him then took his arm as they strolled to the bench. A shiver of pleasure shook him at her touch. "You've created a magical night, Etienne. It seems you have a success."

"Yes, thank God." He drew in a breath and lifted his face to the elaborate gilded ceiling. "I had a lot riding on this show. Fortunately, I had a tons of help."

She joined him on the cold stone seat.

"Thanks for being a good sport," he said. "Maybe after this season, we could have you work when the speculation has gone."

"Please, Etienne. You know you don't mean that." She removed her hand from his elbow and crossed her arms over her chest.

He looked at her, surprised. "Why do you say that?"

"I'm not stupid. I know there's something going on that you won't tell me. Even though you've been very charming, I can tell you're relieved we're not going to work together. I thought you would at least be honest."

He blinked. How accurately she had read him, but he couldn't explain about Jeanne or his developing feelings for her.

"Is she someone you love? This mystery woman?"

He laughed. "Margot, it is so much more complicated than you can possibly imagine. If you see relief on my face, it's because now you don't have to be tangled up in it. It's not that I don't want you around. I like being around you very much, but it wouldn't be best for you. Please trust me."

She stared at him then nodded. "Okay. I'll believe you just because I want to. I really don't want to think you're the type of person who would intentionally hurt someone." She stood, her face plastered with a forced cheery expression. "So, it was nice working with you, however briefly, and thanks for letting me enjoy the ball a few minutes." She held out a hand.

He hesitantly took it. "Please don't leave now because of me. Stay and enjoy the party at least."

She smiled and released his hand then headed toward the Hall. He wanted to call after her, but it would only prolong the inevitable. Instead, he remained sitting in the corner and tried to convince himself he'd done the right thing.

When he returned to the ballroom, he immediately delved into public relations and socializing with famous clients and the media. Margot avoided Etienne, but she spent time laughing and talking to Gaston and Vivienne. Jeanne remained with that group, although he caught her casting curious glances between him and Margot from time to time.

Except for worry over Elizabeth, which seemed to have been unfounded, the evening was a joyful climax to the stressful events of the previous month. He, Gaston and Vivienne achieved successes, which would take their careers in new directions. Claudette had her body, if not her face, plastered all over Paris. Chloe was ecstatic to belong to a House at the top of the fashion world.

Too soon, the magical evening came to a close. Horse-drawn carriages lined up at the palace entrance and transported tired but happily contented guests to their modern cars and reality.

Margot stayed until the end, appearing to have a great time with Vivienne and Gaston. Fortunately, no one had seen through her costume. Speculation about the mystery woman seemed to have subsided now that the show was over. Etienne hoped they could go about their lives and move beyond the drama of the past weeks.

***

Jeanne breathed a sigh of contentment. He'd done it. The night was a success. Etienne said goodbye to the last guests, and Gaston picked through the remains of food on what he called 'Vivienne's fantasy culinary mountain.' Vivienne and Margot laughed about some observations from the ball, while George and Francois spoke softly in a far corner.

"I guess I'd better call it a night. My car's in the Pl. de Léon Gambetta, so I can forgo the carriage ride," Margot said to the redhead. "Thanks for the lovely evening."

An eerie laugh echoed through Jeanne's head as though resounding from a loud speaker. She glanced about, fear coursing through her. It was the same laugh she'd heard at Gaston's. "She is here," she yelled, frantic. "It is Elizabeth!"

Francois and George hurried with her toward Etienne. Francois yelled, "Take her quickly in one of your motorized carriages. Run! George and I will try to keep Elizabeth from following."

A figure materialized in the ballroom - an old woman with gray hair, wild eyes and lips stretched in a horrible grin. "You won't get away from me this time," she shrieked. She swept forward, her glittering eyes focused on Jeanne.

Let's go," Etienne yelled. He called to Vivienne and Gaston, "Stay here." To Margot he said, "I need your help. You said your car is close?"

"Yes, but wha—"

Etienne grabbed her arm and pulled her along a tangle of side halls and through the doors to the group entrance.

Jeanne followed close behind, checking over her shoulder

in fear that nearly froze her. Shouts and more loud laughter chased her, urging her on.

"What's going on?" Margot yelled but kept running.

Etienne kept a hand on her elbow. "Just get us in your car and out of here as fast as you can."

They burst through the doors with attendants staring after them then headed left to the parking area. A beep sounded as Margot pushed something small in her hand. Etienne got in the passenger side, and Jeanne moved into a cramped back seat.

"Hurry," she yelled, "Hurry!"

Margot glanced into the back, her eyes popped wide. She started the car and jammed it into gear. Gravel sprayed as her tires spun before gripping the loose stones and plunging forward. The car fishtailed but soon straightened, and they sped away along the Rue de Reservoirs.

Jeanne looked back. Elizabeth emerged from the doors, followed by Francois and George. They crossed in front of the angry spirit. Jeanne screamed in horror.

"What?" Etienne glanced at her.

"She is behind us. She came out of the doors. Oh, God. Hurry!"

"Drive as fast as you can," he said to Margot.

She nodded, her face pale in the moonlight. The car went faster. They raced along the road running beside Versailles.

"Here. Turn on Rue Carnot." Etienne pointed to the right.

"My God, she is getting closer!" Jeanne put her hands to her cheeks.

Francois and George fought to fly in front of Elizabeth as they had planned. It helped. The frustrated spirit wailed like a banshee as they succeeded in slowing her. She vanished.

"Thank goodness." Jeanne collapsed.

"What happened?" Etienne exclaimed.

"She's gone." She checked to make sure.

Francois waved for them to continue.

"What now?" Etienne asked.

"Keep going." She breathed a sigh of relief. "Just keep going."

Chapter 29

"Where to?" Margot asked as they reached the main road and she accelerated, heading for Paris.

"The atelier," said a female voice from the backseat. "Francois and George will know to find us there."

In a determined voice, Margot asked Etienne, "You want to tell me who's talking? And what the hell just happened?" She glanced in her rearview mirror. Neither the night nor the backseat offered answers.

He took a big breath and let it out. "Just get us to my office. I swear I'll tell you everything then. Everything."

She glanced at him, his face drawn and pale, then shook her head and turned her attention to the road. They continued to Paris in silence.

He led her up the spiral stairs to his office. She glanced around his darkened workroom, expecting something to jump from the shadows. Nobody said a word.

She settled on a chair, her legs shaking. He pulled his laptop to the front of his desk and took the chair beside her. He typed as he talked. "Remember the face of the model?"

"Yes."

"I told you those features came from a painting by Gaston. That's true. Gaston painted several versions, and I digitally placed the face onto photos of my fitting model's body. You saw her tonight. Her name is Claudette."

"I met her. Gaston introduced us."

"The part that you don't know is how Gaston came to paint that face." He finished typing, clicked on a picture and turned the screen her way. It showed a painting of a young woman, by Vigee Le Brun. She wore a flowing white dress with a red shawl and carried a basket of flowers on her head.

She stared at the picture and read the caption. Confused, she glanced at Etienne. Certainly it was the same face. But that could not account for the lifelike quality of those paintings.

"That's Jeanne." Etienne pointed to the computer screen. "This is the face of my model."

"Gaston copied a painting?"

"No. Jeanne is here with us. She was in the backseat of your car. She's a spirit."

She raked agitated fingers through her hair. There was no denying that something odd was going on, but she wasn't quite ready to believe in ghosts.

"Jeanne?" He twisted around and held out a hand. "Come tell Margot about yourself. It's time."

She swallowed and glanced around the room. Nothing moved.

"Etienne is telling you the truth," a voice sounded to her right.

She startled then shrank in her chair. Goosebumps rose on her arms.

"We met by chance. It is a rare case where a living person can see a soul, but Etienne can see me and so can Gaston. There is something else important for you to know. You are my great granddaughter, five generations down."

She froze, staring at Etienne. He nodded, and Jeanne began the long story of how they met, how they'd worked together to pull him from ruin, and how she'd recovered much of her memory including the sad pain of her past. At the part where Elizabeth attacked, a sound below interrupted.

He headed for the stairs. "I hope it's the rest of the gang arriving."

Margot stood and paced, trying to come to terms with this fantastical story. It was unbelievable, yet no other explanation accounted for what had happened. She now understood Etienne's reluctance to tell her before. She would've thought he made a fool of her.

"Margot?"

"Yes?" She turned toward the voice.

"I want you to know that I was so happy to find you. I am so proud of you and what you have made of your life. It has made up for so much of my past and the mistakes I made."

She smiled slightly and slumped into her chair. "Thank you. That's very nice to hear. I wish I had known more about my ancestors after what you've told me. What a rich history is behind me and I never knew. Although I must say, I'm glad I'm not really related to the crazy woman who came after us tonight."

Jeanne laughed. "Yes, I must say I was happy to learn that as well. She was not always like that. When I was a child, she was a loving and devoted mother. Only in later years did her madness and paranoia develop."

She sat back in the chair. Slowly, the trembling in her hands and legs calmed, and the shocking tension of their escape eased.

***

"Jeanne, are you all right?" Francois and George emerged from the stairs and hurried to her side, their expressions grim.

"Yes, I am fine. Are you two unharmed?" She hugged them both, relief flowing through her.

"We are safe." Francois shook his head. "But I was worried. Elizabeth seemed determined to reach you. What madness!"

"What an adventure," George exclaimed. "I never thought to see anything like it."

Margot shrank in her chair, her eyes darting.

Jeanne urged Francois forward. "Margot, this is my father, Francois, and my friend, George. They helped save me tonight."

"Um, nice to meet you," Margot said slowly, uncoiling from her pose of fright. "Sorry I can't see you."

"My dear, it is such a pleasure to converse with you." Francoise bowed. "As I am sure Jeanne has told you, we are very proud to acknowledge you as family."

Margot smiled. "Why, thank you."

"I am very pleased to meet you also," George added. "I hope you were not hurt during your escape. I must say, that was excellent driving on your part."

"Thanks." Margot gave a nervous laugh. "I'm starting to think ghosts are pretty cool once you get past the initial shock of disembodied voices. At least you three are."

"Jeanne, you're okay." Gaston stormed in, followed by Vivienne whose eyes shone large in her pale face. Etienne came in and sagged with a weary smile.

"Gaston, Vivienne, are you both all right?" she asked.

"Yes, yes, we're fine. But we were so worried about you," Vivienne exclaimed. "What a horrible fright. I couldn't see her, but if she looked like she sounded, she must have been terrifying."

They spent the next hour recounting experiences, exclaiming over the ordeal they had survived, and bringing Margot up-to-date on their unusual friendships. She instantly became part of the group, although she retained a slightly dazed expression.

In the early morning hours, Gaston and Vivienne headed home. They said good-byes and waved as they left.

"What are we going to do about you?" Etienne leaned toward Jeanne.

"What do you mean?" she asked.

"How do we know Elizabeth won't find you here?"

"We cannot know what knowledge souls have in Everlasting," Francois said. "Certainly they retain some memory of their past and recognize the souls they knew. How extensive is their knowledge of the living world? It is unclear. From my experience with the two souls who came to warn me, I had the impression that they only kept knowledge of the past. That is why, when I went away from the Louvre, I went someplace unfamiliar to me in my living existence."

"So, Elizabeth may try to find Jeanne in places she either knows were linked to Jeanne in the past, or somewhere she has followed her to in the present," George deduced.

"Then there's a chance she knows of this place," Etienne said.

"There is a chance, I suppose," Francois mused.

"We need to take you somewhere you've never been." Etienne rubbed his chin. "Unless you know of a sure way to stop Elizabeth."

"The only thing that will deter Elizabeth is if Jeanne's soul is no longer here. Otherwise, in her mad obsession, I believe she is going to keep trying," Francois answered.

She went to Etienne's side, unease settling over her. "I am afraid. I do not want her to take my soul now that I have such happiness."

"I know, Jeanne. I know," Etienne said softly. "I'm trying

to think of a good place for you to hide."

"She could stay at my place," Margot said.

Jeanne's heart leapt. Was this a sign Margot wanted to know her better? Joy warmed her through and through. "That is very kind. But I am not sure you should be involved in this. I do not want anything bad to happen to you. We have already caused a great deal of disruption in your life."

"Look, you've never been to my townhouse. It's somewhere you can stay for a while until Etienne and your friends come up with another plan," Margot said decisively. "Besides, you're my family. In a very weird way, of course, but still family. I want to help."

"She's got a point," Etienne said.

She glanced at George and her father. They both nodded.

Relenting, Jeanne said, "Very well. If you are certain you want to do this."

Margot nodded. "I'll go get my car. We'll take a wild ride through the city for good measure then head for my home. How does that sound?"

"That is a good plan, my dear," Francois said. "Thank you for this generosity. I want you both to be safe."

"We will follow you outside, and keep a lookout until you are gone," George said.

Jeanne shared a glance of uncertainty with Etienne, but she followed George down the spiral stairs with Francois close behind.

***

Etienne trailed further behind, his thoughts racing. Having Margot involved left him uneasy, but he couldn't argue with her logic. Jeanne would be safest with her for now. A sense of *déjà vu* enveloped him, but how could he have experienced something like this before? He dismissed the feeling and followed.

Outside, haze settled in the pre-dawn hours. Coolness of the night met the warming kiss of coming sun. Margot pulled her car to the curb, and Jeanne floated into the passenger seat. Jeanne blew him a kiss, but her eyes remained sad.

Etienne walked to the driver's side, and Margot rolled down her window. He put his hands on the top of the door and leaned down. "Be careful, both of you. Call me and let me know you made it safely, okay?"

"I will," Margot said. Her green eyes clouded with worry. She glanced behind then put the car in first gear.

He stood away, and she sped into the early morning gloom. He stared after them for several minutes. What if they couldn't find a way to stop Elizabeth? How could they save Jeanne? And now he worried Margot took a risk. His stomach churned. The two women, so much alike, stirred his protective instinct.

"Etienne," Francois' voice said beside him. "George and I are returning to The Louvre. We know the way."

"Okay." He nodded. "Do you think there's any way to prevent Elizabeth from taking Jeanne?"

"Unfortunately, no. I believe she is safe for the time being, and we have some time to investigate further. May we return tomorrow to check on Jeanne's situation?"

"Of course. You're welcome here any time."

"Excellent. If we discover anything new, we will share it with you immediately."

"Good. I hope you can come up with something."

"Very well. Until tomorrow."

Etienne pulled out his cell to call a taxi. Exhaustion sapped his strength. He wanted to go home and crawl in the bed. Tomorrow he would try to make sense of this chaos.

Chapter 30

Margot weaved her Mini Cooper around the streets of Paris at a fast pace for thirty minutes until satisfied nothing followed. She called Etienne when they arrived at her apartment. Although he expressed thankfulness for their safety, he sounded anxious to end their conversation.

After showing Jeanne around her place, she left her in the living room with family photos, and headed for bed.

Drained emotionally and physically, she fell into her bed with a huge sigh as the cool sheets enveloped her. She rubbed her burning eyelids and yawned. A lingering sense of disbelief made her think morning might reveal that this night had been a dream. Ghosts, evil spirits, relatives from beyond the grave; it was a tad much. Fortunately, her busy mind did not overcome her exhaustion, and she fell into a deep, dreamless sleep.

When she awakened, the sun rode high and the haze of earlier had burned away. She rubbed her eyes and squinted at bright light peeking through her blinds. She pulled on a pair of leggings and a T-shirt then groggily made her way into the kitchen.

"Jeanne?" she called as she prepared coffee. "Where are you?"

"I am here, Margot." Jeanne's voice sounded near the couch. "I have been looking at your photos. You have a lovely family."

"Thanks. I guess they're your family too, actually."

The ghost laughed. "You are right. On your mother's side anyway."

She fiddled in the kitchen until the coffee brewed. She poured a cup and walked into the living room. "Seems we made it through the night without any visitors."

"Yes, thank God. I must tell you again how much I appreciate you letting me stay here."

She sat in the armchair and sipped her coffee. "Well, I have to admit, I have an ulterior motive."

"You do?"

"Yes, it's not every day a person is able to converse with a dead relative. I'd love to hear more about your life and the history of our family. After some of the stories from last night, I'm curious about what occurred. You know, you were in the middle of a fascinating time in history."

"True," Jeanne admitted. "It did not seem that way then, but I can see your point now, looking back on it."

"So, fill me in. I want to know everything." She pulled her feet under her and settled into her chair. The ghost fascinated her. Even though she couldn't see her, a connection existed. Perhaps it was the family connection. If she closed her eyes, she didn't have an eerie sensation.

They spent several hours talking. Jeanne recounted tales of her life, and added what she'd learned from Francois and Vivienne's computer.

"Do you think your Etienne from the past is somehow reincarnated to the current Etienne?" Margot asked.

"I do not know. Vivienne asked me the same thing. I told her it did not really matter to me. What is done is done. I do not want to stir that memory any more. I am content to live in the present."

"But, you, ah, you love him, right?" She glanced at her coffee cup.

"Margot?"

"Yes?" She looked up.

"You love him, too, do you not?" Jeanne's voice held a note of curiosity.

She turned away, hot from embarrassment. Was her interest that transparent?

"It is okay. I understand," the ghost said softly. "How could I, who loves him so dearly, not acknowledge his appeal?"

"I'm sorry. I didn't know about any of this when I met him. It's clear he loves you, so don't worry. I'm not trying to butt in or anything," she replied.

"Perhaps it would be better if you did," Jeanne said, a hint of bitterness in her voice..

"Why?" she asked sharply, clutching her cup.

"I feel such love for him that I must recognize how hopeless it is for him to be in love with a spirit."

217

"But he so obviously adores you," Margot protested.

"Ah, but to know what it feels like to have the tender touch of a lover, to hold him and kiss him. I am depriving Etienne of these things. He can never experience them with me. I am beginning to think you came into our lives for a purpose. Maybe Etienne is meant to be with you. If I fade, it would be a comfort to know you are there for him."

She couldn't speak. Jeanne spoke the truth, but Margot couldn't step in and try to take Etienne from her. She couldn't consider something so unthinkable.

"I can't make someone love me," she finally said. "He loves you."

The room tell silent. She finished her coffee and went to her office to check e-mail and return calls. This was the first day she didn't have a message from a reporter asking about the mystery model. Maybe that story was dead after last night's show. She smiled.

She kept picturing Etienne's face. She shook her head, determined not to explore those thoughts. How easily she could fall for him. But she wouldn't do anything to hurt Jeanne.

As a distraction, she searched for information about her new relatives on the Internet. She also looked up Vigee Le Brun and read her history. What an amazing and prolific painter she'd been. There was a site listing her paintings, and she scrolled through, impressed by the number. She studied the beauty of her works, marveling at her tremendous talent, and yet baffled by the crazy attempt on Jeanne last night. As with many artists, she supposed there was a fine line between genius and madness.

With her business duties complete, she returned to the kitchen and made a sandwich. She called to Jeanne, "You know you're a great houseguest. You don't eat, drink or mess up the place."

The ghost's laugh floated back from the living room. The she asked, "Have you heard from Etienne?"

"No. I should call him. Do you think it's possible he or your friends can think of a way to defeat Elizabeth? I mean, is there a way to get rid of an unwanted spirit? Obviously, we can't kill her. She's already dead."

Jeanne's voice sounded sad. "Francois was right. She will

only be deterred when my soul is no longer here."

"What does that mean? Where could your soul go?"

"If I faded to Everlasting, she would not be able to carry out her plan."

"You told me fading only happens when your time is right. You can't control it."

"Exactly. When a soul fades, we fade. It is our time to go."

"And there aren't any other, oh I don't know, dimensions or something you can go to as a soul?"

"Not that I know of, no. Wait. Once, Francois warned me about walking through the living. He said that if I stayed joined too long, I would become stuck."

"Now that's interesting, but can it help us? How does something like that work?"

"He did not know for sure, only that I would go into the living person and not be able to come out. Perhaps I would go nowhere, or maybe one of those *dimensions* like you said. Other than that, I do not know."

"Is that like stories of possession? Is that true?"

"Francois said possession is caused when a soul talks into the ear of the living in a soul voice to induce a suggestion. If it is an evil deed, that is possession. No one knows what happens after a soul is stuck."

"Hmm, that's interesting." There had to be some way to keep Elizabeth from stealing Jeanne's soul. She deserved better.

Learning of Jeanne's past life horrified Margot. Poor soul, stuck in a bad situation. She didn't want to fade and be with the spirits of her past, but if she stayed with the living people she loved, Elizabeth could steal her soul and damn her to eternal madness. "There's no solution."

"You are right. I fear I am doomed to unhappiness," Jeanne replied, her voice breaking.

She shook her head. She wanted to help the ghost. Even the short time they had spent together had convinced her of Jeanne's character. She was smart, witty and compassionate. A person she would love to have as a living friend, and certainly a relative of whom to be proud. She retrieved her cell to phone Etienne for news, but it rang in her hand.

"Can you bring Jeanne to The Louvre?" Etienne asked.

"Ah, yes, but isn't that supposed to be dangerous for her?" Confusion stalled her.

"I agree, but George came to me, very upset. It's something to do with her father. He says Jeanne needs to come right away." Etienne's voice held an edge.

"Okay, I'll bring her by there. We'll take a taxi so we don't have to park. That will be faster."

"I'm coming too. George said to tell Jeanne they're in the *Galerie d'Apollon*. I'll meet you there."

She relayed the information to Jeanne.

"Of course, we must go at once," Jeanne said, her voice cracking. "George would not ask me to come unless it was an emergency. Something must be dreadfully wrong."

She pulled on a pair of jeans, grabbed a jacket and her purse and headed out to find a taxi.

Chapter 31

Margot urged Jeanne ahead as she entered a short line at the museum entrance. Jeanne hurried through the halls to the *Galerie d'Apollon*. When she entered the gallery, George stood to one side, watching Francois wander among glass cases inspecting their contents.

Her friend gave her a look of relieved welcome and gestured with his head toward the older soul.

"Father?" She went closer. "Are you okay?"

He continued his perusal.

"Francois? Father?" She moved in front of him to force his notice.

"Ah, Jeanne, dear. There you are. How are you, my darling?" His eyes appeared unfocused and vague.

A flush of alarm spread through her. He spoke in barely a whisper, and looked pale and tired. Could a ghost become sick? She glanced at George who sadly shook his head.

"Father, listen to me. You look terrible. What is amiss?" Fear shivered through her like a icy snake.

He stared into the distance but turned slightly her way. "Jeanne, nothing is wrong. Everything is right. It is just my time. I feel it. My time has finally come. I am sorry I cannot stay and look after you, but George will be here to help you." He looked off again and wandered to another case, a slight smile curved his lips.

She glanced at George, dismay filled her soul like a dark cloud. "He is fading," she exclaimed. "My God, no. I do not want to lose him. I cannot. What are we going to do?" She wrung her hands, frantic.

"Do? Why, we can do nothing, Jeanne. If it is his time, he will go."

"But I just discovered him as my father. We were so happy." She broke down in despair, staring at the dear figure as he became even more transparent, like a spirit glimpsed through a cloud. A black hole formed in the pit of her soul at thought of living without him.

"Jeanne, listen to me." George took her arm and turned her to face him. "He is not like you. He wants to go so he can be with Gabrielle. He will be at peace in Everlasting."

"No, no, no," she said, pushing his hand away. Somehow she had to stop it. It wasn't fair to lose him so soon. She needed his wise support, and most of all she needed his love. He was her father in all the ways she'd ever wanted. With him gone, her heart would break. It also meant her time was probably near as well.

"Jeanne, you must not be upset. You know it is what he has wanted for a long time. What is wrong with you?" George took her shoulders and gave her a shake. "Do you not want what is best for him?"

She gripped her hair in either side of her head in dismay. Couldn't her love keep him here? Wasn't that enough? It was selfish, she knew. But it wasn't only about losing him. "It's like I'm reliving my past. I can't stand the wretchedness."

"He wants to be with Gabrielle. You must not grieve. He'd want you to be happy."

"Happy?" She clutched her chest where despair crushed her in its heavy cold grasp. "I can't be happy for this. George, think about it," she cried. "He is fading because he is finally fulfilled. He found his daughter and had a happy time with her. He knows the truth now. Gabrielle had his child and saved her from the revolution."

"So, what is wrong with that? He was hoping for a resolution of the past." George reasoned, his brows coming together.

"What is wrong? I shall tell you. It means I could fade, too. I have found my true father and mother. I helped Etienne. I saw the daughter of my descendants. I am happy. What if it is my time to fade now? I do not want to fade and be with the people I was with while alive. I want to be here with this Etienne, and Gaston and Vivienne." She put her hands over her face, terrified. "It is too much to lose. It's too much."

George shook his head.

"Francois," she cried and ran to his side. She tried to take his hand, but he smiled fondly at her and wandered away. She clutched her cold fingers in fists, filled with hopelessness.

Margot and Etienne arrived, and she gave them a glance

but turned to her father. George whispered in Etienne's ear.

"What's happening?" Margot asked Etienne.

"It's Francois. He's fading," he replied curtly. He gazed at Jeanne. "I don't like her being here. It's too dangerous."

"I will protect her," George said with a firmness that reached his eyes.

Jeanne turned her back to them and followed her father. Her shoulders slumped and a strange blank numbness overcame her grief. There was nothing she could do. He would be gone soon.

She followed, fighting the soul-wracking anguish. Helpless and hopeless. His filmy figure wavered and she clapped a hand over her mouth in horror. No. No. Please.

George came close. Their procession became a ghostly wake as her father floated through the passages of his beloved Louvre, gazing at beautiful works of art one last time. Etienne followed with Margot, both silent. Francois' image grew more and more transparent. He floated into the Salle Napoleon, and scanned the room where he had counseled so many souls. He rotated and gazed in their direction, a wistful smile curving his lips, and then disappeared.

She stifled a cry with her hand and crushed her head to George's shoulder. He wrapped his arms around her as they shared their sorrow. George's mentor and her father, gone forever. A gaping hole remained in her heart with his passing.

She closed her eyes and tried to compose her agitation. "Thank you for being with me."

"Francois is content now," he said, stroking her shoulder. "We should be happy for him."

She nodded, aching with sadness. "You are right. I have to try to be happy for him. But I am scared, George. I do not want to fade. What will I do if it starts with me?"

"I do not think there is anything you can do," he replied. "But you should not stay here in The Louvre. I only called because I knew you would want to see your father before he went. You should go back to Margot's apartment now."

"Thank you, George. Thank you so much." She joined Etienne where he stood with Margot. Her arms hung limp at her sides and her knees trembled.

"I'm sorry," Etienne said softly.

"I'm so sorry, Jeanne. I know you'll miss him," Margot consoled.

"Yes, he will be greatly missed," she agreed, lowering her head. She allowed them to usher her to a taxi. She endured the ride to Margot's in silence, the shock of his passing left her empty.

Once inside her apartment, Margot offered her sympathy. "Francois seemed like such a gentleman."

"He is, or was. He helped so many. His fading confirms what we thought. Once resolution of the past is achieved, fading takes place."

"Do you think *you* have resolution?" Etienne asked.

"I do not know, though a lot has been revealed in the last few weeks," she replied.

"But you don't want to fade."

"No, I do not. I want to stay here with you. I was never happy before. Now I am and I do not want that to change. Why should I have to spend eternity with Bernard, Elizabeth and the Etienne who failed me? It is a prison sentence, not a content eternity."

"I don't want you to fade either," he said.

"There is nothing you can do to stop it," she said, sadness darkening her thoughts. Her heart broke in a million shards that stabbed her inside. "Souls have no choice in the matter."

He turned to Margot who stared at him with compassion.

"I have to go," he said after a second, looking at the floor.

"Why?" Jeanne asked, as a chill swept over her. "Can you not stay with me?"

"No, I can't deal with this right now. I don't know how to help you. I don't know what to do," he replied. His eyes met hers and anguish shone in his gaze. Then he strode out the door.

She and Margot stared after him.

"What happened?" she whispered, confusion and hurt swirling within her. "Why did he leave?"

Margot sighed. "I need to explain about men. You see, they need to fix problems. If they can't, they feel like failures. Etienne wants to help you but doesn't know how. He can't face feeling like a failure, so he ran away."

"How do you know this?"

"I read about it in a book about men and women and how

we're different."

None of this made sense. Bernard had left her. Her uncle had left her. Today, her father had left her. Abandonment made her entire body ache. "Am I only a problem that cannot be fixed?" Her voice caught on a sob.

"Of course not. He'll come back eventually. He has to go to his man-cave and think about it for a while and then he'll feel better."

"His cave? He is going to a cave?" Her head began to ache.

"Not a real cave. It's figurative. He needs to go somewhere he can be alone and think things through." Margot pointed a finger to her head.

She'd come to depend on Etienne. With Francois gone, she'd lost an important source of information and guidance. She couldn't lose Etienne, too. She settled on the couch. The pain of missing her father almost crushed her.

"Give Etienne some time. He loves you. He'll be back." Margot offered a kind smile then went to the kitchen. A few minutes later, she returned with a plate of left-over roast chicken and a glass of white wine. She returned to her seat.

"Jeanne?"

"Yes?"

"Good. I didn't want to sit on you." Margot sank into the big arm chair. "Are you okay?"

"Just sad," she replied. "I mean, I am happy for my father because it is what he wanted, but his loss is great. Not only to me but to the souls who relied on his advice and counsel."

Margot chewed for a while then put her plate aside. "I just had an idea." She sat forward in her chair, excitement shining in her eyes.

"Tell me."

"You told me that you and Etienne visited a medium named Madame Renee. That's where you met your real mother."

"Yes, that is right."

"Well, it seems to me that she has a lot of experience in matters relating to the afterlife. Maybe we should pay her a visit and seek her advice." Her fingers gripped the arms of her chair as she slid forward.

"That is a wonderful idea. When can we go?"

"I suppose I should call her and make an appointment." Margot took her cell phone and performed a search. "Here it is. She's listed under psychics." She grabbed a pen and pad of paper from a side table and wrote the number and address.

"You must tell her it is for me. She wants to help souls."

Margot connected to the number on her cell phone and left a message along with her number. She hung up, lips pressed in a straight line. "I was hoping she'd answer. I really feel like she can help us."

"You may be right. Surely she has gleaned experience and knowledge dealing with souls over the years. I am so glad you thought about calling her."

Five minutes later, Madam Renee returned the call. Margot grinned and gave Jeanne a thumbs-up then hit END. "She'll see you right away. We're to come over at once."

Elation, mixed with hope, burned inside her. Margot grabbed her purse and they headed out the door. Maybe this was the break Jeanne needed.

Chapter 32

Margot handed the taxi driver his fare then climbed the steps of Madame Renee's house. The door opened before she reached it, and the psychic motioned her in. Wrinkles of worry marred her forehead. She wore a flowing caftan in shades of yellow, orange and green. Her hair tangled in a clip on top of her head that left strands hanging at odd angles and lengths.

"Come in, Jeanne. And you are Margot?" Madam Renee looked at her after giving the air beside Margot a quick, worried inspection.

"Yes, and thank you for seeing us so quickly. Jeanne has told me about her previous visit to you, and we thought you might be able to help us."

"I'm happy to assist any soul in need, if I can. What you told me on the phone sounds very disturbing."

"Madam Renee, your kindness is much appreciated," Jeanne added as they followed the psychic to a draped room with table and crystal ball.

"Please, have a seat." The medium closed curtains across the door and motioned to chairs. She settled in one across from them and folded her hands together on top of the table. "Now, tell me how I can help. You said something on the phone about an angry spirit?"

Jeanne said, "Yes, it is the woman I thought was my mother until Etienne and I came to see you. She comes back from Everlasting, searching for me. We believe she seeks to take my soul before its time. I am very afraid."

The older woman's lips drew a grim line and her brow lowered. She did not answer immediately.

"We hope you might know some way to stop her," Margot added.

"Unfortunately, I do not." Madam Renee shook her head. "The evil of such souls has its roots in insanity. There is no reasoning with that. There are souls who haunt the living because they are angry, afraid or unresolved, but there are ways to reach them and help ease their struggles. But this is another matter entirely."

"So calling to Elizabeth and trying to convince her to stop won't work," she said, disappointment sapping the small burst of energy created by her idea of visiting the psychic.

"I would never try to reach a spirit of that type. When I connect with a spirit, I share a level of consciousness for a brief time. I would never invite unpredictable danger to attempt contact with a mentally deranged soul," the older woman stated, clenching her hands on the table.

She frowned, deflated. She'd hoped for a way to contact Elizabeth and convince her to cease her quest to steal Jeanne's soul, but she understood Madam Renee's reluctance. She imagined it compared to trying to convince a serial killer not to take his next victim. She brainstormed for another option.

"Perhaps you will fade before she can accomplish her plan," Madam Renee suggested to Jeanne.

"That fate would only be the lesser of two evils, I am afraid. I cannot imagine happiness with the souls of my past now that I have experienced so much happiness in the present with Etienne and his friends."

"You're certain you can find no peace in your past, my dear?" the medium asked gently, stretching a hand across the table toward an empty chair.

"I am certain I allowed myself to be a victim then. Now I have recognized that I have talents and can have loving, positive relationships. I do not want to go back to being the old Jeanne. Watching my father fade made that fate real."

"I have another question," Margot interrupted as an idea struck her. "What do you know about when a soul melds with a living person? What happens?"

Madam Renee's eyebrows arched. "Why do you ask?"

"It's something Francois told Jeanne, but he didn't know what happened to the soul. Would the soul still exist? Would an evil spirit be able to steal the soul if it had melded with a living person?"

"Well, of course the evil spirit could no longer steal the soul since the soul would no longer be a free-form spirit. But what happens to the soul? I can't say for sure. I've heard of it happening

228

with no apparent harm to the living, but other than that, I have limited experience in the matter."

She let out a big breath. The medium's knowledge brought them no closer to a clear solution. "Okay, well, thank you very much for seeing us and sharing what you know."

"I'm afraid I wasn't much help," the other woman said as she rose from her chair, her brow furrowed.

"At least we have more information to consider," Jeanne replied. "Thank you, Madam Renee."

"As always, I'm happy to help a soul in any way that I can. If you think of any more questions, feel free to call me," she directed to Margot.

"We will, thanks." She smiled and shook the medium's hand. Then she and Jeanne left.

***

When Jeanne returned to Margot's apartment, Etienne paced the sidewalk before the building. His face lit up when she arrived.

"I'm so sorry," he said as he rushed to her, contrition and worry splashed across his features. "That was stupid to leave you like that. Where have you been? I've been calling Margot's cell."

"Sorry," Margot said. "I turned it off when we went in to see Madam Renee."

"I am glad you came back," Jeanne said, a glow of love warming her.

"Madam Renee?" He took a step back.

"Let's go inside and we'll tell you what happened." Margot headed for her door.

"Jeanne, do you forgive me?" he asked.

She smiled. "Of course I do. I know this is an incredibly difficult situation for you. I appreciate your sticking with me despite my problems."

"Jeanne, I love you," he said. "Of course I'm going to stick with you. And I'm not going to run away again."

Her soul swelled with the feeling of love she sensed emanating from him. She was so blessed to have this relationship. But she had guilt too. Ever since she'd suspected Margot had feelings for him as well, she couldn't help considering that Etienne should love a living person. She was selfish but incapable of unraveling the complication of their bond.

They went inside, and Margot sank into the arm chair. Her head fell back and her eyes closed.

"Why did you go to the psychic?" Etienne asked as he settled on the couch beside Jeanne.

"It was Margot's idea, and a good one. I had not thought of enlisting Madam Renee's aid. Given her experience with spirits, it made sense to see if she knew something that could help us."

"Was she able to help?"

Margot raised her head. "She confirmed what we knew but offered no new solution."

He looked down. "That's too bad."

"Do not worry, Etienne. I will be safe here with Margot. Let us talk about something else. I have had enough sadness today. Tell us about the results of your show."

He brightened. "I'm pleased with the deluge of orders and inquiries about when a *prêt-a-porter* line will be available. On top of that, I have an interview with *Vogue* set for tomorrow morning and *Elle* in the afternoon. Seems like House Etienne has returned from the dead."

"That's wonderful, Etienne. I am sure Chloe is ecstatic. Are you really ready to start working on a ready-to-wear line?" Jeanne smiled.

"Chloe being ecstatic is an understatement. I never knew a person could talk on so many phones at the same time. I think ready-to-wear will have to wait. We're too busy right now. Gaston called me a while ago. He has an offer for an exclusive show with the largest gallery in Paris as soon as he builds his collection of work. He said Vivienne has had calls from editors from three food magazines and two from investors wanting to back her in her own restaurant. She has your camera bag, Margot. You left it in when we had to escape last night."

"That's a relief. I'd forgotten about it in all that happened today. Thanks for letting me know. So, last night was a big success for everyone regardless of the final drama," Margot said.

"Yes, thanks to Jeanne," he replied.

"I wish I could see my friends," she said wistfully. "I miss them so much after the loss of my father. But I am afraid to go to Gaston's after what happened the last time with Elizabeth."

"Why not have them come here?" Margot suggested, sitting up. "Tell them to come for dinner," she said to Etienne. "I'd love to see them as well, and I can download my pictures if Vivienne brings my bag. Then she can see the proofs and let me know if she needs any enhancements."

"That is a great idea," Jeanne exclaimed. She longed for a visit to help her forget the day's events. With everyone together, she was happiest.

"Okay. I'll call Gaston when I get to the office. I have work to finish and then I'll come for dinner." He rose. "Take care, you two. I'll bring wine when I return."

Margot laughed. "Thanks. I doubt I have enough here for Gaston."

"Good-bye. I shall see you later," Jeanne said, blowing him a kiss.

After he left, Margot went to the kitchen and looked though her cabinets. She remained quiet and pensive.

Jeanne wondered if she could find peace in her past as Madam Renee had suggested. She explored this idea, but thoughts of her past only brought revulsion. Fading would solve two problems, however. It would prevent Elizabeth from stealing her soul. And, although difficult to contemplate, it would free Etienne to love a living person. Maybe that person could be Margot. If he loved Margot who was part of her in the familial sense, would it make the sting of loss more bearable? Pain of losing him squeezed her heart, but she refused to dismiss the idea. His happiness was as important as her own.

Margot prepared lasagna and put it in the oven to bake. She poured a glass of red wine and returned to her arm chair, her brow slightly wrinkled.

"Are you okay, Margot?" Jeanne asked.

"Yes. I've been thinking about something." She shifted in her chair and pulled her legs under her. "I want to talk to you about it."

"Of course. Please tell me."

"I've been thinking since we left Madam Renee's. There seems to be only one possibility that could save you from both

Elizabeth and fading to Everlasting." Margot took a swallow of wine and paused.

"Really? I heard no such solution. What are you thinking?" She blinked in surprise. Had she missed some element of their meeting with the medium?

Margot's lips turned down, and her gaze intensified. "That you can join with a living person."

"That is not a solution," she protested. "We do not know what actually happens. Furthermore, I cannot walk into a living person without her permission. That would be wrong."

"What if a living person gave you permission? Madam Renee did say there was no apparent harm to the living person. She just didn't know what happened to the soul."

She gasped, taken aback as it dawned on her where Margot's thoughts led.

Margot stood and paced then returned to the couch, her lips pressed in a firm line. "I want you to meld with me."

"What?" She floated in the air, shock running through her.

"It's the only solution if you don't want to go to Everlasting. It would save you from Elizabeth."

Jeanne shook her head. "You do not know what you are saying. There is no knowing how this could affect you."

"I've been thinking about it all afternoon. I want to do it. You're my family and a good person. It couldn't be bad to have your soul in me. Instinctively I know it. Why else were we brought together in this strange manner?"

She sank to the couch, emotion crushing her in its grip. She couldn't believe Margot's generosity. She had to suppress a flicker of hope. She couldn't accept such a sacrifice. "No, Margot. I appreciate your offer more than you can ever know, but it is too much to ask of you. I ruined my life. I cannot ruin yours. We must muddle on and hope another option presents itself."

"But—" The doorbell announced the arrival of their dinner guests.

Jeanne sagged, relieved at the distraction. Margot's offer was too tempting.

Chapter 33

Etienne smiled as Gaston's bellowing laugh filled the apartment, intermixed with jazz from Margot's stereo. Vivienne leaned over the laptop on Margot's table and viewed pictures of her food from the ball. They both smiled and exclaimed over different aspects of the photos. Jeanne beamed as she glanced at them, and Etienne joined her on the couch.

She quietly told him about Margot's proposal. A knot formed in his throat, leaving him unable to comment. On one hand, he didn't want to lose Jeanne. On the other, he couldn't justify putting Margot at risk. There was too much unknown.

"At least you seem safe from Elizabeth here," he said.

"Yes, I am thankful for that," she replied.

"Maybe we could ask Madam Renee to bring back Francois. He may have more knowledge now that he's in Everlasting."

She shook her head. "I do not know. It is possible I suppose. I hate to bring him back now that he is with his beloved Gabrielle after so much time apart. It seems cruel."

"Here," Gaston interrupted, handing him a glass of wine. "No more gloomy talk tonight. Let's celebrate."

"Gaston's right," Jeanne said. "We did not have a chance last night. Tonight we should toast our good fortune in whatever form it takes."

He raised a glass in toast with his old friend. It was true their destinies now headed on a different path compared to a few months ago. It felt good to be back on top.

Vivienne joined the group, and Margot went into the kitchen to remove the lasagna from the oven. He glanced at her and wondered at her selfless offer. She met his gaze over the bar, and they shared a brief smile before she returned to her preparation of the meal.

"Have you decided on a job from your many offers?" Jeanne asked Vivienne.

"I'm still considering, but one of the investors is a woman who wants to go into a restaurant venture as a partner. She would provide the financing, and I would provide my expertise with food and newfound publicity. When I talked to her on the phone, we really got along well, so that's a good opportunity."

"I still want to do the gallery showing of your work, Jeanne," Gaston said. "What do you think?"

She grinned. "If you really want to. Yes, I would love it."

"Good. I have a friend with a small gallery who would be willing to do me a favor. I'll work on the arrangements."

"But are you not busy on your own work?" she asked.

His friend made a dismissive gesture. "It only takes some phone calls. Vivienne is going to help, and so will Etienne."

"I can help, if you need it," Margot added from the kitchen.

"Thanks," he said. "We can certainly use another hand."

Margot carried a stack of plates to the table, and Vivienne helped by setting out silverware and carrying food from the kitchen.

A shriek of terror ripped through the apartment. Etienne turned and froze.

Jeanne gazed at her arms, her face a mask of horror. "It's happening. I'm fading!' She stared hopelessly at him.

"No!" he cried.

Her form became more transparent.

"No! She's fading."

Margot ran forward, stretching out her hands, face pale. "Jeanne! You have to join with me. Now, before it's too late."

"No, I cannot," Jeanne screamed. "I cannot do it."

"Yes, you can! I want it, I told you so. There's no time," Margot urged.

"Jeanne!" both Gaston and Vivienne called in desperation.

She looked to Etienne, but he could not tell her what to do. Anguish ate his heart. A shiver of horror shook his very soul.

"It's the only way." Margot moved further into the living room. "You know it. I don't want to lose you. Please. Do it for me."

Jeanne glanced at Margot then Etienne. She gave a small cry. Her eyes pleaded forgiveness and, as the last of her essence faded from view, she walked into Margot.

Margot gasped and stiffened. Her eyes went wide and glazed. Then she sank to the floor.

Etienne rushed forward, wrapping his arms around her. God, would he lose both of them? It was more than he could bear. His heart felt ripped in two. Her face paled and her skin grew cool. He lifted her in his arms and carried her to the couch. Gaston and Vivienne came close. Margot's head rolled back, and his fingers encountered a chill in her limbs. Fortunately, the pulse of her heart against his chest assured him she still lived.

***

A blast of chill enveloped Margot as the ghost entered her body and did not leave. Then everything went black.

Suddenly, she was a young girl sitting on the floor and playing with a pretty doll. By a window, her mother stood painting. Occasionally, Mother would glance at her and smile before returning to her work.

"Do you love me?" She stared at her pretty mama with her curly brown hair and trim figure.

Laughter lit her mother's eyes. "Of course, my precious Juliette. Why would you ask such a thing? You are my little treasure. Come give me a hug."

She ran and put her arms around her mother's knees, pressing her face against the white apron she wore over her gown when she painted. It smelled of oils and turpentine.

Her mother smoothed her hair and kissed the top of her head. "There now, go back to your doll and play. Mama has work to do," her mother said indulgently then picked up her brush to resume her painting.

In an instant change, she was a teenager. Her mother painted. They sat in opulent hotel room her mother had rented for them in Italy. A richly dressed woman sat on a chair by the window, and her mother painted the woman's portrait.

She put down her needlework and strolled over to inspect the painting. Her mother looked up at her approach, gave her a quick smile then turned to her canvas, absorbed in her endeavor.

"Pretty," she commented, head tilted to one side.

"Hmm," her mother said, eyes not leaving her work. "Have you finished the slipcover, Julie?"

"No, I am tired. I shall finish it later," she replied.

"Go ahead and finish it. You know we are leaving for Russia in a week."

She sighed and returned to her embroidery. How dull this was. She wanted to try painting like her mother. Later, when her mother rested, she took paint and created her own painting. Maybe if she had talent, her mother would pay her more attention.

A blast of white covered her vision. When the view cleared, she rode in a sleigh. Horses pulled her and her friends through a heavy snow, which had fallen overnight. Warm furs covered her friends, Katerina and Bernard. She and Kat laughed in delight at the brisk ride. Bernard gave them a slight smile of indulgence. His attention remained on the reins and keeping the horses away from drifts on the either side of the road.

"Have you told your mother?" Kat gave her a mischievous look.

"No," she exclaimed.

"Why not?"

She sighed heavily. She'd enjoyed the ride, but Kat had brought up her mother and ruined her pleasure. "She will not like it. She does not think I should marry Bernard and has decided we have all turned against her. I cannot make sense with her anymore."

"You will have to tell her soon. Is she not planning to leave Russia next month?"

"That is what she said. Let us not speak of it right now. I wish this ride could last forever." She laughed and linked arms with Kat who appeared more than willing to partake in her forced merriment.

Scenes came and went quickly. Confronting her mother's anger. Marrying Bernard. Bernard's command to stop her painting. Her return to Paris. Etienne dancing with her at Versailles then making love to her. Her mother's rage over their affair. Selling her meager possessions to stay alive, and finally her sad ending, sick and alone. The scenes flashed faster and faster into a blur, and then the darkness consumed her.

She slowly opened her eyes and found Etienne leaning over her, tears brimming in his eyes. Behind him, Gaston held Vivienne who sobbed against his chest.

"Wha, what happened?" she muttered. She rubbed her head

and pulled to a sitting position. A shiver of cold shook her and she rubbed her arms.

"Margot, are you all right?" Etienne grabbed her shoulders, relief lighting his voice.

"Oh, my God! Margot," Vivienne cried. "We thought you might die."

"I think I'm okay." She waved Etienne away and glanced around. "Jeanne's gone?"

"It looked like she went into you. Do you know what happened?" He rose from the floor where he'd knelt beside her.

"I'm not sure. I felt a chill through my body then I blacked out. I had visions. They were scenes Jeanne had described to me of her life, but more realistic, as if I was Jeanne. As if it all happened to me. Then everything vanished and I woke. How long was I out?"

"Not more than a minute, but you had us worried." Vivienne came around and sat on the other side of her, draping an arm around her shoulders. "Are you sure you're okay? Maybe we should call for an ambulance."

"No, I'm okay. I think so anyway." She blinked. Her skin warmed and she felt the same as she had before Jeanne started to fade.

"What happened to Jeanne?" Gaston asked.

She searched her consciousness, but she had no sense of another presence. She did, however, seem to have completely absorbed all of Jeanne's memories. "I'm not certain. I have her memories, but I don't feel anything else."

A muscle twitched in Etienne's jaw. He poured a glass of wine. When he faced her, his lips quivered on an unconvincing upturn. He brought the glass and handed it to her. "Here drink this."

She smiled her thanks and sipped. Relief filled her that Jeanne had listened and joined with her before fading. Was she happy inside her now? She hoped so. But how would her friends deal with this change?

Vivienne rubbed her hands together and stared at her. Gaston moved to a chair at the dining room table, head down.

Etienne took his friend's glass and refilled it, then poured one for himself. "She's gone," he said, taking a chair beside the big man.

Gaston nodded morosely. "I can't believe it. It was so sudden. Now she will never see her art appreciated."

"You should still have the show," Margot said. "As a memorial now. Jeanne would like that."

"I will. I just wish she could be there to see it. It would make her happy."

"Maybe in some way she will know, wherever she is." Etienne glanced at Margot, his expression wary.

"I'm sure of it." She nodded, wrapping her arms around her chest. A twinge of uneasiness invaded her, however. One thing Jeanne loved more than anything was being with her new friends. What if they didn't include her in their group after this? Would Jeanne really be happy with that future? She bit her bottom lip.

Gaston gave her a speculative glance and scratched his chin.

"Of course she will know." Vivienne hurried to sit beside her on the sofa and grasped her hands in her own. She threw a meaningful glance over her shoulder at her lover. "We can't forget Jeanne just because her presence is no longer visible."

Margo breathed a sigh of relief that did not entirely dissipate her uneasiness. "Thank you."

"Sure, sweetie." The redhead released her hands and stood. "We should go. Margot needs to rest and deal with this internal change."

She rose and ran her palms down her thighs. Maybe sleep would be a good thing. Tomorrow she might be able to think more objectively about the future.

Gaston mumbled something and lumbered to his feet. He hesitated, shuffling his feet, then gave her a hug. "Goodnight, Margot and uh, and Jeanne."

Vivienne gave her an apologetic smile and kissed her cheek. "Call us if you need anything."

"I will. Thanks."

After Gaston and Vivienne left, Etienne lingered. He asked, "Are you sure you're okay?"

She forced a smile, suddenly uncomfortable in his presence. "Yes, seems I'm fine. I don't feel any different. Don't worry about me. You need to get some rest, too."

He lowered his head a moment, his face wan. "I'll call you tomorrow and make sure you're all right."

"Thank you, that's kind." She pushed aside her own feelings and placed a hand on his shoulder. He'd lost his love. Her gut wrenched for him. "I'm sorry, Etienne. I know how much you loved her. It's okay to grieve."

He raised his head and gave her a half smile then patted her hand. He left, wrapped in a somber air.

Chapter 34

Margot had a cup of coffee, surprised she'd slept well after what had happened. She'd anticipated dreams or further visions from Jeanne's life. If Jeanne existed in her, however, she did not make her presence known. Margot could only hope that she was safe and at peace wherever she'd gone.

She made another pot of coffee and checked her e-mails. She couldn't shake a desire to contact George. She wanted him to know Jeanne was gone, and there was a hope she'd not met the fate of her past. The compulsion sent her forward with optimism. She hurriedly dressed and headed to The Louvre.

She walked under the giant, glass pyramid and gazed around with new perspective. She'd visited the museum many times, but Jeanne had lived here for hundreds of years. Now it felt familiar, like home. Instinctively, she headed for the Salle de Napoleon. Like visiting a gravesite, she wanted to return there for a time of remembrance in Francois' honor.

The museum didn't have crowds yet. She wove between a few people and went to a rope partition that kept the visitors from the display. Inside, figures in varied period dress reclined and sat on extravagant historic display furniture. Five or six souls sat surrounding a man, as if he held court. She gasped. These were ghosts.

"George?" she whispered, uncertain.

He glanced in her direction. A bewildered look was soon replaced with one of pleasure. He excused himself from the group and came toward her. She moved aside so they could converse out of earshot of passersby.

"Jeanne? Is that you?" He studied her face.

"It's me, Margot. I came to tell you some news. Jeanne is gone." She explained about the previous night and how the merging had occurred.

"My God, Jeanne faded," George exclaimed.

"Yes, I was frantic. I had been trying to convince her to join with me, but she thought it would put me in danger."

"But she agreed?" He appeared fascinated and relieved at the same time.

"Yes. We were desperate. She didn't want to go and we didn't want to lose her. I don't know if she would have decided to if the fading hadn't come so suddenly."

"No Everlasting?" George placed his forefinger over his lips.

"I can't tell. I have her memories, though. And now I can see spirits. I have to believe she's here in me somewhere." She touched her palm to her chest.

"That is exceptionally interesting, I must say. I wonder what Francois would have thought," he murmured, rubbing his chin.

"He would be happy," she replied. Deep inside her an assurance welled that must come from Jeanne.

After a bit, he nodded. "Yes, he would be very happy, I think. I will miss Jeanne so much. I have lost a mentor, and now my best friend. But both have gone on to better places."

"I came to say good-bye," she said. "I know it's what Jeanne would've wanted."

"I am glad you came. I have taken up Francois' mission and hope to have some purpose in helping other souls. Since there have been no revelations from my past, I am no nearer to fading. I shall carry on here. Maybe something will turn up eventually."

"George, from what Jeanne told me, you'll do a wonderful job filling Francois' place," she said sincerely. "In fact, that may be your purpose to fulfill before fading."

"Thank you. Stop by now and then, will you? It will remind me of Jeanne." He gave her a sad smile.

"I'll do that. Take care," she replied, directing a small salute at Jeanne's old friend.

He smiled then floated to his group. He looked at home there.

Margot left and arrived at her place. She needed to catch up on her old life. The foray into fashion had been interesting and exciting. She had new friends as a result, and a new family history to explore. The exciting interlude had ended, and she prepared to return to her boring existence.

She turned on her laptop and plunged into numerous e-mails she hadn't had time to read in the last few days. She had several job offers, so she would make calls and meet with prospective clients. She sighed. Yep, back to normal.

The doorbell rang. At her door, she gazed through the peephole and took a deep breath.

Etienne.

She slowly opened the door, struggling to control a rush of anticipation crowded by fear. Part of her didn't want to face him after the drama of last night. She was attracted to him, and she wanted him to be attracted to her as well. Jeanne's memories had become hers, and she didn't know what that would mean to the relationship she wanted with him.

"Hey," he said, his face drawn. He didn't meet her gaze.

Other than looking tired, he looked great. He wore his typical black jeans and a white linen shirt, which showed his physique to perfection. She swallowed against her difficulty.

"Hey, yourself. Come on in," she said, motioning with one hand.

"I wanted to check on you. Are you okay?" he asked as she led him into the living room.

"I went to The Louvre this morning," she told him as they sat on the couch.

"Why?"

"I had a feeling I needed to tell George about Jeanne. Guess what? I can now see ghosts. I guess there was some change in me. Surely Jeanne is in here somewhere."

He didn't reply. His eyes darkened, shadowed with sadness. "Is George okay?"

"He's upset at losing her, of course, but happy Jeanne was able to avoid fading to her past relationships. It was a better fate than being attacked by crazy Elizabeth, too. He's going to carry on with Francois' work of helping souls. I think that's really great."

"It is. Jeanne would be pleased, and so would Francois," he said. Tones of pain and sadness lowered his voice.

"How are you doing?" Her desire to hold and comfort him almost overwhelmed her. She shifted in her seat.

"I'll be fine. I'm busy, so that helps. The aftermath of the show is a welcome distraction. I barely have time to breathe, much less think."

She nodded, averting her gaze and fighting a need to throw her arms around him.

Etienne let out a sigh. "Vivienne wants us over for dinner next week so we can plan the show for Jeanne's paintings. I'll call you and let you know when it is."

She smiled. "I really want to help. Please do."

"Okay, and uh Margot?"

"Yes?"

"I want to thank you, for...well, for what you did for Jeanne. That was an incredibly kind and selfless act. So, thank you."

"There's no need to thank me, Etienne. I did it for her. She deserved help. I was the right person, that's all. In a way, I have a feeling it was fate."

He paused then murmured, "Yes, you were the right person."

"Have some wine," she offered, handing him a glass. Her hands shook a bit, but she shoved them in her lap.

He took it and smiled at her. "Thanks." He raised it in a silent toast then took a big swallow.

She tried to think of the right words to discuss how they would interact in the future. Not knowing left her uncomfortable. He loved Jeanne, but she hadn't missed signals that he was attracted to her as well. Was it because she looked like Jeanne, or did he distinguish her as unique? She hoped for a chance at friendship, at least. Jeanne would've wanted that.

"What are you going to do now?" Etienne took another sip of wine. His gaze met hers, easier now.

"I have lots of photo shoot offers. Back to normal, right?" She tried to smile but failed. To cover her nervousness, she went to her stereo. She selected a CD and placed it in the player. The sounds of Edith Piaf emerged, and he glanced at her.

"She's one of my favorites, too." Margot shrugged. It was the song he had played the night she had ended up at his apartment, *I Regret Nothing*.

His gaze grew intense, burning. He placed his glass of wine on the coffee table. His nostrils flared on a breath. He rose and strode toward her, stopping only inches away. She could feel his tension, thick and charged with electricity. Her breath caught in her throat and she quivered, aching for his touch.

"Margot," he said in a ragged breath.

"Yes," she whispered. His closeness made her lose her ability to think straight. Her heart fluttered.

"This is crazy."

She shook her head, breathless at his proximity and the desire unmistakable on his face. She ached for his touch more than ever. If he didn't touch her soon, she'd be unable to control her impulse to wrap her arms around him.

"I keep trying to make sense of this. Why I met Jeanne. Why I was witness to the other strange occurrences over the past month. What if it happened so Jeanne could be saved? I have to believe that. I have to think she's somewhere special now, safe from her past and from Elizabeth. It's left a big empty hole in me. I feel so completely empty." His voice thickened with emotion.

She sighed and ran her tongue over her dry lips that tingled in need of his mouth on hers. "Who knows how the universe works? I don't pretend to. I suspect things have a way of working out the way they're supposed to. In a way, yes, I think everything happened so Jeanne could be saved. So Francois could fade. So George could find his place helping souls. But we're still here, living, and we have to go on living. We can't deny the results any more than they could."

He locked his gaze to hers. "That's just it. Where do we go from here? Is there some special purpose I'm supposed to fulfill because of this? Is there some legacy from Jeanne we're involved in now?"

"I don't know." She took a deep breath and let it out. Frustration and desire urging her comment. "Dammit, I'm crazy about you. If that's some legacy from Jeanne, then so be it. We're alive, Etienne. Living people need relationships and love. I want you. I like the idea of needing you. That's reality. Everything else is just speculation."

"You're crazy about me?" His eyes flickered with a dawning of hope.

"Yes." She burst out laughing and retreated a step to keep from knocking into him. "Yes, you dope."

His gaze turned tender as he searched her eyes. He trailed his fingers from her forehead to her chin. "That night in my apartment, I felt guilty because of my attraction to you. I didn't sleep last night. I beat myself up. Like you said, I think this was meant to happen. Jeanne was meant to be saved. Francois was meant to fade. I can't deny my feelings for you. She led me to you. The thing is, you're a part of Jeanne and she's a part of you. I watched her enter you." He swallowed. "I want you, but I don't want to betray Jeanne's memory."

She took his hand and kissed his knuckles. "I understand. I feel the same. We have time to explore this. If it leads to love, then it's meant to be. No matter what, Jeanne will always be a part of us."

He nodded. His arms encircled her waist, and he pressed her against him, his hands caressing the small of her back. They molded perfectly. His strong chest against her breasts, his hips tight to hers. She let out a shuddering breath and circled her arms around his neck, resting her head on his shoulder. Like it was meant to be.

He kissed the top of her head and sighed. "Yes, she will always be with us."

***

In the most remote corner of Margot's consciousness, Jeanne experienced a warm swell of contentment. Margot and Etienne had discovered each other, as she wished. Margot didn't need awareness of her presence. With her benevolent act, Margot had saved her from both Elizabeth and the fate she'd dreaded. She gave her a safe haven. Now Jeanne could rest. She hadn't realized how tired she was. Oblivion enveloped her, and she slipped into the sleep of souls, safe and at peace. She was finally happy, wrapped in Etienne's arms.

Peut m'arriver n'importe quoi
J'm'en fous pas mal ...
J'etais heureuse, et prête.
(No matter what happens now
I couldn't care less ...
I am happy, and ready) - Edith Piaf

La Fin

Go here to listen to the song, *Non, Je Ne Regrette Rien,* by Edith Piaf: http://archive.org/details/EdithPiaf-21-30

Reread the section on Page 187 where Etienne dances with Margo in his apartment and play this music in the background. It's an interesting experience...

Even though many aspects of the history and actions of the historical figures in this novel are from my imagination, they are interspersed with numerous facts regarding Elizabeth and her daughter. If you become fascinated with that time in history and the interesting people who lived through the terror of the French Revolution, you might enjoy knowing more.

For more information on Elizabeth Vigee Le Brun check out this site:

http://en.wikipedia.org/wiki/%C3%89lisabeth-Louise_Vig%C3%A9e-Le_Brun

Paintings of characters mentioned in this book:
Self portrait of the artist:
http://www.batguano.com/vlbsp1782d.jpg
The artist and her daughter Julie:
http://www.batguano.com/vlb10.jpg
Marie Antoinette: http://www.batguano.com/maversai.jpg
Jeanne: http://www.batguano.com/julielebrun.jpg
Francois: http://www.batguano.com/vlbvaudreuil.jpg
Gabrielle: http://www.batguano.com/vlbdpolinacc.jpg

Visit my website for news about new books and my sailing adventures! www.laranance.com

More Books by Lara Nance:

Mysteries:
Murder in the World Below
The Secret of Angler's Creek

Paranormal Romance:
Memories of Murder
Dealers of Light
The DraculaVille series:
Discovery in New York
Danger in Los Angeles
Destiny in Transylvania

Steampunk:
The Airship Adventure Chronicles:
Revenge of the Mad Scientist
Rescue from the Baron
Attack of the Automatons
Short story – The Asylum Prodigy

A Clockwork Angel – steampunk short story.

Made in United States
Orlando, FL
07 November 2022

24307108R00137